Mamas' Drama

By

Nanette Marie

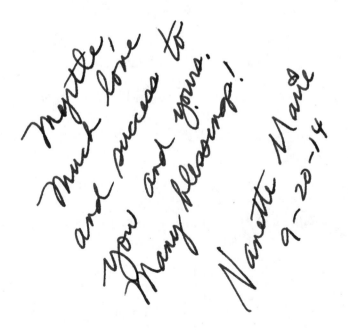

MAMAS' DRAMA

Published by Real Good Press, P.O. Box 297984
Columbus, Ohio 43229.
www.mamasdramaplaybook.com.
Library of Congress Cataloging-in-Publication Data
Nanette M. Hodge

ISBN 978-0-692-02765-3

Cover design by Mitchell Stanford
Interior design Mark Stevenson
Photo by Donald Sgontz @ DSg Photography
Edited by Sheri Chaffin

This book is dedicated to my handsome son, Chad Hodge, and my pretty granddaughter, Dominique. Chad, having you stand with me, support me and believe in me during this phenomenal journey gives me the strength and courage I need to keep going. Reminding me to laugh is a real good thing, too. And yes, "I'm your Mama who wrote this!" (lol). Dominique, my Sweetie Girl, thank you for confirming that this work is divinely ordered by wanting to play your Maw Maw. I love you both dearly, and thank God for you daily.

To my beautiful mother, Margaret; my father, Fred Sr.; and my sister, Beverly; who walk around heaven all day. Mama, you nurtured me in your womb and gave me life; and I am forever grateful. Daddy, thank you for loving me. Beverly, I did it, Sis--I told our story! I love you all, and will see you again one day.

Acknowledgements

"I can do all things through Christ, who strengthens me." (Philippians 4:13). Thank you God for revealing my purpose, and giving me favor to write this book.

To my "bestest editors" and friends—Lisa Earley, Sharron Kornegay, Janette Patterson, and Arlinda Perryman—your honesty was instrumental in helping to shape this book. Jackie Woodward-Marable, the countless hours and loving patience you showered on me as we read each word was priceless. Thanks for keeping me grounded when I started to spiral. I love and appreciate all of you "bestest editors" for impelling (sometimes it felt like you were impaling) me to complete this book. Your suggestions, comments and sidebar conversations were essential to pull the truth and artistic license out of me. Our gatherings, meals, love and laughter kept me encouraged during this journey.

My heartfelt gratitude to my dear and precious friends and family members who support and love me. To everybody who contributed their attention, time and talents to breathe life into this book and my plays, I am so grateful.

To my director, actors and production crew—watching you take my words and birth them on stage is just amazing!

I love and cherish each and every one of you. Be blessed!

Introduction

"Now, Thomas will always be your daddy, but Mr. Clarence is your real father."

Have you or someone close to you heard similar words at any point in your lives? I was inspired to write this book, which is based on a true story, as I lived well into adulthood before I was told the truth about my biological father.

Mamas' Drama explores the subject of the "mama's baby, daddy's maybe" condition, which occurs when the identity of the father is questionable. Whether in the family's past or present, this condition runs rampant; but discussions are avoided because of shame, blame, and pain. *Mamas' Drama* focuses on the females' participation in keeping secrets and telling lies about children born from extramarital affairs.

I was divinely ordered to write this book. In 2007, I attended the National Black Theatre Festival (NBTF) for the first time. My mama passed at home in Columbus, Ohio while I was in Winston-Salem. I ignored the voice inside, and didn't recognize her departure at that time was a sign for me to write about her life. When I attended the NBTF in 2009, I spoke with a festival staff person, and it became crystal clear that I was to write my Mama's story. I wrote and produced the play, "Mamas' Drama" which debuted in 2011 and toured theatre festivals nationally in 2012 and 2013. My biggest thrill came when it was selected for the Readers' Theatre of New Works at the NBTF in 2013. I had come full circle, and could feel Mama's spirit of pride during the reading of the play about our lives.

My hope is for readers to realize that those born into situations where paternity is questionable are generally told the truth by someone; and it can, and does hurt. I speak to and for those, who, like me, grew up surrounded by a shroud of secrets and lies about the identity of their biological father. My experience is not unique, and my prayer is that if you have been affected by the "mama's, baby, daddy's maybe" condition, whether directly or indirectly, that you find not only entertainment, but comfort and healing within. Hopefully you will recognize that you are not alone, and healing can begin.

Now, the mayor awaits you at Millie's doorstep. So get comfortable and turn the page, if you would be so kind.

Nanette Marie
April 8, 2014

CHAPTER ONE

Millie Stewart walks slowly through her home as she meticulously inspects each room to ensure everything is in impeccable order. The business has been immensely successful for five years, proof that her careful preparation pays off.

Standing at Millie's doorstep, Clarence McElroy adjusts his hat as the streetlight catches his reflection. Even though he is the mayor of Harriman, Tennessee, he keeps his street representation intact. He has cultivated a smile that melts the hearts of most women so they keep in mind that he is finer than Wedgewood china. He eludes confidence as tall as his six feet, two inch frame.

Being a lawyer and mayor for nine years is impressive, especially for a man barely 35 years old. The tailored, three-piece ecru-colored suit he wears reveals his apparent success. Unlike most men in their Sunday best, his textured striped vest does not fit snugly; it fits just so to suggest his firm, athletic body underneath. A silk Italian ivory neck tie lies on top of a crisp, starched white shirt that would make any dry cleaner proud. His tan hat is slightly cocked to the left, with a feather placed precisely on its right side. The tan shoes he wears glisten as though he spit shined them while waiting at the door.

Clarence gives his distinctive knock. Millie, who knows the sound well, peeks into the mirror before sashaying to the door while finger stroking her hair to make sure each strand is in place.

"Hello Mayor, how are you?" she purrs, an involuntary blush tinting her cheeks as he steps across her door's threshold.

Clarence flashes his inviting smile, "I'm fine, Millie, and you?" His eyes linger, devouring her from head to toe. "I can already see you're fine," he pronounces in that sly way lady killers say so charmingly. She catches herself enjoying his advances and turns quickly to walk back toward the living room.

Millie has to be mindful that people are present, and she and Clarence are both married. He and his wife, Leslee, have two children—a son and daughter the same age as her two older children. As mayor, he risks losing it all every time he comes here—her home by day and after-hours place by night. Many townspeople speculate as to why a man in his position would frequent the illegal business. But he disregards them, and they don't dare ask him directly.

Millie, tall and slender, is an attractive 32-year-old housewife, mother and businesswoman—a disciplinarian by day and savvy entrepreneur by night. She is poised as she entertains her customers—as efficient at running her after-hours business as she is her household. Millie wears a red and black sequined skirt and top which frame her body and dance when she walks. Her patent leather black tee-strap shoes and sequined red and black hat complement her party outfit. Ready to please the customers who please her pockets, she mingles from guest to guest, laughing and talking while encouraging them to eat and drink.

Josephine, the oldest of Millie and husband Thomas' three children, regularly helps her mama with the customers. Petite and pretty, Josephine is an obedient, lively and inquisitive seven-year-old who loves people. Millie's seamstress talents are displayed in Josephine's yellow and white polka dot dress, with matching bloomers and hair ribbons. Josephine moves quickly, counting money and serving food and drinks as well as her mama. Millie has carefully trained her how to properly handle the customers so they will come back again and again.

Josephine gets a nickel when they make good money; and when she works extra hard, Millie sometimes gives her as much as a whole dime. Allowed to spend her money however she wants, she often buys gifts for her younger brother and sister. She keeps a smile on her face, as the customers always talk about how pretty it is. A few customers slip her a penny or two and tell her not to tell her mama, but she always does because her mama will not tolerate secrets.

It is 1929, but prohibition laws don't deter people from coming to Millie's place for the moonshine and food lauded as "a taste of heaven right here on earth." Whether sitting or standing, the guests find pleasure in each other, the music, food and liquor—especially Millie's home-made moonshine. She prides herself on her uniquely-flavored moonshine, with peach being the most popular. The dining room and living room tables overflow with food and beverages. A glass Mason jar with a hole hammered in its metal top serves as the tip jar. Millie prominently displays it on the cocktail table in the living room; the few nickels and dimes inside are visible reminders for customers to contribute.

From the corner of the living room, the music blares as the Victrola plays "Cottontail." Guests become livelier as they keep up with each other's conversations and the music's rhythms and beats. Clara, Millie's longtime friend, is celebrating her 40th birthday. She dances the Charleston in the middle of the living room—her royal blue flapper dress swaying rhythmically. The men seated on the sofa sip their drinks and eat their food eagerly, without missing any of Clara's seductive gyrations. A man and woman at the dining room table seem oblivious to their surroundings as they laugh and talk with each other. The atmosphere becomes even more festive as "Old Yazoo" now plays on the Victrola.

Clarence's eyes follow Millie's every move. She glances at him, seemingly reading his lustful thoughts. As if trying to deflect being exposed, he whispers, "Where's my daughter?"

Millie senses his embarrassment and chuckles. "Clarence you see her over there with a customer. Josephine, come over here baby." Josephine smiles as she walks over to them.

"Hello Josephine, you look very pretty. How are you this evening?" Josephine says that she's fine, and thanks him for the compliment as she eyes the small bag he holds in his hand. But instead of handing the bag to her, he reaches into his pocket, something he normally does when he is going to give her money. She wonders how much it will be—pennies, a nickel, a dime—or if she will hit the jackpot and get a whole quarter. A quarter is more than her mama gives her for an entire month, sometimes two.

After what seems like an eternity, Mr. Clarence pulls out the coin and hands it to her. A quarter—she hit the jackpot! She thanks him and quickly places it in her sock. He hands her the small bag and she peers into it; happy to see her favorite candy, peanut butter cups. Josephine thanks him again and opens one to eat. She remembers her manners and extends the bag to him, but he graciously refuses. He is pleased that she shows such good manners. Josephine is grateful for the money and gifts Mr. Clarence gives her. Other customers give her pennies and small gifts at times, but he brings her money and gifts all of the time.

Millie is annoyed with Clarence for taking up too much of Josephine's attention, and motions for her to come and help with the other guests.

"Yes, Mama," she says politely, and excuses herself from Mr. Clarence, offering a sweet smile that mirrors his.

"That's fine, Josephine," he says, as he walks over to take his usual seat in the armchair. The customer sitting there gets up the moment the mayor heads in his direction. It is an unspoken rule that the chair belongs to the mayor whenever he is present.

A forceful knock at the door startles everyone, disrupting the party. Millie doesn't say a word or even look at Josephine when she motions for her to grab the tip jar. Josephine immediately runs to her bedroom; the jar tucked snugly under her arm.

Millie opens the door, and standing on her porch are two stern-looking police officers. She recognizes Officer Bob, who withholds complete familiarity and introduces Officer Bill. In a cordial tone, Millie asks, "Officers, why did you knock so hard?"

Officer Bill looks around as he enters as if on a high-profile investigation. In an agitated tone he remarks, "It's against the law to sell liquor and food you know!"

Millie, fully aware that her connection to the mayor protects the operation of her business, is not affected by his unfriendly attitude, "I know that officer, but I'm not selling anything. We're just celebrating my friend Clara's birthday!" She points to Clara who smiles and waves. "Now there is no harm in having a birthday party is it?"

Officer Bob, who routinely patrols this area and is aware that the mayor is a frequent visitor, responds, "No, Millie, there's no harm, as long as you're not selling anything." He emphasizes to Officer Bill that nothing illegal is going on and they can leave. He then acknowledges the mayor's presence and prepares to make a quick exit while trying not to be obvious. "Well hello, Mr. Mayor. How are you this evening, sir?" The mayor nods and looks over at Josephine as she enters the room and stands next to her Mama.

Officer Bill is surprised to see the mayor, and attempts to hide his awkwardness by making small talk. "Umm... umm...that chicken smells mighty good!"

Millie smiles at him, "Well, do you want some of this good smelling chicken—or anything else good?"

Officer Bill looks past Millie and smiles at Josephine a little too long for both Josephine and Clarence's comfort. "No, Millie, not right now, but I may want something later." Josephine smiles sheepishly at Officer Bill, but cringes once he turns his head. She cradles herself, hoping no one sees the uneasy look on her face.

Clarence loudly clears his throat, a warning for the policemen to leave. Bob nudges Bill, and looks at the door. As they turn to leave, Officer Bill says condescendingly, "Well, you folks enjoy your party. We'll see you the next time." Millie escorts them to the door, as Clarence makes a mental note to order the chief of police to take Bill off patrol for a couple of weeks, and to remove him from that area. Millie closes the door and wastes no time getting the party back into full swing.

"Umm...these chicken, greens and potato salad are going to taste real good with some more moonshine. Josephine, baby run to the basement and get another jug of peach shine."

A relieved Josephine answers, "Yes, Mama! The jug's kind of heavy, but I can carry it all by myself."

Millie reminds her to bring the tip jar and put it back on the table for their guests. She then smiles at her customers; enjoying the fact that its mere presence suggests they feed it as they feed themselves.

Clarence grimaces as he's walking up to Millie. "I saw the way that cop looked at Josephine, and I didn't like it."

"I noticed him, but he won't try anything stupid. He saw you and knows who you are. If he had any ideas, I'm sure they cleared out of his head the moment he realized it was you sitting in the chair."

Clarence raises his voice, "You'd better not let anything happen to my daughter!"

Millie is aggravated by his outburst but remains calm. "Look, she's my daughter and nothing's going to happen to her. Now lower your voice, I don't want anybody to hear you—especially Josephine."

"Don't tell me what to do, woman," Clarence says in his most mayoral tone. "She's going to have to hear and know that I'm her father one day, and you'd better make it soon! I told you to tell her before she turns eight. You may be married to Thomas, but Josephine is my blood—and don't you forget that!"

Millie silently counts to ten to keep her temper in check. "How could I forget? And why is it so important that I tell her anyway? You said you wanted to keep her a secret—so why do you want to tell her now?"

Thoughts about his father's sudden passing, and the void it created in his heart when he was only eight pass through Clarence's mind. He made a vow at his young age that he would always be close to his children, as his longing to see his father alive never stops. Although Josephine wasn't born under ideal circumstances, she is his blood, and he loves her dearly.

He snaps at Millie, "You don't need to know why; you just need to tell her. Do you understand me?"

Millie foregoes the subject, "I have customers to attend to right now. Why don't you sit down and let me get you a drink?"

Clarence walks back towards the armchair which remained empty. "Bring me my whiskey so I can get back home to my family." Millie rolls her eyes and gets his drink. She hands it to him, holding her hand out, palm facing up. In a patronizing tone she remarks, "That's a quarter, please."

Millie becomes nervous as Clarence locks eyes with her and takes his time reaching into his pocket. "Okay, woman here's your quarter." He hands it to her, pauses for a moment, and pulls out a nickel. In the same patronizing tone she used, he quips, "And here's a nickel for your tip jar."

"Thanks, Mayor, I'm going to serve my other customers because I am truly tired of serving you." She saunters away, switching provocatively, as she is fully aware that he is watching her every move. She struggles constantly to control the deep-seated yearning she has held for Clarence since meeting him 10 years ago. A twinge of guilt surfaces as she thinks back to intimate moments they spent in secret.

Thomas' fascination for Millie began in the second grade. His focus on her instead of his class work made him oblivious to his teachers, which often landed him a seat in the principal's office. The starry-eyed Thomas was consumed with puppy love, determined he would marry Millie one day. Even though they were childhood sweethearts, as they grew up, Millie related to him more as a good friend. During high school she had several boyfriends, but he was always there, loving Millie and waiting for her to love him back.

Thomas was a hard worker, and got a job at Parker's Steel Mill right after their graduation from high school. Being in love with Millie all of his life gave him the courage to act on his feelings, and he proposed to her. Minnie Kirksey, like most women in their time, wanted her daughter to marry a good man who would take care of her; and encouraged Millie to accept his proposal before somebody else took him. Minnie certainly didn't want her daughter to end up without a husband and become a burden or embarrassment to the family. Millie told her mama she didn't love Thomas like she thought a woman should love a husband; but Minnie reassured her that their love would grow once they got married. Since Thomas was a good man and her best friend, she followed her Mama's urging and accepted his proposal.

Millie's marriage was one of convenience; and instead of being true to her heart, she married Thomas to please her mama.

They had celebrated their one-year anniversary when Millie's best friend, Nana, asked her to work on Clarence McElroy's campaign for mayor. Nana wanted to meet a good man, and working on campaigns was an acceptable way to accomplish her goal. Millie was spending her evenings alone as Thomas's graveyard shift had him working overtime from early evening until 7a.m. the next morning. She decided it would be fun to work with Nana on the campaign. Clarence McElroy had a flirtatious nature and made playful overtures to Millie, which she found amusing. It wasn't long before his flirtations became more deliberate. Millie was flattered, as he epitomized the perfect man— educated, successful, attentive and handsome. The enticing smell of his cologne and immaculate manner of dress further intrigued her. She allowed herself to be vulnerable and open up to him fully during their private conversations.

Clarence's charm won over Millie's good sense, and they shared a few stolen kisses. The kisses became deeper and longer, leaving them breathless and wanting more. The intensity of their kisses and the lustful looks they exchanged, evoked such passion that Millie became beguiled, and embraced her desire for Clarence. They acted on their forbidden attraction to each other just months after meeting. The moments of intimacy still haunt her, and she recalls every detail about their first evening in the fancy hotel not far from Harriman. Whispers of desire, electrifying touches, and passionate kisses accompanied them on the drive to satisfy their insatiable longing for each other.

Their actions once inside the privacy of the room proved surreal. Spending hours making love in every fathomable—and some unfathomable ways—left an indelible imprint in Millie's body and soul. She vividly recalls the wonder of his deliberate long, slow, wet kisses from her head to her toes. The breathlessness she felt from the passion that arose in her almost rendered her unconscious. As they made fanatical love, Millie found unbridled pleasure in the ethereal orgasms she reached, feeling much like she would imagine an out-of-body experience would feel. Their connection was not just an intertwining of bodies; Millie felt her soul connected with his soul. She was captured by Clarence Eric McElroy, hook, line and sinker; and was undeniably and shamelessly under his spell.

Many years have passed, but she still feels the passion of their intimacy as if they remain in the hotel room. For Millie, the sparks ignited during Clarence's campaign never died, and the embers reignite each time she sees him. Their romantic interlude was brief, but not brief enough. As fate would have it, Clarence became Josephine's biological father during one of their few surreal encounters. Damn it, she thinks.

Mamas' Drama

CHAPTER TWO

It is an unseasonably warm September afternoon. The trees, slightly kissed with the colors of fall, frame Unaka Street; now bustling with people enjoying the Indian summer-like weather. The Depression looms on the horizon, but has yet to have a noticeable impact on the lives of people in the small town. They live as if nothing is about to change.

Millie loves their three-bedroom Victorian home, which is much more spacious than the one bedroom they bought when they first married 10 years ago. The oak table in the dining room is covered with an ivory lace tablecloth which perfectly matches the ivory and gold-trimmed swag lamps in the living room. Her embroidery talent is impressively displayed in the fashionable pewter-green curtains. She takes pride in knowing no other home in Harriman has any more class than hers.

Millie and Thomas carefully selected the paintings which grace the walls of their living and dining rooms. Oil paintings of the Harlem Renaissance—replete with swinging bands, crooning singers and carefree dancers—reflect their love of art and music. A painting of their favorite musician, Louis "Satchmo" Armstrong, hangs in a place of honor behind the richly-colored emerald green sofa.

Millie cleans the kitchen after serving her family a bountiful breakfast. Unlike some of their neighbors, they are blessed to enjoy three square meals daily. Their hearty breakfast of buttermilk pancakes, sausage, eggs, grits and biscuits slathered with butter, leaves them happy and satisfied. Josephine keeps a watchful eye on her mama while she helps prepare their delicious meals. Her mama has taught her it is essential to become a good cook to please her future husband. The air in the ample, bright, sunshine-yellow kitchen fills with mouth-watering aromas as they prepare the delicious food for tonight's customers.

Thomas Sr. especially enjoys waking up to the traditional Saturday breakfast; not only because it is the best food in town, but because Saturday breakfast signals his last night on the graveyard shift before his day off from the steel mill. An average-looking man, Thomas Sr. is rugged and quiet-natured. He is a dedicated family man and is totally devoted to Millie. Very much the patriarch of the Stewart family, he relinquishes full reign over the household to her, for he knows when mama's happy, daddy's life is real good. Like many marriages, theirs has had a lion's share of challenges, but he is content that he and the love of his life have weathered the storms and remain together.

They are proud of their children, Josephine, Thomas Jr. and Betty. Josephine is her "daddy's girl" and lives for his attention and affection. She dreams of becoming a fashion designer; her clothing designs express knowledge well beyond her seven years. Six-year-old Thomas Jr., shy and quiet natured like his dad, took his good looks after his mama. He is content spending hours reading and playing with toy cars and marbles. Betty, a rambunctious five-year old, is the baby of the family. She is candid and speaks her mind; much to everybody's chagrin. Jealous of the attention Josephine receives from their daddy, Betty constantly competes for his affection.

Josephine finishes her kitchen duties and heads down the street to her second favorite place, her old home, which is now Grandma Kirksey's home. Minnie, a tall, stout woman at five feet, eight inches, appears even taller because of her added girth. Josephine loves visiting her maternal grandmother. Minnie Kirksey comes from a long line of southern preachers; her grandfather, daddy and husband were all men of the cloth. She is the first woman in her family to preach in the pulpit, and gives her all when she preaches the word.

Minnie is aware of her anointing, and preaching has been her calling since she can remember. She is comfortable being the only female pastor at Love Zion Baptist Church, and is appreciative to Pastor Jordan for allowing her to give the sermon every fourth Sunday. A serious-natured woman, she finds great joy and laughter when telling her granddaughter Bible stories and about her childhood memories. Expecting Josephine at any moment, Grandma peers out the living room window, and sees her approaching. She opens the door and welcomes her with a bear hug so tight, Josephine knows her grandma is delighted to see her.

Josephine lived in this home until she was four, but it looks and feels completely different. Grandma's furnishings are such a stark contrast to her parents' home, that Josephine thinks they are as old as Grandma. The curtains are tattered, but Grandma refuses Millie's offers to sew new ones. There is no doubt Grandma loves Jesus; the framed paintings look like they jumped straight from the pages of the Bible onto the walls. The life-sized painting on the living room wall depicting Jesus on the cross seems so real that Josephine sometimes imagines she hears voices from the crowds. A large golden cross holds a place of prominence on the small dining room wall.

The face of Jesus covers the majority of the sofa cover on the grayish-white sofa that was once an eggshell color. Grandma sits in her rocking chair and motions for Josephine to sit on the sofa. Because the face of Jesus is so large, Josephine inevitably ends up sitting on Jesus' face. She looks down and says a silent "excuse me" to Jesus.

Grandma offers her a piece of the family's sweet potato pie, which she eagerly accepts. Josephine loves the stories Grandma and her mama tell about the females from previous generations and how they passed along the cherished recipe. Grandma recounts the story about her great grandmother teaching her to bake the traditional pie when she was Josephine's age. Josephine has heard this story for what seems like a million times, but she always reacts as if it is her first time hearing it.

Grandma adds the peach slices Josephine requests to a glass of freshly-brewed ice tea. Josephine has heard customers at her mama's parties talk about how tasty the peach shine is, but she doesn't dare tell Grandma that's why she wants peaches in her tea. Josephine thinks Grandma is ashamed of Millie for having the house parties, and doesn't want Josephine to be around the likes of the carousing and unsaved folks. She has heard her mama tell Grandma to not talk about the parties to Josephine, or anybody else for that matter. And although Josephine has tried to share some of the funny things that happen, Grandma starts praying and won't listen to her.

Josephine finishes the pie and sips her tea as Grandma shares what she is going to preach about tomorrow. "Precious flower, the Lord put it in my spirit to talk to his people about Barak. Read Judges 4, verses 6 through 12 and Judges 5, verses 1 through 6 for me please." Josephine reads the verses slowly, and isn't surprised when Grandma wants her to read parts of them again. The spirit of the Lord comes over Grandma and she begins to hum and tap her foot, briskly rocking back and forth in her chair. "Precious flower, I love the way you read God's words. It fills my soul with joy!"

Grandma never writes notes for her sermons, and Josephine has always been curious as to why. She figures now is a good time to ask, especially with the spirit coming on. "Grandma, you never write your sermons down—how do you remember what to say?"

"I don't need to write them down. God allows me to remember them so I can spread His word. All I need is my sweet granddaughter to read the good book to me."

"Grandma, can you read and write?"

She holds her head up and sits in a proud posture, "I can read and write a teeny bit, but you don't have to know how to read and write to talk to others about God, baby," she says convincingly in her preacher's voice.

Josephine wonders if she has the gift of anointing since she reads the Bible to Grandma, but prays she doesn't start speaking in tongues the way Grandma does. Josephine doesn't understand how anybody knows what that gibberish means. After reading the verses a couple more times and listening to Grandma preach some, preparation for the sermon is complete. Grandma recounts stories about her childhood, as Josephine hangs on to every word. Hours seem like minutes and it is time for Josephine to return home. She walks up the street, feeling like she's on cloud nine, after having her grandma's attention all to herself. On her way home, she smiles when she thinks about waking up and seeing her daddy up and about first thing. He usually sleeps in most Sundays; but he always attends church when Grandma Kirksey preaches.

That evening, like clockwork, the frolicking party guests arrive at Millie's, and eat, drink and dance to their hearts' content until the early hours of the morning. Josephine is exhausted and relieved when she is permitted to go to bed. She enjoys the customers, but would prefer to be asleep or creating her fashion designs. But her mama relies on her, so she is happy to help.

The Stewart family is in good spirits on their way to church. They walk the two blocks slowly so the praying Pastor Kirksey can keep up with them. The 20 pews in the quaint little church shine like welcoming beacons for its congregation and visitors at Love Zion Baptist. Colorful stained glass windows sparkle as if newly polished, and the sun shines through the intricate panes. Live plants line the altar, and a table in the middle holds a pair of candles flanked by a large black Bible. The pulpit podium is adorned with a rich purple cloth with an ornate gold cross at its center. Grandma Kirksey now sits tall in the pulpit; the spirit of anointing surrounding her.

The family sits on the second pew so Josephine is close to the pulpit when she stands to read. She has barely slept and is nervous about reading. She is seated between her mama and daddy, and Betty sits on the other side of their mama. Thomas Jr. sits on the other side of their daddy. Millie stares blankly at her mama as she prepares to deliver the sermon, but her thoughts dwell on the after-hours business. A tired Thomas Sr. fights to stave off sleep.

Pastor Kirksey has a regal air about her when she steps up to the podium. "Welcome to the house of the Lord! We are going to have a mighty spirit-filled time today as we feed our souls with the word! Now, I want you to stay with me while I talk about Barak. Josephine, would you kindly read Judges 4, verses 6 through 12." Thomas Sr. perks up as Josephine stands and reads clearly and loudly. Once finished, she sits down and snuggles close to her daddy, content to be at his side.

Betty makes the sounds of each animal she draws, and Millie has to remind her to be quiet. Thomas Jr. is his usual quiet self as he plays with his toy car. Thomas Sr. nods off, awakens several times and looks over and smiles at his children. Josephine smiles back at her daddy, as she watches his every move. Betty smiles back at him, but wrinkles her nose at Josephine. Thomas Jr. is preoccupied with his car and doesn't notice his daddy. Millie glances up at her mama from time to time, but pays more attention to the children to make sure they behave. She thinks about Clarence, hoping the next time he visits that he wears the

Zizanie cologne she loves to smell on him. Millie's thoughts remain on Clarence until Betty brays like a donkey. Millie gives her a mean stare and tells her to hush the noise.

Pastor Kirksey's forehead is dripping wet from perspiration and her glasses are askew from the forcefulness of her delivery. The napping Thomas Sr. awakens abruptly when her deep baritone voice begins singing "The Old Rugged Cross," while extending the call to discipleship. Reverend Jordan prays a prayer of protection, and church service ends. Grandma beams with a sense of accomplishment as she receives appreciation and love from the departing congregation. Hungry and tired, the family leaves church in anticipation of Sunday dinner. Thomas Sr., fully awake now, tells his mother-in-law how much he enjoyed her sermon. She looks at him questionably, "Well Thomas Sr., I'm surprised you heard anything since you were asleep most of the time."

He tries to defend himself, "Mother Kirksey, I heard enough to know that it was good indeed. And with all those folks shouting and screaming—it was Holy-Ghost filled!"

Mother Kirksey is wise enough to know further conversation about his sleeping is futile, and asks him if he learned about Barak. His automatic response is "yes," but he prays she doesn't ask him to tell her what he learned. Millie reminds everybody to hurry so they can get home to Sunday dinner. She doesn't need to remind them twice, as they all look forward to the scrumptious Sunday feasts she prepares every Lord's day.

Minnie has worked up an appetite as big as she is tall, and asks Mille what is on the menu. Pork chops, greens, macaroni and cheese, potato salad, rolls, and much to her delight, sweet potato pie are today's fare. Minnie takes pride in her daughter's excellent cooking ability and readily admits Millie cooks some dishes better than she; especially the family's prized sweet potato pie. She offers Millie praise, "Your meals are gifts sent straight from the Lord. I'm ready to eat dinner and relax the rest of His glorious day." She then looks at Josephine with loving eyes, "Josephine you read real good today. I think you get better every time." Josephine blushes and thanks her grandma.

Betty chimes in, "I want to read in church, too." Grandma assures Betty that she will when she learns to read a little better. Betty rolls her eyes at Josephine, "Okay Grandma, I'll keep reading because I'm gonna read better than Josephine!"

Millie has a short fuse for Betty's competitiveness, "Betty, quit running your mouth and just be glad you can read at all. Josephine's older and reads all the time, that's why she does so well."

Thomas Sr. agrees, "Your mama's right, Betty. You need to read a little better and then you can read for Mother Kirksey, too." Not wanting to leave Thomas Jr. out, he asks if he wants to read during his grandma's sermons. Thomas Jr. responds, "no" as soon as the words leave his daddy's mouth. He doesn't like to read and is not the slight bit interested in reading aloud in church.

Thomas Sr. says a prayer of thanks before the family devours dinner. A tired, but satisfied Mother Kirksey is pleased when Millie gives her a sweet potato pie to take home. Once she leaves, they turn on the radio and listen to Amos and Andy while playing their favorite card game, Cooncan. Thomas Sr. thinks again about how grateful he is that it is Sunday and he doesn't have to leave his family to go to work tonight.

Millie appreciates the break from the after-hours customers, but cleans greens in preparation for tomorrow night. She thinks about Clarence being so insistent that she tell Josephine he is her biological father. He has never been so demanding before, and she can't figure out why it is so important to him now. After spending too much time thinking about it, she doesn't come up with anything that makes rhyme nor reason. And Clarence is not the least bit inclined to tell her. She decides to tell Josephine tomorrow the secret she's held for almost eight years. She dreads that moment, as it will break Josephine's heart, as she is so fond of her daddy. Millie tries to diminish the thoughts of Clarence, and turns her focus to what she's going to wear tomorrow night. But, even though she wishes he would leave her mind, the thoughts persist. Perhaps it's Josephine's resemblance to her daddy that keeps him on her mind. And perhaps not.

Mamas' Drama

CHAPTER THREE

Fall takes a diversion from the Indian summer-like weather, and it is a bit chilly on this October evening. The Stewarts enjoy family fun while Millie puts the finishing touches on dinner. Josephine and Betty dance to the songs from the "Grand Old Opry" playing loudly on the radio. Josephine is having a great time as Betty tries to out dance her older sister, who by far is the better dancer. Thomas Sr. and Thomas Jr. laugh at the girls. Eventually Thomas Jr. blows all caution to the wind, joins in and dances with his sisters.

Thomas Sr. laughs heartily as he sees his son behave like a six-year old instead of the serious-minded boy he is most times. Millie comes into the room and is amused at her brood. She relaxes for a few minutes, thoroughly enjoying their antics. Once the song ends, Josephine runs to her daddy and sits on his lap, already missing him since he'll soon be leaving for work. She rubs his arms and traces the outline of his face with her fingers. Thomas Sr. calls her his special angel, hugs her and kisses her forehead. Josephine relishes every bit of attention she receives from her daddy.

Betty wants his attention. "Josephine, get off of daddy's lap, I want to sit there." Josephine refuses to move away from the most favorite person in her world, and tells Betty to get away. Betty is determined to take her place on his lap and retorts, "He's my daddy, so get off of him!"

Thomas Sr. intervenes, "Betty, you both are my daughters, and I don't want to hear my little ladies talking in that manner. Remember, we're a family, and we love each other. Josephine, baby, scoot over to my right leg, and Betty, you can sit on my left." Betty pouts, and Thomas Sr. is silent as she resignedly shares his attention with her sister. Thomas Jr. doesn't vie for his daddy's attention, as they always do "men stuff" together—fishing being one of their mainstays. He wishes his sisters didn't fight so much, and is often the peacemaker, with Betty being by far the hardest one to pacify.

Millie's break is short-lived when the pressure cooker whistles loudly from the kitchen, signaling the cabbage is ready. She summons the girls to come and help, and instructs Betty to set the table and Josephine to help serve the food. Thomas Sr. and Thomas Jr. continue listening to the radio as the women do the women's work.

While in the kitchen, Millie speaks to Josephine in a hushed tone, "Josephine, you're almost eight years old now, and we need to have a woman-to-woman talk. After dinner we'll get someplace quiet—just you and me. And what I tell you is for your ears only, do you hear me?"

Josephine is leery and thinks she's done something wrong, as it's rare for her mama to whisper. And she has absolutely no clue what a woman-to-woman talk is. She shakes her head yes as she really doesn't want to talk, afraid her vocal chords won't emit a sound.

Millie senses Josephine's nervousness and reassures her she is not in trouble. "Now, you can keep a secret, right?" Josephine shakes her head yes again, but her mind cannot fathom why her mama is so serious. Is this secret that important? She knew, like it or not, she would find out soon enough.

The family sits down and eats to their hearts' content, the children being careful not to talk with their mouths open, as Millie doesn't tolerate improper table manners. When her daddy stands up, Josephine, who had momentarily forgotten about the talk with her mama, suddenly remembers. A sick feeling rises in her stomach, and she wishes her daddy wasn't leaving.

Thomas Sr. rubs his belly, "Millie, that dinner was so good, it hit two spots instead of one!"

Millie knows her husband is appreciative of her cooking, but reminds him that Josephine was very helpful and is becoming quite a good cook. Thomas Sr. compliments Josephine, who is happy her mama said something that is nice and isn't a secret. It makes her feel extra special to receive compliments from her daddy, but she wishes her mama's secret would just go away without her having to know it.

Millie and the girls clear the dishes from the table while the males settle back on the sofa. Thomas Sr. has to get ready for work, and is grateful to have a job, especially with the talk about a Depression. Thomas Sr. is proud of his wife for running the successful after-hours business which has allowed them to afford a lifestyle that most of the men he works alongside at the mill envy. At work while she runs the business, he enjoys her entertaining stories about the customers. He is aware that Clarence visits regularly, spends time with Josephine and brings her gifts. At times it bothers him that Clarence is Josephine's daddy, but he is satisfied Millie was honest about her indiscretion. He avoids thinking about their affair, as he intends to live the rest of his days on earth with the love of his life—Millie Stewart.

Millie and the girls return to the living room, and Thomas Jr. asks if he can go over to his friend, Arthur's house to play. Millie looks at him and thinks about it for a few moments. "You can go, but don't let that boy get you in trouble. You'd better not climb on the roof or do anything else foolish with him. Just last week I saw him jump off the garage before his mama could get the words out of her mouth to tell him not to. He's lucky he didn't break anything. I hope she broke that switch on his behind when she whipped him."

"And I haven't forgotten when he rolled across the street in his new Easter suit; I wanted to whip his butt for his mama. I don't know what gets in to him, but you'd better not let him talk you into joining in on any of his shenanigans. And you get home before it gets dark." He heads toward the door before Millie can change her mind as Thomas Sr. retreats to the bedroom to change into his work clothes.

Millie tells Betty that after her daddy leaves, she can set up the tea set so she and Josephine can have a tea party. This reminds an already uncomfortable Josephine that they're going to have a talk. Josephine shudders as she can't imagine what her mama has to talk to her about. Thomas Sr. returns from the bedroom and kisses the ladies of his heart.

As he walks toward the door, Josephine runs over and hugs him tightly. "Daddy, I love you so much! I know God loves me 'cause he gave me you. You're the bestest daddy in the whole world!" Not to be outdone, Betty runs over and boots Josephine with her hip, knocking her aside so she can hug their daddy. He chuckles and tells Betty he loves her too.

"Well, I want some of this good loving," Millie says, and kisses him. "Be careful at work, Thomas. I'll see you early in the morning."

He grabs his lunch pail and hat, and wishes Millie luck with the customers. Trying to outshout each other, Betty and Josephine holler, "goodbye, Daddy" several times to the top of their lungs.

Thomas Sr. is barely out the door when Millie reminds Betty to go to her room. Betty is happy Josephine looks so uncomfortable and sneers as she leaves. Josephine is confused and doesn't understand why her Mama wants to have a woman-to-woman talk with her. Maybe it's because she's having a birthday soon. But she'd rather not be a woman just yet because it seems too confusing.

Millie sits on the sofa and motions for Josephine to sit down beside her. She talks in an unusually soft tone, telling her how much she appreciates her help with the household chores and party customers. Josephine smiles when Millie mentions how much Josephine spoils her daddy by scratching his head and rubbing his scalp with grease. She also tells her that she is a blessing to Grandma Kirksey. Josephine doesn't know why her mama is saying these nice things to her, but she loves doing things for them—especially her daddy.

Millie laughs nervously, and Josephine becomes even more uncomfortable. "Move over a little closer to me, baby. I want you to listen to me real good because I need you to understand what I say." Josephine reluctantly moves closer, wishing with all her might that her mama would just tell her the darn secret and be done with it.

Millie clears her throat, "Now we're a family—you, me, your daddy, your brother and sister. You're our first born—came along two years after me and your daddy were married."

Josephine beams, proud of her status as the oldest child. Her brief moment of happiness ends abruptly as Millie's pause seems endless. Josephine looks over at her mama and notices she is uneasy. "Now,

22

Josephine, you know Mr. Clarence who comes to Mama's parties, right?"

"Of course, Mama. He's so nice—and he's rich! He always brings me candy and money—and buys me pretty dresses too."

Millie stands and paces around the sofa. "Well, baby, I know you really love your daddy, and he loves you very much too. Now, Thomas will always be your daddy, but Mr. Clarence is your real father."

Josephine doesn't understand this woman talk at all. "Ma'am?" she says in bewilderment.

"I said daddy is still your daddy, but Mr. Clarence is your real father."

Totally confused, she asks, "Mama, if Daddy is my daddy, how can Mr. Clarence be my father too? I don't want Mr. Clarence to be my father. Mama, I don't understand!" Tears swell up in Josephine's eyes, but Millie's tone turns frigid as she repeats the devastating, unwelcome truth. Josephine struggles to understand what her mama's words mean. Is she really saying her daddy is not her daddy? That can't be true! Tears pour down her face as she protests, and asks if Mr. Clarence can stop being her daddy if she doesn't take any more gifts.

Millie's frustration intensifies and she doesn't muster an ounce of compassion; "The gifts don't matter, Clarence and I made you, not Daddy and me."

Millie heads to the bedroom to get ready for the party customers. She reiterates to Josephine that she better not say anything to anybody about Mr. Clarence—especially her daddy. "This is our secret. Now you wipe your face and get up to your room for that tea party with Betty." Josephine can't make her body move. "Do you hear me talking to you?" Feeling like her world just stopped, Josephine is unsure if she's speaking aloud as she acknowledges that she hears.

Millie leaves the room, and Josephine falls to her knees, sobbing, "God, I love my daddy so much. He tells me I'm his special angel. But God, Mama just told me Mr. Clarence is my daddy too; but I don't want anybody else to be my daddy! Just because Mr. Clarence gives me things, does he have to be my daddy, too? God, if I don't take them anymore, can Daddy be my only daddy again? Please tell me because I don't understand. This hurts me so much!" Josephine is still crying as Millie calls out to her to get to her room. She wipes her eyes, and a voice she doesn't recognize as her own, whispers, "Yes, Mama." In a trance-like state, she walks toward her room, hoping Betty is in a friendly mood. She prays that if only for a few minutes, she can escape this nightmare. Her world is totally upside down; her little heart is broken.

CHAPTER FOUR

Josephine is eight years old today and is blossoming into a beautiful young girl. Her mama baked her favorite buttermilk chocolate cake with cream cheese icing. The family sang "Happy Birthday", and as a special celebration, they went to the ice cream parlor. Josephine was delighted as she was expecting the vanilla ice cream her mama usually makes.

It is early evening and the party guests will soon arrive. The smell of Millie's freshly-brewed batch of peach moonshine is heavy in the air, enticing the customers to drink more of the intoxicating liquor. When the customers drink more alcohol, they eat more food—which means more money for Millie. Josephine is especially excited as customers usually give her pennies for her birthday—and if she's lucky, a few might give her a whole nickel.

Josephine and Betty play Cooncan in their bedroom, and Josephine is winning the hand. As usual, Betty is upset about losing; plus she knows Mama is going to call Josephine to help with the guests soon. Josephine sees the storm brewing and tries to pacify her spoiled sister. "Betty, if I get a nickel tonight I'll give it to you if you quit being so mad." Betty likes it when her big sister bribes her.

"You always get money from the party guests. It's not fair that you get to help Mama, but I don't. It's just not fair, Josephine!"

Josephine has heard this countless times. "Betty, Mama decides who helps her, and I always share the money I get with you. Mama gives you money too—and you don't have to work like I do. It's hard waiting on the customers sometimes. They start drinking that moonshine, and get loud and say and do things I wish I didn't have to see or hear. I just pretend like I don't see them."

Betty thinks about the gifts Mr. Clarence always gives Josephine and is envious. She hears the grown folks say that he is Josephine's daddy, but she really doesn't understand how that could be. It seems strange for Josephine—or anybody else for that matter—to have two daddies.

Darn it; it's just not fair—Josephine always gets more of everything. "Why does Mr. Clarence always bring you money and presents but never brings me anything?"

Josephine prays Mama will call her so she can escape Betty's wrath. "I always share with you, and you get to wear the dresses he buys when I outgrow them. Please, Betty, it's my birthday. Let's be happy and not talk about this anymore. Please, pretty please?"

"Okay, but I still don't like it! And Josephine, why do you stay up under Daddy so much? Every day, you're up under Daddy! He's my daddy, so you stay away from him."

Betty's stinging words hurt, "He's our daddy, Betty, and I love him, and I love you too. Let's play another game of Cooncan." She hugs Betty, knowing she is going to let her win so they can be happy. Josephine wishes her mama hadn't told her about Mr. Clarence. She hurts because the daddy she loves and adores isn't her real father, and she doesn't feel any differently about Mr. Clarence.

The customers are having a good time when Clarence arrives, clean as the Board of Health in his charcoal gray, two-piece double breasted suit. His stylish brown hat and shoes, and his light gray tie complete his polished look. He feels real good as he anticipates Josephine's reaction to the birthday gifts he brought. Millie hears his familiar knock, and as she saunters toward the door, checks her hair and smoothes her dress so it will fall perfectly in place when he sees her.

She is overly cordial, "Hello, Clarence. How are you?"

He walks past her. "I'm fine, Millie. Where's Josephine?"

She tries not to take his hastiness personally, but she spent extra time choosing the purple flapper dress she knew would appeal to him; certain he would come tonight. Hell, he didn't even give her his usual head-to-toe once over! She collects herself, "In her bedroom."

Millie calls for Josephine, who enters the room looking doll-like in her flowered pink dress. Her beautiful long black hair, adorned with pink bows, has been straightened. Millie uses the hot comb on her hair only on special occasions. Josephine loves her long, flowing locks—a welcome change from the confining braids.

Mr. Clarence smiles, a deep sense of pride overtakes him. "Happy birthday, Josephine! You're extra pretty today. It's hard to believe you're eight already—seems like it was only yesterday when you were born." Millie rolls her eyes and walks away.

Mr. Clarence has two bags, and one is much larger than the other. Josephine tries to imagine what is in them, and begins to talk excitedly. "Mr. Clarence, I'm so happy! Me, my daddy, mama, my brother and sister went to the ice cream parlor, and I had a great big sundae all by myself. My daddy even let me have three scoops! My stomach's still full of that good-tasting ice cream." She looks around to see where Millie is to make sure she doesn't overhear before she whispers, "Don't tell Mama, but it tasted even better than the ice cream she always makes."

Clarence delights in seeing his daughter so happy, and laughs robustly. "I'm glad you enjoyed yourself and the ice cream; sounds like you're having a fun birthday. Here's something else for your sweet tooth." He hands her a large bag filled with her favorite candy.

"Wow, this is a whole lot of peanut butter cups. It'll take me a long time to eat these. Thanks, Mr. Clarence!"

Clarence knew he bought far too many, but he wanted to treat his daughter extra special for her birthday. "Well, just don't eat too many and get a stomach ache."

Josephine waits patiently while he fumbles to get the gift out of the large bag. He finally pulls it out, "I think you've been wanting these."

She can hardly believe her eyes. "Marionettes! I love marionettes! Thanks, Mr. Clarence!"

Mr. Clarence says he has something else for her. Something else? Peanut butter cups, marionettes and something else too? He is so rich! He tells her to hold her hand out and reaches into his pocket. Her shaking hands carefully place the marionettes back in the bag. When Mr. Clarence pulls his hand out, it is filled with coins that look like they may be quarters. She wonders how many he's giving her—four, maybe five? She holds her hand out, preparing to use both hands if necessary. Mr. Clarence counts the coins one by one as he drops them into her hand. She has to use her other hand to hold the coins as he counts all the way up to eight! She squeals in total delight and catches herself as she doesn't want her mama to hear her and get mad. "Eight quarters! I'm rich! Oh, thanks, Mr. Clarence!" Josephine is beside herself—eight quarters is more money than she gets from her mama and tips in a whole a year—maybe longer!

Her hands are still shaking when Mr. Clarence gives her a little black cloth bag to put her coins in; which she does one by one, thinking that she is now as rich as he. Mr. Clarence gets down on one knee and takes her hand into his. "Josephine, when I'm over here, you can call me Daddy if you want. You know I am your daddy."

"Yes, Mama told me, but I don't want to call you daddy—I only call my daddy that."

A disappointed Clarence stands back up. Accustomed to having his way because of his prestige and power, he thought she would want to call him daddy. He collects himself, "Okay Josephine, maybe one day you'll want to—and you can—but only when I'm over here."

An excited, grateful Josephine hugs him before heading to her bedroom. "I'm gonna go hide my money so nobody can find it but me! Thanks so much for the all of the wonderful birthday presents, Mr. Clarence!"

Millie doesn't allow much to escape her, especially when it comes to Clarence, and has kept her eyes and ears on them while tending to her customers. She walks over, "Did I hear you tell Josephine to call you Daddy?"

"Yes, but only when I'm over here. And did you see her hug me? That was the first time she's ever done that." He struts like a peacock on display. "She's getting used to me being her father."

Millie is disgusted. "Why did you tell her that? Thomas is raising her, so he is her daddy. I don't want you making it hard on Josephine.

She has enough to deal with—people always tell her she looks different than her brother and sister—like it's something she did to herself. Now you want her to call you Daddy? If you love and care about her, just let her call you what she's comfortable with—Mr. Clarence. She doesn't need any more heartache—especially from you. She knows you're her biological father, but Thomas will always be her daddy. Clarence, we're her family."

"I'm aware of that, Millie. But I'm not going to pretend she's not my daughter. I won't deny her—after all, she is my blood!"

"Clarence, please lower your voice. That looked like a lot of money you gave her. How much was it?"

"Eight quarters—one for each birthday."

"Clarence, has the last of your good sense left you? That's far too much! I'll have to tell Thomas the customers were extra nice and gave her money to explain away all those quarters. That's going to be hard to believe with the economy being so tight. Or maybe I'll just make sure she only spends them ever so often. Why did you give her so much money on top of those expensive marionettes?"

"Because she's my daughter, and I wanted her to have them. But did you see her hug me?"

"Yes, I saw her. She's happy and is just being grateful, that's all."

Clarence doesn't say anything for a few seconds—his eyes linger on Millie's body as he looks her up and down. He walks behind her and stands close, softly stroking her cheeks with his finger. "Alright, woman, but we were good together though, weren't we?"

Millie jerks away, too upset to care about his flirtation. Clarence's look turns to one clearly of dismissal, and he waves his hand in the same manner. "Give me a glass of whiskey so I can get back home to my family."

She extends her hand, palm up, "That's a quarter, please."

He taunts her with his teasing smile, "Here you are." Holding eye contact, he reaches into his pocket again and pulls out another coin. "And of course, here's a nickel for your tip jar."

Unaffected by his attempts to disarm her, Millie retorts, "Thanks, Mayor. I have to go check on my other customers." She walks away, and in an effort to aggravate him, intentionally makes him wait a few minutes before taking his drink to him. She walks up as he's working his charm on a beautiful younger woman who has been flirting with him for some time. Clarence is nonchalant as he accepts the glass. Millie glares at the woman, who excuses herself and hastily slips away. Millie then walks toward her other customers without uttering another word. Clarence motions for the woman to come back over, but she smiles and stays safely on the other side of the room. He laughs and remains seated in his chair, drinking his whiskey.

Josephine hides away in her room, daring to take some time to enjoy her marionettes. She thinks about all of the things she can buy with the money, and carefully hides the coins so Betty won't snoop and find them. It'll take years to spend this much money! Her mama calls her and she hurriedly goes back out, hoping she isn't mad at her for taking so long.

CHAPTER FIVE

Several days later, Josephine and Shirley, her bestest friend since they were toddlers, are at the general store. Shirley is the same age as Josephine and is plain-looking, shy and somewhat gawky. She is quiet around most people, but talks incessantly to Josephine. Josephine told Shirley about Mr. Clarence being her daddy, and she agreed to keep her secret. Bruce and Yolanda West, Shirley's parents, are neighbors and friends with Josephine's parents. The Wests and Stewarts have remained close since the Wests moved to Unaka Street. Bruce works the graveyard shift with Thomas Sr., so he doesn't go to Millie's after-hours place; but Yolanda goes once in a while.

"Shirley, I'm glad you came with me. I have to get these things for Mama, and I can spend some of my birthday money."

"I was happy to get away from my little brother. He's a real stinker sometimes—almost as bad as Betty. Well, maybe not that bad, but bad enough." They both laugh, knowing their comments about their younger siblings are not exaggerations.

Shirley is curious as to how much money Mr. Clarence gave Josephine for her birthday. "Josephine, what did Mr. Clarence give you for your birthday? I bet he gave you lots of money since he's rich!"

Josephine giggles, "Shirley, Mr. Clarence gave me marionettes! Yes, he really got them for me. And he gave me a huge bag of peanut butter cups. They'll last for months, even with me sharing them!"

"I know you're happy! You've been wanting the marionettes for a long time! And that sounds like a lot of candy. Did he give you money, too?"

Josephine squeals, "He gave me the candy, the marionettes and eight quarters!"

"Eight quarters?! Mr. Clarence is really, really rich to give you that much money! My parents told me it's bad times and a lot of families are poor. Wow, Mr. Clarence is rich alright."

Josephine hisses "shhhh," and puts her finger across her lips so Shirley will lower her voice. No one is standing close to them, but Josephine is not going to take any chances. "Mama said not to let anybody else know I had the money—especially daddy. It'll take me forever to spend it."

"Gee whiz, I wish I had two daddies, then I'd have lots of money too! And I haven't told anybody else that Mr. Clarence is your daddy either—just like I promised."

Josephine's smile vanishes, "Shirley, I wish he was your daddy and not mine. I don't want two daddies, but since Mama was with him, I have two. I wish she had just been with my daddy. It hurts when everybody says how different I look from my brother and sister, and sometimes people even ask me if we have the same daddy. Nobody understands how I feel inside. I didn't ask for two daddies. I love my daddy, and I only want one. Please don't say that to me again, Shirley."

She didn't mean to upset her teary-eyed friend; Shirley was just impressed with her bounty. "I didn't mean to hurt your feelings. I just wish I had the money and gifts Mr. Clarence gives you, that's all. But I won't say anything else about you having two daddies. Okay?"

"Thanks, Shirley. Hey, do you want 10 cents to spend on something?"

Shirley does a happy dance. "Ten cents?! I would love to have 10 cents—that's a whole lot of money! Wow, now I'm rich! Thanks, Josephine!"

"You're welcome. What are you going to buy?"

Shirley's mind races as her eyes dance around the store. "I don't know for sure—I can probably buy 20 things with that much money. Let's look around!" They browse for a few minutes, and Shirley goes to look at dolls while Josephine goes to find the items on her mama's list. After seeing how happy Shirley is about the money, she'll share with her more often. Her mama told her to spend only one quarter every three months, and even though she's glad she has the money to share, she's still not happy Mr. Clarence is her father.

Josephine walks to the fabric section and notices a familiar face. Mr. Clarence is standing with a woman and two children. They're dressed fashionably, like the other rich people in town. The children stand quietly while the woman looks at fabric. Josephine smiles, walks up and speaks, "Hello, Mr. Clarence." He looks at her as if he has never laid eyes on her before, in this or another lifetime.

"Excuse me, but I don't know you," he says as if she's a vagrant asking for a handout.

"Mr. Clarence, I'm Josephine…uh, Millie's daughter. How are…."

Clarence cuts her off mid-sentence. "Don't bother me—can't you see my family and I are shopping? I don't know you or Millie. Move away from us. Go on now, quit bothering us."

Josephine is confused. Is this the same man who was at her house on her birthday a few days ago, asking her to call him daddy? How can he act like he doesn't know her—she's in the store spending one of the quarters he gave her. "But, Mr. Clarence."

Clarence is perturbed, "But nothing. I don't know you. Move away so my family and I can get back to our shopping. Go on little girl, move along."

Stunned, Josephine is appreciative that the legs she can no longer feel beneath her move her in a direction away from him. As she turns to walk away, she mutters, "Oh, uh, okay." She doesn't understand why he's being so mean—he is always so nice at her mama's parties.

Clarence's wife, Leslee, is standing only a few steps away. She walks over to him, "Clarence, who is that child? She seems to know you and was confused when you told her to move away. How uncanny that she's wearing the same dress our daughter is wearing, but only in a different color. And who is Millie?"

Clarence calmly responds, "I don't know the little girl or Millie. Leslee, I am the mayor, and people do know me."

"She didn't call you Mayor; she called you Mr. Clarence."

He looks around for a distraction, "Don't bother me with this foolishness, woman. Look at that red hat over there—it looks like it was made just for my baby." He kisses her on the cheek to further garner her attention.

Leslee, who is more than willing to end the conversation about the little girl, coos, "Oh Clarence, I think it should belong to me. Let's go over there so I can try it on. I think I need a new pair of shoes too."

Clarence smiles, "Whatever you want dear, whatever you want."

Josephine finds Shirley, as tears stream down her face. She tries to tell her what happened, but Shirley can only make out that she saw Mr. Clarence. "Josephine, why are you crying? You see him all the time." In between sobs, Josephine tells Shirley what happened. "He said what?!"

"He said he didn't know me and to stop bothering him. Do you see how hurt I get for being born? I don't know why God punishes me so much! I didn't ask for two daddies."

Quiet, shy, Shirley has become angry, crazed Shirley. "Mr. Clarence shouldn't have treated you that way. Do you want me to go and kick him? You know I will! She hugs her friend while looking around for Mr. Clarence like a sharp-eyed hawk. Where is he?" She hopes to land her eyes on him so she can march right up and kick him in his shins as hard as she can.

"Shirley, I just want to go outside. We can come back in a little while. I just want to get out of here."

"Okay, Josephine, just try not to think about Mr. Clarence. I love you, so think about me instead of him, okay?"

Josephine wonders what would have happened if her mama was there. She knew Mr. Clarence would have spoken to both of them, because he certainly wouldn't have ignored Millie Stewart. No, he wouldn't have ignored or mistreated her if her mama was there.

They are standing outside when Mr. Clarence and his family come out. Josephine doesn't look at him, and has to hold Shirley back from making good on her promise. They go back inside and get the items on Millie's list, and Shirley buys something for her and her brother. Josephine doesn't feel like shopping for herself; she just wants to get back to the love and safety of her daddy and mama.

CHAPTER SIX

It is the fourth Saturday in October, and Josephine is on her way to her usual respite—Grandma's house. She hasn't slept well since seeing Mr. Clarence at the store two weeks ago. The scene replays in her mind like it is on a movie reel; the shock feels fresh over and over again. Mr. Clarence is always so nice when he comes to her mama's parties. She wonders if he's nice because he's around the party guests, or because he's around her mama? It certainly can't be because he's around her; if so he wouldn't have acted like he didn't know her. She's doesn't know what to think, and is hurt and confused.

Josephine has thought about telling her mama what happened, but she's afraid she will get mad. She knows how happy her mama is when Mr. Clarence is around, and she doesn't want her to think she did anything to make him act so mean. She thinks about talking to her daddy but is afraid of what he would think. The short walk seems like forever, but she finally arrives at Grandma's house and is relieved to see Grandma's smiling face when she opens the door. "Precious flower, you are truly my angel." Grandma always makes Josephine feel so special.

Grandma has noticed Josephine hasn't been quite her happy-go-lucky self lately, and can see an unsettled look in her eyes. "Baby, tomorrow I'm going to preach about taking your pain to the Lord. God doesn't want you to be in pain—whether it's in your body, your heart or your mind. God wants you to be happy and feel joy."

Josephine can't believe her ears. God must have told Grandma she is in pain. She feels her grandma will understand. "Grandma, I'm in a lot of pain."

"What's wrong, my sweet flower? You look just fine to me."

"Grandma, I have pain in my heart."

"In your heart? The doctor needs to come over and take a look at you! Did you tell your mama? How bad does it hurt, baby?"

"My heart doesn't hurt in my body. My heart hurts because of Mr. Clarence."

"Has Mr. Clarence done something to you? You know you can tell me." Her heart races like a pack of wild stallions as she anticipates Josephine's response.

"I don't want Mr. Clarence to be my father—I only want my daddy to be my daddy! I try not to think about it, but since Mama told me, it just hurts a little all the time. And when I see Mr. Clarence, I feel ashamed of myself. I smile and act happy, but I don't feel good inside. People always say I look different than Thomas Jr. and Betty, and that hurts too. But Grandma, when I look at my daddy, that's when it hurts me most. I don't want Daddy to stop loving me because Mama got me with Mr. Clarence. In my heart he's not my real father—Daddy is!"

Grandma is relieved it isn't a physical condition, but sees that Josephine is hurting. "My precious granddaughter, your true father is God. It doesn't matter how you came to this earth. He made you in His image and loves you because you are His special child. So don't let your heart hurt anymore, baby. You're the most precious child I've been blessed to know. God doesn't want you to feel pain; He wants you to feel joy!" Pastor Kirksey gets wound up and starts preaching like she's in the pulpit. Josephine tunes out, wishing her grandmother would just listen and not preach all of the time.

"Me and Shirley were at the store right after my birthday, and I saw Mr. Clarence with his family. I went up and spoke to him and he acted like he didn't know me, and told me to get away. He said it twice. And when I said I was Millie's daughter, he said he didn't know Mama either. It hurt me so much. He's always nice to me when he comes to Mama's parties, but he was so mean at the store. It's like I'm special to him sometimes, and other times I don't matter at all. When he came to our house on my birthday, he told me I could call him Daddy. But I told him I only call my daddy that." Josephine starts to cry, and Pastor Kirksey has to say a silent prayer as she struggles to keep her Christian side intact. How dare he treat Josephine so cruelly!

"Honey, don't you worry your pretty little head about Mr. Clarence.

He acted foolishly and never should have been so cruel to you." She puts her ample arms around Josephine and cradles her head to her chest while trying to soothe her.

"Grandma, I can't make the hurt go away." Josephine continues to cry, and Grandma holds her close, stroking her hair and rubbing her arms.

"Just think about the people who love you and how happy they make you, precious granddaughter. Don't let the bad things get the better of you. God loves you, I love you, your mama and daddy, your brother and sister all love you. A lot of people love you, so you don't need to be sad, baby."

Josephine wishes she didn't feel sad, but she does—awfully sad. "Grandma, it still hurts." She wants to stop crying—she wants to let the pain go, but the crying and the pain stay.

Grandma generally knows what to say and do, but is at a loss for words. She wishes Millie had stayed within the confines of her marriage. "Try to stop crying, baby, you're loved so much. Remember, God doesn't make mistakes—you're His child and He loves you, as we all do. Please stop thinking about Mr. Clarence; he is a foolish, foolish man to treat you like he did. And don't you worry, baby, vengeance is mine, saith the Lord! He'll deal with Mr. Clarence, yes, He will." Grandma holds Josephine, gently strokes her face and hair, and tells her to trust in God. She rocks and hums softly to her.

She doesn't ask, but wonders if Josephine told Millie. On second thought, she is certain that if Millie Stewart knew, the explosion would be such that the entire sky in Harriman, Tennessee would be lit up like fireworks on the Fourth of July. "Come on baby, let's read the scriptures so we can hear what God wants you to hear. Remember, you're His child, and He will carry you through this and everything else that hurts."

Minnie Kirksey feels a twinge of guilt because she drove Millie to marry Thomas, knowing she wasn't in love with him. She did what every loving mother would do to make sure her daughter had a good life. Thomas is a good man, an honest, hard-working man, who loves

Millie without end. Minnie knew her daughter wasn't in love with him; but prayed Millie would grow to love him as her husband.

Minnie recalls seeing a change in Millie when she began to work on Clarence's campaign. A demure person all of her life, Millie began dressing provocatively and wearing heavy make up. She became distant toward Thomas; the absence of affection toward him was evident to her mother. Minnie's prayer was that after the campaign ended, Millie would grow closer to the man she married. Instead, when it was over, Millie seemed to have a void in her life. Minnie heard about Millie and Clarence's affair; and though she was a person of the cloth, she was ashamed of her daughter. When Josephine was born, Minnie saw the fruit of Millie and Clarence's passion the moment she laid eyes on her granddaughter.

Josephine settles down and starts to read the verses for Grandma. She is still baffled about how Grandma knows the Bible so well. "Grandma, how do you know which verses to tell me to read if you don't know how to read?"

"I memorized the books when I was a little girl. Your Great Grandpa Michael would read them to me when I was about three years old, and I'd recite the names, numbers and the verses back to him, word for word. I can't do that with every verse now, but I pretty much know where they are and what's in most of them. Now, read the verses I gave you real slow for me, baby."

Josephine starts to feel a little better as she reads, and Grandma explains the meaning of the verses. Grandma then prays for God to make Josephine's broken heart whole again. "Remember, Josephine, He can and He will fix it for you. God can fix everything and everybody!" She prays again, and Josephine closes her eyes real tight, praying for God to take her pain away.

Grandma goes to the kitchen to get Josephine's peach ice tea. Josephine realizes she sat down without apologizing to Jesus for sitting on His face, and does so immediately. Her mood lifts after a few sips of Grandma's special tea and the humorous stories about the good ole days. All too soon, it is time for her to go back home. Josephine hopes Mr. Clarence, who hasn't been over since she saw him at the store, doesn't come to their house tonight, or ever again. In spite of what her mama says, he's not her real daddy anyway—her daddy, Thomas, is.

The Saturday night party customers arrive, and Josephine is too busy to think about Mr. Clarence. She enjoys the customers, and some of them who haven't been there since her birthday give her money. Their home is crowded—it seems like everybody in Harriman is there tonight, except for Mr. Clarence. Josephine overhears one of the customers ask her mama about him. Millie sounds sad when she says he hasn't been by in a couple of weeks. Josephine hopes her mama isn't sad because she thinks Josephine misses him; because she doesn't—not even a little bit.

The next morning the Stewart family and Pastor Kirksey walk to Sunday morning service. Pastor Kirksey takes her seat in the pulpit, and the family takes their respective seats in the pews. She is anxious to preach her sermon on joy and pain; hoping Josephine listens carefully, even though she heard it yesterday. When Grandma calls on her to read, sadness overwhelms Josephine; and she struggles, stumbling over some of the words.

Grandma reassures her from the pulpit, "That's alright, baby, take your time." Josephine looks at her mama, who stares disapprovingly at her. Thomas Sr. pats Josephine lightly on the back. She clears her throat, and regains her composure, hoping to avoid another mean look from her mama. She is already in pain, and doesn't want to have to contend with her mama being angry on top of it.

Josephine sighs with relief after finishing; then sits down and lowers her head, glancing up only at her daddy. Thomas Sr. hugs her and whispers that she did a wonderful job. She snuggles up against him and takes a quick glance at Millie, who still has a disapproving look on her face. Thomas Sr. looks at Millie, his eyes clearly communicating for her to look elsewhere. Millie turns her attention to her mama, who is thoroughly enraptured in her sermon. Familiar thoughts of good times with Clarence invade Millie's mind, and she finds a place of contentment.

As is their customary Sunday routine, the family enjoys a tasty dinner. Grandma, tired from preaching but satisfied from Millie's meal, returns home, and the Stewart family relaxes in their living room. Millie has been somewhat distant to Josephine since church, and Josephine doesn't want her mama to stay mad about her messing up. She is going to tell her what happened at the store, and hopes it will help her mama understand that she's hurt about what Mr. Clarence did. And maybe it would help explain why Mr. Clarence hasn't been to the parties.

When she and Millie are in the kitchen cleaning the dishes, Josephine finds a moment of bravery. "Mama, something happened when I went to the store a couple of weeks ago." She takes a deep breath and shares what happened, careful not to leave out any details. She even mentions that she and Mr. Clarence's daughter were wearing the same dress, but in different colors.

Millie is surprisingly compassionate when she responds, "Josephine, I'm sorry. I had no idea. Clarence is wrong, and has no business treating you that way. Don't you worry, I'll be sure to talk to him." In a calm, cool and collected manner she adds, "You shouldn't have kept this to yourself. I could tell something was wrong. And, baby, if anybody ever mistreats you again, be sure to tell me as soon as it happens. Don't keep it to yourself, okay?" Josephine nods her head, astonished at her mama being so nice. "Now, you just go on in there with your daddy and the kids and enjoy the radio program. I'll finish cleaning the kitchen. Go on now."

Josephine starts to ask her mama if she is sure, but after she saw the expression on her face, which looked like she wanted to hurt somebody, she did what she was told. Josephine removes her apron and gets out of the kitchen as quickly as her legs could move without running. Once Josephine is out of ear range, Millie, in the lowest audible tone she could muster, curses Clarence Eric McElroy—and his mama—for having him. She now knows why he hasn't been over. But why would he stay away—certainly not out of fear. After all, he is the big time mayor of Harriman, Tennessee! She welcomes the few pots she has left to scrub, as it gives her something constructive to do while she continues to cuss and pull herself together. Clarence wouldn't appreciate anybody treating his other children like that, and he isn't going to get away with treating her daughter like that, either. And on top of hurting Josephine, he denies knowing her too? Damn him!

Mamas' Drama

CHAPTER SEVEN

The children stay at home while Millie and Thomas Sr. go to the general store. They are in the living room listening to "Happy Days are Here Again" on the Victrola. Thomas Jr. and Josephine are having fun playing a game of Cooncan, and Betty is playing with her dolls. Betty grows tired of her dolls and wants to play cards. Josephine tells her to wait until they finish their hand and then they will deal her in on the next one. Betty is in a bratty mood and takes full advantage of the adults being absent. She walks over to Josephine and Thomas Jr. and annoys them by singing loudly as they try to talk to each other. Josephine and Thomas Jr. do their best to ignore her, but hurry to finish the hand so they can deal her in and keep the peace.

Josephine wins the hand, jumps up and shouts, "Cooncan! Some coons can't and some coons can!" Betty immediately accuses her of cheating.

Thomas Jr. speaks up. "Betty, she didn't cheat. She won fair and square—she even beat daddy last time!"

Betty jumps up and calls Josephine a spoiled daddy's girl. Josephine laughs and tells her to calm down. "I don't know why you're laughing, Josephine, Daddy's not really your daddy anyway! He's me and Thomas Jr.'s daddy—but he's not yours. You're always hugging on him. Stay away from my daddy! Go hug Mr. Clarence—that's your daddy!"

Josephine can't utter a word as she fights the tears that are swelling up in her eyes.

Thomas Jr. rises to Josephine's defense, "Shut up, Betty, you don't know what you're talking about!"

"Yes, I do!" Betty retorts. "I hear Mama and Daddy fussing, and Daddy says Josephine ain't his—she's Mr. Clarence's. I hear it with my own two ears." She looks at Josephine, "I bet Daddy only pays you attention because he feels sorry for you. He doesn't really love you, and neither does your real daddy. So now!"

Thomas Jr. gets angry, "Betty, you better be quiet! Daddy loves us all!"

Josephine speaks, wishing this is the last time she has to have this conversation. "Betty, Daddy is my only daddy in my heart. And when you say mean words like that, it hurts me. Losing a card game shouldn't make you want to hurt me. I know you don't understand—it happened to me and I don't really understand. But I really love my family, and it's not my fault about Mr. Clarence."

Betty continues her rant, "Daddy always gives you all of the attention all of the time. I wish he'd pay more attention to me, 'cause I am his daughter!"

Thomas Jr. becomes so angry he shouts, "Betty, shut up right now or I'm gonna hit you real hard!" He lunges at Betty, but Josephine jumps in between them to shield her.

Josephine is crying, "Thomas Jr., please don't touch her. Betty, you are my little sister, and I love you. I'm not going to be mad, but I want you to be nice and stop saying mean things."

Betty has a change of heart when she sees how badly her big sister is crying. "Okay Josephine, I'm sorry. You're the best sister ever!" She hugs and kisses Josephine on the cheek. "I'm going to my room and draw," she says as she moves well out of Thomas Jr.'s reach.

Thomas Jr., who usually has to be reminded to give a hug, hugs his big sister like there's no tomorrow. "Josephine, you know Daddy loves you more than anything. Don't let Betty hurt you—she doesn't know better, and she's just jealous."

"Thanks, Thomas Jr., but what hurts me more than anything is that I want Daddy to be my real daddy. I just hate it that Mr. Clarence is my daddy."

Thomas Jr. feels helpless because he can't change things for her. "Don't worry about Mr. Clarence or his snooty family. We're your real family, and we love you. Please stop crying."

"I love you too," Josephine whimpers while in her brother's comforting arms. She is glad her mama and daddy aren't home because she would be crying buckets of tears; especially if she saw her daddy. She wishes she felt this safe and loved all of the time.

It has been three weeks since Clarence has seen Josephine. He misses her, and has apologized many times in his head, but knows he needs to apologize in person. She is only an eight-year-old child, and she is his blood. He hates that he mistreated her, and needs to redeem himself. He is well aware that Millie will be enraged, and is hopeful customers are there so she will have to be relatively civil. He hasn't stayed away because of Millie; he's stayed away because he knows he hurt Josephine, and it's going to be a challenge to face her. His only other option is to not see his daughter; and that option is no longer acceptable.

He takes the usual inventory of himself before knocking. Unfortunately for him, no other customers have arrived, and when she hears his knock, Millie instantly becomes angry. She flings the door wide open; and doesn't pay one bit of attention to his sharp Palm Beach suit or his smell—nothing about his fine ass matters to her at that moment. She lights into Clarence with reckless abandon, angry about the way he mistreated his daughter and denied knowing her. He listens, as he knows it is fruitless to interrupt. "You were the one who insisted she know you're her father, and you said you wouldn't deny her, but you did! And you said you didn't know me? Ooh, I want to call you names, but there are far too many of them!"

Clarence is apologetic and calmly responds, "Millie, I didn't want Leslee to see her resemblance to our daughter. On top of looking like each other, they were wearing the same dress."

"I don't give a damn about your wife or what she sees! You shouldn't have treated Josephine that way, Clarence. She didn't deserve that, especially from you!"

"I told you I don't want my wife or my kids to know about Josephine."

Millie, getting angrier by the second, retorts, "Why not, Thomas knows!"

Clarence remains calm, "You are lucky Thomas stays with you. If I tell Leslee, she would leave me, and I don't want to lose my family. You should understand, Millie. What you and I did, we can't change—we had an affair and Josephine is the result. Hell, I only know she's mine because she looks so much like me."

Millie mutters through clenched teeth, "Look, Clarence, I'm trying not to cuss you out. I know full well what happened—you didn't make her by yourself! I'm only concerned about how it affects Josephine! You wouldn't appreciate anybody talking to your other children like that, now would you?" Clarence doesn't respond, as he doesn't want to fuel Millie's anger. "Josephine didn't make this mess, and I'm tired of her getting hurt. So for the record, if you ever do that to her again, I'll bring her to your precious home, and we'll all talk about you being her biological father. You better quit playing games with my daughter's heart. And you'd better not hurt her again, either. It's enough Clarence, enough! And you can say you don't know me, but you'll never forget what you and I did, especially in that hotel room."

Clarence tires of Millie's ranting, "I don't like threats, Millie. And what we did in that hotel room is over!" He walks through the living room, and as he gestures his hand around the room, he issues her a warning. "I could make sure your little after hours place gets raided, and you go to jail. It is against the law you know, and I am the mayor! So don't you dare threaten me, Millie Stewart! And you better not show up at my home either. I just told you what I'd do, and trust me I will have you put in jail if you cross me. Now, we'd hate for Josephine to have two daddies but no mama, wouldn't we?"

Millie is perched to respond, but Josephine enters the room, so she rolls her eyes and walks away. Josephine is polite, but indifferent when she speaks to Clarence. He collects himself before speaking. "Hi Josephine, I brought your favorite candy, and I picked out a special dress for you."

Josephine usually looks forward to his gifts, but today she only wishes for him to leave. "That's alright, Mr. Clarence. I still have lots of candy from my birthday, and I don't want a new dress."

Clarence's guilt deepens, and he is sincere as he apologizes. "Josephine, I came to apologize. I hurt you, and I'm awfully sorry. I know it's hard for you to speak to me when I'm here, but not speak when I'm with my family. But unfortunately, that's the way it has to be right now."

His apology doesn't make sense to Josephine. "Mr. Clarence, you're the mayor, and everybody in town speaks to you, and you speak back. Why am I different? I didn't do anything wrong."

Clarence is awkward as he tries to find an answer that would make her understand. "Because I'm married and have a family. I'm so sorry if that hurts your feelings, but it's just the way it has to be."

"Well, it hurts my feelings a whole lot! You told me to call you daddy when you're over here, but then you tell me not to speak to you when you're with your family. I don't understand, Mr. Clarence! I'm your child too, even though I don't want to be! I wish you and mama never made me!" She storms out of the room, crying her heart out.

Millie walks over and gets so close to Clarence that she feels his breath on her face. "Do you see how much you hurt her? Are you happy now?"

Clarence doesn't want to hear Millie's mouth—he knows he's hurt Josephine, and he feels terrible about it. "I apologized and I tried to explain it the best I could. But I'm not losing everything that's dear to me because of you or Josephine. You make sure she understands she's not to speak to me when she sees me with my family."

Millie tries to reason with him. "Clarence, she's only a child. You could at least speak to her—she will always call you Mr. Clarence."

He walks to the door, ending the conversation before Millie starts to rage again. "I don't like hurting her, but I'm not jeopardizing everything either. And remember, Millie, if you get any ideas about coming to my home—your next home will be a jail cell. Goodbye."

Millie slams the door and mumbles "asshole" to the man that is now on the other side of it. She calls teary-eyed Josephine into the room, and they sit on the sofa. "Baby, I'm so sorry about Mr. Clarence. You have to suffer because of something I did. I can't tell you how much I hurt because I've hurt you. I love you, and I'm glad you're my child."

"Mama, that's the first time you ever told me you love me."

Millie is so upset that she doesn't react. "And to make sure Mr. Clarence doesn't hurt you anymore, if you see him outside of this house, just act like he's not alive. Okay, baby?"

Josephine feels better, especially after hearing her mama tell her she loves her. "Okay, mama," she says, as she reaches out to hug Millie, who initially turns away, and then turns back to hug her.

Millie realizes why Clarence could be so adamant that Josephine not speak to him when he is with his family. The resemblance of their daughters is striking. She thinks he is afraid that his highfalutin Leslee may notice it even if Josephine is only around for a moment. But she can't figure out why Clarence wants Josephine to call him Daddy, even if it is only at her home. She wishes she knew, but she can't make sense out of his nonsense. Millie holds Josephine until a knock on the door interrupts them as the party guests begin to arrive. Josephine is in second heaven—her mama held her and told her she loves her. Millie stands to answer the door and thinks about how sharp Clarence looked, and smiles in spite of her anger. She still hasn't figured out why she is so beguiled by him. Those few nights of making sweet and unbridled love to, with and on him has penetrated Millie's soul forever.

CHAPTER EIGHT

Hard times prevail in 1934 as the Depression and the downturn in the economy take even more of a devastating toll on the nation. Harriman, Tennessee and the Stewart family are no exception. Parker's Steel Mill recently laid off half of their 700 employees; and the outlook isn't much better for those who remain employed. Thomas Sr.'s 20 years' seniority doesn't save him or his long-time friend and neighbor, Bruce West, from the lay off.

The Great Migration of people moving from the South to the North is an option many families choose for an opportunity to survive the struggling economy. Bruce's relatives have told him about the booming industries and job openings up North. The Columbus Malleable is an iron-casting company that has recently been built and is hiring.

"Thomas, my relatives up North say they're building new factories and hiring workers there. I'm driving up this week to see if I like the city, and if I can get hired on. If I do, I'm relocating my family. From what they say, there are plenty of jobs to be had. Do you want to go with me? My relatives like Columbus, Ohio, but warn that it gets cold in the winter. But they say you get used to the change in weather over time. One thing I know, I'd rather be cold with money, than warm and broke. Are you interested in going?"

Thomas is apprehensive, but decides to take Bruce up on his offer. "Well, it won't hurt to look into it. I'll have a tough time convincing Millie to leave, but I need to make sure we survive this Depression. The mayor is supposed to find me a job, but I don't want a handout from him. I can take care of my own family. When do we leave?"

Bruce chuckles, "How about in two days? By that time, Millie may be speaking to you again after you break the news to her."

"You know my wife well; she's a strong-willed woman, and runs the household, but I'm the head of my family. I'll go up North with you; I need to find a job."

He was confident while talking to Bruce, but Thomas knows it's going to be tough to get Millie to leave Harriman. Prohibition remains in force, but the moonshine business survives even in a bad economy as people seek an escape from their problems. But these past few years haven't been very profitable for Millie's after-hours business. The family can't survive solely on money from the illegal operation, which could be shut down anytime Mayor Clarence McElroy withdraws his protection. Thomas accepts his responsibility to keep his family secure and will do whatever is necessary to make sure he earns wages to support them.

He thinks long and hard as to how best to approach Millie. Certain she won't leave her mama, he plans to take Mother Kirksey with them. She has been very good to him, and is the mama he's missed since his own passed when he was barely 16. Plus, it's always good to have a praying woman nearby.

Thomas approaches Millie after dinner. "Millie, you're aware that the factories here and in neighboring towns are closing. I need to get another job. I don't want to lose everything we've worked so hard to get. People are leaving Harriman and relocating to other states to find jobs. We may have to leave as well."

Millie has been thinking for some time that Thomas would reach this point. "Clarence is looking for a job for you, Thomas. I'll call and ask him when you can expect to be working. It should be soon."

Slightly annoyed, Thomas responds, "Millie, I'm a man, and I can find my own job and take care of my own family. We may have to relocate up North, though."

"Up North? Do you mean north of Harriman or in another state up North?"

"Up North in another state, Millie—like Ohio."

"I'm not moving to another state, Thomas—Harriman, Tennessee is my home. I was born here, and I plan to die right here!"

Thomas expected her reaction. "Millie, I've been looking for work, and all the industries are drying up. Bruce has relatives in Columbus, Ohio. They say the factories up there are hiring, and I'd have a real good chance of getting a job."

"Well, I don't want to leave Harriman, and I'm certainly not going to leave my mama."

"I wouldn't expect you to leave Mother Kirksey—I don't plan to leave her either. I plan to take her to Ohio with us."

Millie can only internalize the other reason she doesn't want to leave Harriman—even after 14 years, she hasn't let go of her desire for him. The precious hours she spent with Clarence are etched in her soul as if tattoos. But she knows that when her husband puts his foot down, he will do what he feels is best, regardless of her protests. "Well, I don't like the idea of leaving, but we do have to survive."

Thomas is relieved, as she didn't resist as much as he thought she would. "Yes, we do. I'm going to Ohio with Bruce in a couple of days. We'll be gone for a week to apply for jobs and look for housing if we are hired."

"Well, you go on up North and see if that's where we're supposed to live. I'll pack some food to take on the road with you." She doesn't think Thomas will find a job, but he needs to find that out for himself. She dismisses the thought of leaving Harriman just as quickly as their conversation ends. The following day, she calls Clarence and reminds him to find work for Thomas as he promised, but doesn't tell him about Thomas going up North to look for a job. After all, Thomas is not going to really find a job and move them all the way up North.

After two restless nights, Thomas Sr. and Bruce are ready to travel to Ohio. Mother Kirksey prays a powerful prayer, and after hugs and tears from their wives and children, they leave early Sunday morning on the eight-hour drive. They apply for jobs at The Columbus Malleable on Monday, and search for housing before the ink dries on the applications. Prayers are answered when they are told two days later that they are both hired. With the help of God and Bruce's relatives, they find homes down the street from each other on the east side of town.

They are unable to find Mother Kirksey a home in the same neighborhood, but she can live with Thomas Sr. and Millie until they find her a suitable place. He doesn't think Millie would want to run an after-hours business in Columbus anyway, as she could easily run amuck with the law without the protection of the mayor. Given that the children are older, the business would not be a good influence on them anyway; and if Mother Kirksey lives with them, her religion and Millie's alcohol business would not mix. But Thomas is not going to cross that bridge right now, and feels it will all work out. He thinks about how challenging the move will be for Millie, and hopes she will be happy in their new location.

Thomas and Bruce call their wives to tell them about the blessing of finding jobs and housing. Millie is lackluster upon hearing the news; but Thomas understands she will need time to adjust to the thought of leaving Harriman. Millie hangs up, calls Clarence, and asks him to come by. She wants to tell him about the move before he hears from other people in the small town. Clarence asks her if something is wrong, but Millie tells him she needs to talk to him in person, and preferably before the customers come this evening. Clarence commits to coming by, and hopes she isn't planning to go on a rant because he hasn't found Thomas a job. Even as mayor, he is challenged to find jobs for anybody as the factories continue to close and times get harder. But it will be good for him to see Josephine ahead of the rowdy customers.

Millie composes herself before opening the door, as she anticipates Clarence will give her pure hell about moving Josephine away. Clarence is his usual dapper self in his dark brown Italian designer suit with matching accessories. The cream colored shirt sets well with the chocolate brown—both the man and his clothing. He greets Millie with his usual flirtation, but she isn't responsive. "Clarence, I asked you to come by because I need to speak with you." She swallows the lump in her throat, "As you well know, Thomas is jobless, and my business has been down for some time."

"Yes, Millie, I know just how bad the economy is locally, nationally and beyond. It's rough on everybody, but I'm still looking for a job for

Thomas. Don't worry, I'm calling in a favor, and I'll get him something soon."

Millie sighs, "Well, Thomas got a job up North, and we'll be moving to Columbus, Ohio by June if we sell our home; or by the time school is in session in the fall, even if our home doesn't sell by then."

Clarence feels like he has been sucker punched. "Ohio? That's far north! So does that mean you're taking my daughter with you?"

"Yes, Josephine is moving with the rest of her family."

"I don't want you to move my daughter all the way up North! I've been trying to find a job for Thomas, but there's not much of a market here for blue collar workers."

"Clarence, he's found a good-paying factory job, and we're moving."

"When am I going to see Josephine? Are you sending her back to spend the summers with Mrs. Kirksey?"

"No, Mama is moving with us once her house sells; but you're welcome to come to visit whenever you want to see your daughter."

Clarence snaps, "I'm not giving you permission to move my daughter away, so you'd better find some other way to work this out."

Millie snaps back, "Your daughter? Your daughter? You mean the one you forbade to speak to you in public until a year ago? That daughter? Clarence, she's mine and Thomas' daughter—I had her and we're raising her. So I'd advise you to get off of your high horse and make the most of the time she has left here, because we're heading north. And just for the record, Josephine looks so much like you and your other daughter that folks can figure it out. So you should be happy your little secret will soon disappear from plain sight."

Clarence is livid. "Millie, I've done everything I could possibly do to be a part of Josephine's life. Do you think it's easy to be on the outside? And since you're putting things on the record, put this one on it—I would love to have her around as my other two children are, but because of our circumstances, I can't. Don't you ever give yourself the pleasure of thinking I feel good about not being close to my daughter. I see the confusion and pain she goes through, and it hurts me to my heart."

"Do you think I come to your after-hours place to be around all those irresponsible drunks? Their lifestyle is beneath me! I come because I want to see my daughter. She's not the only one who hurts because of our relationship; her daddy—me—hurts too. I love Josephine, and you taking her away from me is not going to be a relief; it's going to be a loss. I know you have to do what's best for your family, and I will try to get to Columbus from time to time. And when I do, it's not going to be at your after-hours business either; I will be there to visit my daughter!"

Millie is taken back at his display of emotion. "Clarence, I didn't realize until now just how much you love Josephine. I guess there are no real winners in our situation, but I know Josephine came here the way she was supposed to come. And I doubt I will run an after-hours business in Columbus—after all, I don't have any connections with the mayor there. And when you do come to see your daughter, you don't have to see me; I can live perfectly fine without you."

Clarence stares at her in silence, and the all too familiar passion begins to arise in Millie. It is short-lived, as a knock on the door interrupts them. Millie answers the door and lets the customer in as Josephine walks into the living room. An overwhelmed Clarence thinks about how much he is going to miss his daughter, but forces a smile on his face.

The following Sunday, Thomas and Bruce return, jubilant about their new homes and jobs. They have one week before starting to work, and decide it best that their families remain in Harriman at least until the end of the school year. The latest they will move to Ohio is in the fall, so the children can attend their new schools. Thomas and Bruce are hopeful their homes will sell during this time. If not, a realtor friend will keep them on the market until they do.

While in their children's presence, Millie pretends to be happy about the move, but she is heartbroken at the mere thought of leaving her hometown. Not only is Harriman the only place she's known, she has heard about the drastic changes in seasons up North; most especially the harsh winters. Snow and cold are elements she is unfamiliar with, and she is not looking forward to experiencing cool, much less cold weather. Millie loves her familiar surroundings and the year-round warmth. She has heard from others that the Northerners are not friendly, and they talk much faster than people in her region of the country.

Millie tries one final time to convince Thomas to stay in Harriman; however, her emotional attachment to the town could not override the need to provide a secure future for their family. Thomas puts his foot down and makes it window-pane clear that their family is relocating to Columbus, Ohio. He understands her reluctance to leave the familiar, but hopes it has nothing to do with her not wanting to leave Clarence McElroy. He has always struggled with his wife having the affair, and knows she still cares for Clarence. But he loves Millie in spite of her attachment to Clarence.

Millie feels she has been diagnosed with a terminal illness, and is going to miss the people she's known all her life. She finds a bit of happiness that she will remain in her home town for a few months, and plans to enjoy every day she remains. She knew this day could come, but never imagined it would. She was sure Clarence would have eventually found something for Thomas. Damn that Bruce and his northern relatives!

Mamas' Drama

CHAPTER NINE

Thomas Sr. and Bruce pack up as many of their belongings as will fit in their cars to take back to Columbus. They drive to Harriman several weekends to see their families over the next few months, always taking back more belongings with them. Millie's sadness increases each time she shares the news about their impending move. Clarence visits more frequently, three to four times a week, and arrives ahead of the customers to spend time alone with Josephine. Josephine feels awkward seeing Mr. Clarence so often. She misses her daddy, Thomas, and anxiously awaits being reunited with him.

The children are excited about moving to their new home, as they've heard about the big cities up North. They look forward to experiencing the snow and going through the various changes in seasons. Millie is despondent and becomes her customer, as she drinks up her profits. She is not yet able to accept leaving the place she has known her whole lifetime—and the man that is in possession of her heart.

Although it is a blessing that the Stewart and West families' homes sell by the end of the school year, Millie considers it a curse. Minnie's home doesn't sell, but she prays to God, and relies on Him to send the right buyer at the right time. She is grateful, as it will allow Thomas Sr. and Millie more time to find her a home. Minnie loves her daughter, but both recognize that living under the same roof is a recipe for disaster.

It is June, and school is out for the summer. Thomas Sr. and Bruce return to load up their families and possessions to move to their new homes. Millie suggests that she and the children remain in Harriman until the end of summer so she doesn't have to leave her mama. Thomas stands firm and insists they move to their new home as planned. As the financial Depression hits the country, Millie is hit by an emotional depression, with drinking being her main means of escaping.

Millie warily packs their possessions, spending time with each item as if she is leaving it behind instead of wrapping it to take with her. On moving day, saying goodbye to her mama is extremely difficult for Millie; not because she is leaving her, but because she envies her for being able to remain in Harriman. Millie feels it unjust that she is forced to move across the country with the man she married but loves as a friend, while the woman who forced her to marry Thomas stays in the place and with the man Millie loves. Millie hopes that by leaving Harriman, she will finally be free from the spell Clarence Eric McElroy has cast on her. Since finding their new home, Thomas has often thought about how good it will be to have his wife to himself, instead of sharing her with Clarence. Maybe now she can put her heart into loving him like he wants to be loved.

On the road to Ohio, the Stewarts and Wests take their time driving; stopping often to eat the food they packed and take in the scenery of the countryside. Thomas Sr. and the children are upbeat, but Millie is somber for most of the trip. The reality of leaving Harriman hits her like a rockslide. The enthusiasm of the children becomes contagious, and as they inch closer to their new home, Millie makes an effort to join in the chatter and excitement. The flask of peach moonshine that accompanies her helps her make it through the road trip to, what is for her, an unwanted, unnecessary evil.

Thomas Sr. and Bruce have had several months to acclimate to their new surroundings, and hope their families adjust as quickly as they did. The neighborhood is quite a contrast to their old one. The houses on 20th Street are situated closely together. You can hear the neighbors' doors shutting, televisions and stereos blaring, and loud voices that carry easily through the small, congested neighborhood.

The landscape of the trees is very different from their southern home, as the trees are not as beautiful or plentiful, and in between them are wide, barren spaces. Only a few of the trees on 20th Street are flowering ones, unlike those on Unaka Street that flower year round. Their Ranch-style home is average; not as large or graceful as the beautiful Victorian home to which Millie had grown accustomed. She hopes in time to resign herself to her new surroundings—no longer the quiet, laid-back, country-like atmosphere—it is busy with hustle and bustle, with more people in less space.

The home has four bedrooms, and the children are elated to have their own, especially Josephine. Now she can have peace when she goes to her bedroom. Betty thought she would miss sharing a room, but it doesn't take her long to adapt to having her own space. Thomas Jr. appreciates the shelves his dad built in his bedroom, as they are perfect for his books and science projects.

Days after moving in, Josephine, Shirley, Thomas Jr. and Betty hear about the activities at the community center. Neighborhood kids tell Josephine that Miss Wiley is a wonderful woman who teaches them many different dances—the cha-cha, the Charleston, samba, and even square dancing. She is also a teacher at Champion Junior High School, where the older children will attend in the fall. The girls sign up and attend class the same day. This is a special treat for Josephine, as, other than fashion designing, dancing is her passion. Josephine takes an instant liking to the dances and Miss Wiley. Shirley enjoys the class even though she finds some of the moves challenging. Even Betty has a good time and looks forward to returning. Thomas Jr. passes on the dance classes and joins the baseball team so he can practice to play for the school team in the fall.

Over the summer months Josephine and Miss Wiley form a close bond, and Josephine shares her dream of becoming a fashion designer. Miss Wiley enlists her to design costumes for their summer dance recital. Josephine hopes she's lucky enough to be in Miss Wiley's classes at school in the fall. She feels strongly that if Miss Wiley is anything in the classroom like she is at the community center, she can help make her dreams of becoming a fashion designer come true.

Summer is now past and the children anticipate their first day of school. Josephine and Shirley, now 13, are in the eighth grade at Champion, where Thomas Jr., 12, is in the seventh grade. Betty, 10, is a fifth-grader at Felton Avenue Elementary School. A far cry from the closeness and familiarity of life-long friends in Harriman, they look forward to attending their new schools and meeting new friends. Josephine, who is just as pretty and petite as always, is an intelligent teenager. Thanks to her mama's tutelage, she is outgoing and a real people pleaser. Shirley is a cute teenager, but is still shy. She relies on Josephine to get her involved in activities to interact with schoolmates. She rivals Josephine in most subjects, particularly the sciences.

Josephine is elated that Miss Wiley is her home economics and math teacher. Miss Wiley is one of the most loved teachers at Champion. She is an educator who insists on excellence, and is concerned about her students' academic achievements and personal growth. Firm and steadfast, Miss Wiley adds love and caring to the same spoon she feeds education. She doesn't hesitate to paddle students when necessary to keep their attention and respect. Josephine works diligently to impress her teachers, especially Miss Wiley.

Miss Wiley greets her home economic students, "Good morning, class. Today we are going to learn more about the world of fashion design." She talks about the fashion industries in France and Italy; focusing on French designer, Madeleine Vionnet, and Italian designer, Elsa Schiaparelli. She has Josephine's undivided attention, and no word or detail escapes her captivated ears.

Miss Wiley had encouraged students who wanted to share their designs to bring them in today, and notices Josephine's large portfolio. "Josephine Stewart, would you bring your portfolio and come to the front?" Josephine stumbles as she hurriedly moves to get to the front of the class. "You don't have to move so fast—we're not going anywhere," teases Miss Wiley. Before sharing her portfolio, Josephine reveals that she is wearing one of her creations, leaving her classmates in awe. As she displays her designs, they begin "oooing" and "aahing," suggesting they should be in fashion shows in Paris and Rome. Maybe one day, thought Josephine, as she has many more ideas in her head that are screaming to come out. Other students share their designs, but much to her delight, Josephine's are voted the most fashionable.

After class, Miss Wiley stops her as she is leaving the classroom. "Josephine, not only are you a wonderful dancer, but you really have potential in fashion designing. With proper training your designs could rival international designers. If you would like, I will look into programs that will provide you the training, and you can be the next Vionnet or Schiaparelli. What do you think—is this something you would like to do?"

Josephine is beside herself with excitement. "Miss Wiley, it's my dream to become a fashion designer! When can I start?"

"I'll need to talk to your parents to get their permission, and if they approve, I'll look into it next week." Miss Wiley is impressed by Josephine's talent and eagerness to pursue her dream career, and wants to help in any way she can. She saw Millie and Thomas Sr. a few times during the summer, and observed that Millie has a drinking problem. She hopes she is willing to support Josephine in her desire to enter the fashion world.

"Thanks, Miss Wiley. I love you like you're my mama."

Miss Wiley feels close to Josephine. "I love you too; I'll see you in math class." Josephine isn't sure how her feet touch the floor, but she finds herself outside of the classroom.

After school, she and her bestest friend drink malteds at the ice cream shop. The juke box is blaring "Swing it Girl" and Josephine and some of her classmates do the Charleston in the middle of the floor. After the song ends, Josephine flops down to catch her breath and finish her malted. "Shirley, I am having so much fun—you should have danced with us."

"I'm not ready to dance with them yet, but you're the center of attention. And I really like your dress. Did you design it yourself? I've never seen anything quite like it."

"Yes, I did. Miss Wiley thinks I can be a real fashion designer. She's going to talk to Mama and Daddy about putting me into a design school. Shirley, I could be a famous designer one day, and we'll be rich!"

"I know, Josephine, we can be as rich as Mr. Clarence."

"Shirley, I'm going to be richer than Mr. Clarence. He is a mayor, but I'm going to be an international fashion designer and travel all over the world!" The girls laugh and Josephine looks over and sees the cutest boy in the school making eyes at her.

She nudges Shirley, who looks over at Loren. "Girl, he's cuter than pewter."

Josephine giggles, "He is cute, with that good, wavy hair and those light brown eyes. He must brush his teeth four times a day—they sparkle when he smiles." He glances over a couple more times, and then winks at Josephine. Shirley and Josephine, and probably the rest of the envious girls, see him.

Loren comes over and asks her to dance. Josephine has the best time dancing with him as the other girls watch, wishing it were them. While dancing, she wonders how the boys in France and Italy dance. She plans to find out when she goes over there. That's her dream, and dreams do come true. She looks around and everybody is staring. She feels like she is the center of attention, and she loves it.

The Stewarts and Wests have their first exposure to cold temperatures as their first winter approaches. Thomas Sr. makes the adjustment like he has been in cold weather all of his life. Both families acclimate well; that is, with the exception of Millie. She hates the cold weather and finds it even more of a reason to justify staying inside. Since the move, Yolanda West has tried to encourage Millie to go out with her to get acclimated with the city. Millie rarely accepts Yolanda's act of friendship, preferring to go out only when she absolutely has to go for the essentials—alcohol, food and sometimes church—in that order.

Millie sorely misses her old hometown; she thinks about the Sundays they would sit in church while her mama preached, and how disinterested she was at the time. Oh, how she longs to be back home, sitting on that tiny pew in the quaint little church. And then having dinner afterwards, and making preparations for the next evening for her customers—and Clarence. But all of that is regrettably in the past. Millie doesn't like Columbus, and she hates the cold weather. The liquid she once sold to make profits, she now drinks to drown her misery. Unfortunately for Millie, liquor and misery become her constant and closest companions.

CHAPTER TEN

On this July day in 1937, the Stewart and West families have endured three cold winters and are reminded of the weather they were most accustomed to—hot and tepid. Minnie Kirksey has been in Columbus for two years, and is slow to adjust to her surroundings. Thomas Sr. found her a home one street over, and Minnie is thankful she didn't have to live under the same roof with Millie. She finds the people up North distant compared to the laid-back southern people she has been accustomed to her entire life. Her younger sister, Susan Kornegay, moved from Gainesville, Georgia to Columbus shortly after Minnie made her journey up North. Unlike Minnie, Susan did not have children, although she was married briefly. Susan travels between Atlanta and Columbus to stay with relatives of her deceased husband, who was well-to-do. She often returns to Atlanta when the winter season approaches. Minnie is happy being with her family, and the coldness of the winter weather and the people's attitudes don't deter her from enjoying those close to her heart.

The family joins the neighborhood church, Shiloh Baptist, where Pastor Kirksey becomes an Associate Pastor. She doesn't have an assigned Sunday to preach, but sits proudly in the pulpit each Sunday to assist Pastor Gilyard with the services, whether it is an opening prayer, the collection, or the call to discipleship. Josephine no longer has to read Bible verses to Grandma. Betty feels like she has won a place of honor as she now reads the Bible to their grandmother.

Millie is a homebody, almost reclusive, and rarely leaves the house. She relies on alcohol and sleep to make it through the long days and longer nights, and isn't concerned with adjusting to life up North. She is content with her daily routine of lying in bed, sitting on the sofa watching television, fixing herself drinks, and preparing an occasional meal for her family.

Thomas Sr. has been a line supervisor at the Columbus Malleable for over a year, and knows his decision to relocate was a sound one. He is patient, but wishes his wife would return to the woman she was in

Harriman. Mother Kirksey sends up powerful prayers to accompany his for Millie's return to a happy life. Thomas misses his wife, and she is right there under the same roof, in the same home. Most of her interaction with him or the children is to ask them to do something for her. Thomas misses the days he would come home to a wife who looks pretty and smells nice. He also misses the smell of her home-cooked meals that once wafted through the air, which made coming home all the more inviting. Josephine and Betty now prepare most of the meals. They do a good job, but have a long way to go to cook as well as their mama.

Thomas Jr. is a freshman at East High and plays baseball and the saxophone. Betty is in the seventh grade at Champion Junior High and, along with Josephine and Shirley, attends Miss Wiley's weekly dance classes now held during the school year.

Josephine and Shirley are sweet sixteen and eleventh graders at East High. Josephine still loves fashion designing, but her mama wouldn't allow her to attend a local school for design and adamantly vetoed her studying abroad. Millie told Miss Wiley she needs to stay home to help out with the family. Josephine hopes that once she graduates from high school she will be able to break free of her mama's grip, and go abroad to study her passion for fashion.

Clarence McElroy has not contacted Josephine or Millie in the three years since they moved. Millie gave him the contact information a couple of times before leaving Harriman. She hears from friends in Harriman that he is still the mayor, and as charming as ever. She left a few messages at his office, but he did not return her calls. Millie tries to resign herself that Clarence has decided to follow the "out of sight, out of mind" behavior, but refuses to lose hope that he will contact her or Josephine one day.

Millie was convinced Clarence would keep in touch, especially after his display of emotions when she told him they were moving. Josephine doesn't mention him, and it is apparent she doesn't miss him. Millie doesn't think about Clarence as often, but his imprint is on her heart. In her closet hang the red and black sequined skirt and top and the purple flapper dress, the two outfits he liked most. At times, when no one is around, she puts one or the other on and pretends he is sitting in the armchair, waiting for her to serve him his whiskey. She stands there for a few minutes, feeling the nervousness she felt when his eyes lingered on her body. When the ugly reality hits that he is not there, she drinks his shot of whiskey, on top of her own.

Josephine and Shirley are window shopping outside a clothing store on this Saturday afternoon. Josephine is engrossed in the dresses in the window, deciding how she would modify their designs. Shirley notices an older man staring in their direction—actually his eyes are fixated on Josephine while her eyes are fixated on the dresses. He has a woman and little girl with him, which doesn't make him stare any less. Shirley elbows her and whispers that the man is staring. Josephine is accustomed to Shirley watching for attention from admirers and doesn't pay her any mind. Shirley nudges her several times, forcing her to look over in his direction.

He is older, but is the finest man Josephine has ever laid eyes on. His chiseled features stand out on his dark-complexioned skin, which is baby-butt smooth. Average height, his muscular build is pleasing to the eye. Two gold teeth in the top of his mouth draws you to him like magnets, and glisten when he smiles. His steel grey bowtie and matching grey steel Portis straw hat with the wide black band matching his suit, complement his black shirt, pants and jacket. Josephine is intensely attracted to him, and notices he has a wedding ring on.

"I see him Shirley, but he's with a woman and child, and he's wearing a wedding ring. Don't you see it?" Josephine looks back over at him as Shirley stares him down.

"May be, but he's gazing at you like he's watching a reel-to-reel movie!" Josephine loses interest in the dresses and gives her full attention to the man. They both giggle, and he doesn't take his eyes off of her.

She finally turns back to the dresses, but eagle-eyed Shirley continues to watch him watch Josephine. A few seconds pass and Shirley nudges her again, "Girl, the chocolate man is coming our way."

"You're crazy. He's with his family."

"Not anymore!"

Josephine turns around abruptly as she hears his sultry deep voice, "Hello ladies, my name is George."

Shirley wastes no time warding off the predator. "From the looks of things you're Married George."

Josephine is embarrassed at Shirley's behavior, but tries not to blush as he is even more attractive than she originally thought. His playful smile frames his gold teeth, which intrigue her, and his wide nose adds a rugged touch to his handsome face. George answers Shirley but doesn't take his eyes off of Josephine. "That is true, but not for long. What's your name, pretty young thing?" Josephine blushes and introduces herself and her bestest friend. Shirley gives George a disapproving stare and barely speaks to him.

The matronly-looking woman who is with George, glares over at them, grabs the little girl's hand, and walks in the opposite direction. George doesn't notice or seem to care, as he is enthralled with Josephine. He hardly blinks his eyes the entire time he talks to her, telling her that the woman is his soon-to-be-ex-wife and their daughter, Delores. Josephine gets lost looking into his almond shaped, dark brown eyes and tries to figure out which is more mesmerizing—his eyes or his teeth.

"Josephine, it feels like I've known you all my life."

Shirley doesn't mince her words, "You haven't known her all your life—looks to me Josephine's much younger than you!" Josephine doesn't recognize this person standing there looking like Shirley but acting like her mama. She wants to pull her to the side and tell her to quit being rude, but she doesn't want to walk away from George. Instead, she smiles at him, her eyes flirting without permission.

"Can I get in touch with you somehow? Will you give me your phone number?" he asks an enchanted Josephine.

Shirley cautions her not to give it to him and whispers that he's married and has a child.

George wishes he could make Shirley disappear, but calmly tells Josephine that he and his daughter, Delores, and her mother, Lucile, are shopping for clothes for Delores. He also shares with gullible Josephine that they will soon be divorced. That makes sense to her because she can't imagine him being so rude to a woman he plans to keep in his life. George gazes at Josephine, nervously playing with the brim of his hat. "I don't want to frighten you, but you have taken my breath away. Can I please contact you?"

She thinks about it for a minute. She really wants to give her number to him, but knows she shouldn't—he's an older man and he's married. Plus, her mama would surely detect he's older when she answers the phone, which is every time it rings. "I really can't give you my phone number. You're married with a child, and I'm only 16 years old."

"I am married, but not for long. Can we talk about it more, Josephine? I don't want to let the sight of you to leave my eyes. You are the prettiest woman I have seen in my life. Please give me a chance to talk to you again."

Shirley is aggravated by his comments. "She is not a woman. She's a 16-year-old teenager, and you're much older than she is—you're probably her daddy's age. And that must be your wife that just walked away in a huff, dragging your little girl by the hand."

Josephine is appalled at Shirley's behavior, as she has already made up her mind she wants to see him again. She knows there are many reasons she shouldn't—his age and his marital status are two big ones and the child makes three. But even with all of the reasons she shouldn't, she is strongly attracted to him. She has had boyfriends in school, but she's never felt quite like this before.

"Will you meet me here tomorrow at the same time? I just want to talk to you. I won't keep you long; I just want to see you again. I am taken by the sight of you."

Shirley answers for Josephine, "No, she won't meet you. You're old, and you're married."

Josephine shushes Shirley and tells George that she may meet him, but it could be for only a short time, as she has to help her mama. "Please try your hardest to make it. I will count each minute until I see you again. Meet me right here in this same spot, okay?"

Shirley's glare remains intense and she grabs Josephine's arm to take her friend out of the clutches of the old vulture. "Well, you may be counting for a long time because she's not coming back here tomorrow. Josephine, come on. We need to go. You know your mama said to come right back!" She stands still in her tracks, feeling love struck. Shirley pulls on her arm, "Come on. Let's go!"

She drags her away as Josephine looks back at George, "I'll see you tomorrow, George. Bye bye."

George is smitten. "Goodbye—for now," he sighs and smiles. He looks over at his wife and daughter and shakes his head in disgust as he walks back to a frowning Lucile. He knows he'll get an earful, but he doesn't care; as the only thing he will hear in his mind is Josephine's sweet voice. He removes his wedding ring the moment he returns home. He has met the girl of his dreams, and intends to make her his wife—after he divorces his current wife, that is.

The following evening, Josephine returns to the store where she said she would meet him. George is standing there looking delightfully handsome in his striped seersucker suit with a white shirt and blue bow tie. The color of the band on his foxhound hat is identical to the blue stripes in the suit. He fights his urge to hug her and instead reaches out and holds her hands when she walks near to him. They spend an hour together, which feels like five minutes; and they decide to see each other again. The following day they meet and go for a ride in his 1935 Plymouth. The flaming red exterior matches the burning emotions that brew on the car's interior. Josephine is enchanted by George and can't wait to spend more time with him. She notices the only sign of his wedding band is the tan line on his dark chocolate skin.

George and Josephine steal away several evenings a week, and as they grow closer and closer, the tan line disappears. She knows he is the man of her dreams; and he knows he wants her to belong to him forever. Josephine gives George her heart and her virginity. Over the months that follow, secluded spots are their backdrop as they make love in his Plymouth; and sometimes on the weekends when they can spend several hours together, he drives her to the city limits and rents a room. Her mama and daddy think she is spending time with Shirley; and Shirley, being the bestest friend she is, doesn't spill the beans on Josephine.

Mamas' Drama

CHAPTER ELEVEN

Nine months have passed, and it's April of 1938. Millie and Thomas Sr. do not know Josephine is seeing George. Josephine is no longer that little girl who doesn't keep secrets from her mama; she has learned keeping secrets is a way of life. After all, her mama kept the secret about Mr. Clarence for years, and Josephine still wishes she had kept it forever.

Shirley is visiting Josephine and they are alone; the rest of the family are at the circus. Thomas Sr. forced Millie out of the comfort of her bed, and Betty's incessant begging sealed the deal. "Shirley, it's been too long since you and I have been together."

Shirley has missed her bestest friend, but can't help being sarcastic, "I know, but since George is in your life, you spend all of your time with him. In the nine months you've been seeing him, I can count on one hand how many times we've spent together. I'm glad we at least see each other at school, and he can't come there; they would probably think he's your daddy or uncle anyway."

Josephine realizes Shirley's feelings are hurt because they haven't spent time together, but she doesn't appreciate her snide remarks. "Shirley, don't say such mean things about George. I love him, and I really know how true love feels!"

Love him? Shirley doesn't expect to hear that from her friend, and tries, as usual, to be the voice of reason. "Josephine, you haven't known George that long. You're only 16 years old, and he looks old enough to be your daddy—like he's at least 30. How can you be in love with him? You should have a boyfriend in high school, not an old man your daddy's age!"

"Shirley, he's not that old, plus he told me he's getting a divorce soon."

"Are you sure you want to marry him?" Shirley is disappointed when Josephine shakes her head yes. "George is fine and all, but you haven't known him very long. And you certainly can't believe everything he says."

Josephine defends her man. "I've known him for nine months, Shirley. That's long enough to know I love him."

"Nine months isn't a long time—that's only a school year. You can't learn everything about something in one school year—that's why they teach the same subject for several years. So how can you be so sure you know everything about George? And you call yourself being in love with him? Come on, Josephine, he's almost old enough to be your daddy."

Josephine wants Shirley to stop talking. "Shirley, I love George, and I want you to try to like him. Anyway, I've been waiting until we were alone to share a secret with you."

"A secret? What secret?"

"Shirley, I'm pregnant!"

Shirley gasps and jumps straight up off of the sofa. "Pregnant! How did that happen?"

"I've been with George—and now I'm carrying his child. I'm excited, but I'm afraid to tell Mama and Daddy. I'm really scared, Shirley."

Shirley isn't supportive, but is perturbed. "You should be scared; you know your mama will be furious! You're out there acting like a grown woman, now you really gotta be one. George ought to be ashamed of himself!"

"Shirley, please be happy for me. I love George."

"You love George? Josephine, you're only 16 years old—you're just a teenager! What do you really know about love? Oh, Josephine!"

Josephine is in a dream-like state, "I know a lot about love, Shirley. I know I love him like a woman loves her man. He buys me fabric and other things I need to do my fashion designing. He even says we will go to Paris for me to study after I finish high school, or sooner if we get

74

married before then."

"If you get married before you graduate from high school? Have you lost your mind?! You know if you get married, he's not going to let you go to Paris, let alone go with you! And you're pregnant?! He really has you in a bind now!"

Josephine quips, "Shirley, George loves me, and he wants me to be happy! Mama's gonna be mad, though. She needs me to do everything while she lies in bed all of the time; plus, I help Grandma Kirksey too."

"Why can't Betty help with your mama and grandma?"

"Betty acts like she's ten instead of thirteen and is more of a nuisance than a help. But Shirley, the fact that I'm pregnant will break Daddy's heart! But I really love George, and I want to spend my whole life with him!"

Shirley feels sick inside, "You've gotten yourself into a big heap of trouble this time, Josephine! I hope George gets his divorce and marries you soon. Sometimes it takes a long time. Geez, your parents are going to be so upset! Ooh, Josephine, I wouldn't wanna be you telling your mama!" Shirley trembles with fear when she thinks about how Miss Millie will react to the news of Josephine sneaking around and being pregnant.

Josephine knows it's going to be hell to pay when she tells them. "I don't know when and how I'm gonna tell them. I've got to think about that for awhile. I've only missed two monthlies, so I should have a couple more months before I start showing. And he should be divorced by then, so he can ask Daddy for my hand in marriage."

Shirley just stares at Josephine, trying to figure out what possessed her to get pregnant. Josephine pleads for her bestest friend to understand. "Please be happy for me, Shirley; I love George—he is the man for me."

"Just because you're pregnant, you're trying to talk like you are grown. But if you love him, then I guess the best thing to do is to marry him." Shirley is apprehensive but asks, "Uh, Josephine, you know your mama kept the secret about your real daddy from you. Uh...it is

George's child, right?"

Josephine is insulted by Shirley's insinuation. "Yes, Shirley, it is George's child. I could never be with another man and deceive George like Mama deceived Daddy and me! My feelings are hurt that you're asking me this question."

"I wasn't trying to hurt you, but you know from your own life that it's always mama's baby, daddy's maybe." She nervously glances at her watch and is thankful it's time to leave. "Josephine, I gotta go take care of my brother while my parents go to the picture show." She hugs her, "Is the baby kicking yet?"

"Not yet, but you'll be the second one to feel it when he does."

For the first time in her life, Shirley is happy she is not Josephine. She hugs her friend tightly, almost expecting the baby to kick. "Okay, make sure. See you tomorrow Bestest Friend. Take good care of yourself—and your baby."

Josephine rubs her stomach, thinks about George and sighs with contentment as she envisions their baby and their happy-ever-after future together. "My George and me and baby make three," she sings cheerfully.

Millie was suspicious months ago and figured out Josephine was meeting up with a male, and could tell his voice was older than a boy in high school. She gave Josephine a stern talking to, but surprisingly didn't whip her. The sad reality is that Millie can't harness the energy to whip anybody because the harshness of the alcohol she consumes daily is whipping her.

Josephine is in her third month. The baby has started kicking and her morning sickness is less frequent. Throwing up almost daily was difficult to hide, and she is glad that phase of the pregnancy is ending. Her belly is beginning to swell, and she decides to tell her mama and daddy she's pregnant and George's intention to marry her. Millie and Thomas Sr. are in the bedroom talking; Millie is lying in bed and he is sitting on the side. Millie refuses to get out of bed most days so the family now regularly goes to her bedroom to talk to her. Josephine devises a plan to get Thomas Jr. and Betty out of the house so she can speak to her parents privately. She can't anticipate how her mama will react and wants to spare her younger siblings Mama's wrath. Betty loves ice cream, so she gives Thomas Jr. money and asks him to take Betty to the ice cream shop.

The ice cream shop is the hang out place for the junior and senior high school kids, and Thomas Jr. likes to go and see the girls. He doesn't mind his little sister tagging along, and she won't be much of a nuisance since she will be focused on her ice cream. Plus, the girls make a fuss over Betty, and that brings him welcomed attention. "Betty, Josephine gave me money for us to go to the ice cream shop. Do you want to go?"

"Of course, I do. Thanks, Josephine. Are you coming with us?"

Josephine hopes to avoid a series of questions, "No, Betty. You and Thomas Jr. go on and enjoy yourselves. I need to cook dinner and do laundry."

Betty is her usual inquisitive self when she asks, "Josephine, are you feeling okay? You've been getting sick a lot lately, especially in the mornings." Millie unexpectedly walks into the living room, and Josephine prays she didn't hear them talking.

"I just want to treat you both to something special. Ask Mama if you and Thomas Jr. can go." Millie glares at Josephine while nodding her head yes. They leave quickly to escape the wrath they know can follow the expression on their mama's face. Betty even feels bad for Josephine, because they all know that look is a look of terror in the making.

"What's this about you being sick? I thought I heard somebody throwing up, and you've been awfully tired lately! Just what is wrong with you girl?"

Thomas Sr. overhears Millie and enters the room. He puts his arms around Josephine's shoulder, "Millie quit hollering at her. She has been babysitting and designing clothes a lot lately. Baby, are you feeling alright?"

Josephine tells her daddy her stomach is cramping, and then, calling on all of her strength and courage, she says, "I'm three months pregnant with George's baby."

"What did you say, girl?!" Millie is livid as she paces around Josephine and Thomas Sr. A mountain lion stalking his prey looks like a picture of calmness compared to Millie. Josephine is frightened out of her wits, but bravely repeats herself.

Before Thomas Sr. could anticipate it, Millie grabs Josephine and slaps her across the face. The force of the blow unbalances Josephine, and she falls to the floor while Millie screams obscenities at her. Thomas Sr. fends Josephine from Millie's reach. "Now that's enough, Millie!" He falls to his knees, hugging and protecting a weeping Josephine as Millie goes into a rage. He helps Josephine off the floor and walks her to the sofa as she grabs and holds her stomach. "It's going to be okay, baby. Does George know you're pregnant?"

Millie can hardly restrain herself from slapping her again. It is a blessing that Thomas Sr. is in between them. Josephine glances at her mama, and quickly looks back at her daddy, "Yes, Daddy, he knows.

Millie is still pacing, "So what's his married ass going to do about you? Why did you do this Josephine? Are you trying to get back at me?"

Josephine is afraid, but stands up to her mama. "Mama, me and George are in love, and we plan to get married after he gets his divorce."

Millie screams, "Josephine! He's not going to marry you! Can't you see that?"

Thomas Sr. has grown tired of Millie's tirade and doesn't want to upset Josephine further. "Millie, settle down. Go to the bedroom if you need to calm yourself."

Millie hasn't returned to civility yet, and fails at regaining her composure. "So if he's such a man, why isn't he here with you? And why doesn't he ask for your hand in marriage, like a proper man would do? Oh, I know why, because he's already married!"

"Mama, we'll be married by the time I'm showing, you'll see." Josephine groans, grabbing her stomach, oblivious to the blood that is trickling down the inside of her legs.

Millie sees the blood and remains calm as she walks toward Josephine. "Come to the bathroom with me." Josephine shields herself, afraid of being slapped again. Thomas Sr. notices the blood and gently persuades her, "Josephine, it's okay, baby. You go on to the bathroom with your mama."

She looks down and is horrified to see blood running down her legs. "Mama, what's happening to me?"

Millie's anger changes to concern. "Josephine, come with me. Thomas, call Dr. Johnson."

As she and her mama walk slowly toward the bathroom, a worried Thomas Sr. dials the operator. "Operator, please connect me with Dr. Nathaniel Johnson."

Dr. Johnson visits, and after he leaves, Josephine calls Shirley, who can tell when she hears her bestest friend's voice that something is wrong. Josephine tells her she was just thinking about her, and has something to tell her at school tomorrow. Shirley tries to coax her into telling, but she refuses. The fact that Josephine is calling is unusual these days, as she has been spending all of her time with George. Shirley thinks George has finally told Josephine he isn't going to get a divorce, but doesn't say it. That darn old man! "You sound tired, you should go to bed." Shirley then whispers, "It's probably because you're pregnant." They say goodbye; and after hanging up the phone, the sad reality of losing their baby sinks in even deeper, as Josephine cries herself to sleep.

Dr. Johnson recommends bed rest for Josephine for the rest of the evening. Millie cooks dinner, which is a rarity these days. Betty and Thomas Jr. return home, happy and laughing about the fun they had at the ice cream shop. As Thomas Jr. hoped, the girls were making over Betty while he was making over the girls. They step into the house and the fragrant smell of dinner hits their nostrils. They are surprised to see it is their mama, and not Josephine, in the kitchen fixing dinner.

Millie tells them Josephine is not feeling well and is in bed. Josephine awakens when they rush to her bedroom, almost in a state of panic; as it is as rare for Josephine to be in the bed as it is for their mama to be cooking.

Curious Betty asks, "Josephine, why are you in the bed?"

"My stomach started hurting me real bad, Betty. That's probably why I've been throwing up. I'll be okay. Mama told me to come and lie down."

"Well you must be pretty sick for Mama to let you go to bed—and she's cooking dinner too. I hope you feel better, but I'm glad Mama's cooking. Thanks again for the ice cream treat; I wish you could have gone with us." Thomas Jr. thanks her too, but it has been several months since his mama cooked a meal, and Thomas Jr. is almost sorry he ate ice cream. He wants to stuff his stomach as full as he can as they don't know when she will cook again. Thomas Sr. is sad about Josephine, but is ecstatic Millie is cooking one of her delicious meals. He hopes this is a sign of things to come—the smell of his wife's cooking wafting through their home—divine!

Josephine finally reaches George and tells him about the miscarriage. He is upset and feels badly about not being there with her. He promises to see her tomorrow as soon as he is off of work.

Millie calls Grandma Kirksey, who arrives, Bible and anointing oil in tow, and prays for and anoints Josephine with oil. Josephine is attentive when Grandma warns her to stay away from George. She knows her grandmother is trying to protect her, but she doesn't promise to stay away from him. She's already asking for forgiveness, and doesn't want to tell a bare faced lie on top of that. Thomas Sr. comes in to check on Josephine before going to bed. He holds her for a while before telling her he loves her and to get some sleep. Josephine lies in bed, but sleep couldn't visit—her tears had taken up all of the space.

The following morning, Millie tells Josephine she can stay home from school if she wants. Josephine doesn't want to lie around with her mama, or weep about the baby, and convinces Millie that she is alright. When Shirley sees Josephine, she rushes up to her bestest friend, as she can easily tell she is sad. "Josephine, what's wrong? What were you going to tell me?"

She fights tears, "I told Mama and Daddy I was pregnant. Mama slapped me, and I fell to the floor. Shirley, I lost our baby."

Shirley is stunned, "Oh Josephine, I'm so sorry. Maybe your body is too young to carry a baby; but you'll have a house full one day. Oh my God, did you talk to George?"

"Yes. He's real upset. He thought I lost the baby because I fell to the floor."

"Well, that's why you lost it, isn't it?"

"No, I don't think so. I started cramping earlier in the day and they were getting harder, so I think it was happening then. Mama didn't push me down; I lost my balance and fell, and I didn't fall hard. It was just supposed to happen, I guess." Josephine feels numb as a helpless Shirley, at a total loss for words, remains silent.

"I think Mama is glad it happened because she needs me to stay home to help her. I do everything almost single-handedly while she drinks and stays in bed all the time. I wait on Mama hand and foot, and Daddy and I make sure Betty gets to school; and I have to stay on her about homework. It's good Thomas Jr. can take care of himself. Shirley, I don't even have time to spend on my designs anymore. I don't know if I'll ever get out of Mama's clutches. And just when I think I'm going to have something special, I lose the one thing that was created from love—our baby."

"I'm so tired, Shirley. Other than being around Daddy, the only time I truly feel alive is when I'm with George. The precious moments I spend with him bring me so much joy. I can't imagine being without him. I love him as much as I love Daddy—probably more if I tell the truth. With George, I feel a love so deep I can't explain it to you, or even to myself. I hope you feel this kind of love one day."

Shirley holds Josephine tightly, "Me too. But Josephine, what's your daddy saying about all of this?"

"Daddy is hurt, and he just says everything will be alright. I'm sure he doesn't want me to leave either. It's like Mama's given up on living; she changed when we moved here. I thought she would get back to her old self once Grandma Kirksey came, but she's only gotten worse. I don't know what happened."

"Did your grandma know about the baby?"

"Not until Mama called her last night. She came over and we prayed. Then she put anointed oil on my head and prayed that I not see George anymore."

Shirley knew the answer but thought she'd ask anyway. "Did it work? Are you going to stay away from him?"

Josephine smiles, "Sure it works, for as long as it takes me to meet back up with him after he gets off of work. George and I will marry and have a house full of children. That is what we both want, and that is what we'll have. George fills all the empty places in my heart—nothing and nobody will keep us apart." For some strange reason, Shirley feels Josephine is right about eventually marrying George. She certainly hopes Josephine's life will be filled with joy, as she's certainly had a lot of pain.

CHAPTER TWELVE

George has always been emotionally and physically close to his mama, Rose Emerson. Rose is a petite woman, even more so than Josephine, and stands a mere four feet, eleven inches tall. She is strict but showers George with love and affection, waiting on him hand and foot. George treats his mama real good. The youngest of three boys, he feels he is her favorite son because of his status as the baby. Mama Rose is an avid fisherwoman who taught her boys the art of fishing when they were young. She occupies the other side of the duplex George and his family live in.

James Emerson, who was courting Mama Rose, had to agree to live in the duplex once they married. George made it clear that he would approve Mr. Emerson marrying his mama as long as they lived next door. Mr. Emerson packed up his things, sold his home and moved in the duplex with his beautiful wife, Rose. They were happily married for five years until he passed away.

Mr. Stewart permitted George to court Josephine once his divorce became final, and they have been courting for a year. Their courtship is fruitful, as Josephine is now six months pregnant. Mama Rose loves Josephine and persuades her son to marry her, or, as the older folks say, "make an honest woman out of her."

George is extremely nervous as he drives to the Stewarts' home; hoping Mr. Stewart is in a good mood, and Miss Millie isn't too drunk. He's been sowing his wild oats since his divorce, and figures they have probably heard about some of his indiscretions. But, in spite of his womanizing ways, Josephine is the woman who holds his heart. He wants her to become his wife before giving birth to their child.

George wears a navy blue suit with a multi-colored bow tie on top of a white shirt. His fedora has the trademark band to match his navy blue suit. He blows his breath in his hands to make sure its wintergreen fresh before he rings the door bell. He feels as though he could lose consciousness when Thomas Sr. answers the door. He enters, clears his throat and plays with the brim of his hat.

"Hello Mr. Stewart. How are you, sir?"

"I'm fine, George. Do you want me to get Josephine?"

"Not yet, sir. I'd like to speak with you for a few minutes, if you'll allow me. Mr. Stewart, I love Josephine, and I came to ask for her hand in marriage. I should have asked months ago. Mr. Stewart, can I please have Josephine's hand in marriage?"

Thomas Sr. wants to laugh at seeing this man, who is as close to his age as he is Josephine's, acting like a nervous teenager. He manages to remain serious. "George, I want Josephine to marry you because she is in love with you, and you have her with child again. But your womanizing ways are known by many, and I don't want you hurting her anymore. I want her to be happy. Can you promise you will treat her right?"

"Yes sir! I love Josephine, sir, and I will treat her real good."

George squirms when Mr. Stewart pauses, "Well, it seems the only answer I can give you is yes, you may have my daughter's hand in marriage."

George stammers when asking if he can talk to Josephine. Thomas Sr. laughs and calls for her to come into the living room.

Josephine is radiant when she enters, smiling from ear to ear. George's pulse beats like a track star who just won first place in a heated race. He hugs her, gets down on one knee, taking her hand into his. "Josephine, I love you—you know I love you. From the day we met, I intended to marry you. You're carrying my child, and I want us to raise our family together. I want you to become Mrs. George Edward Price. Josephine Stewart, will you marry me?" She quickly accepts as she has long awaited this day. She is the happiest she's ever been in her life.

George gets up slowly and takes both of Josephine's hands into his. "All I want you to do is to give me a house full of children, keep our house clean and cook me those delicious meals of yours—especially your family's sweet potato pie. Will you do that for me?"

"Yes, George, I can!"

George is happier than he's been in a long time and is glad his mama convinced him to propose. "Pastor Perryman can marry us tomorrow. I told you we'd be using that marriage license soon. Mark is going to be my best man. Are you going to ask Shirley to be your maid of honor?"

"I'll call her after I tell Mama our good news! I know she'll be happy for us." Josephine calls for her mama, "Mama, can you come in here please? It's important!" Millie stumbles in, fashionably dressed in her lavender silk pajamas with matching robe and eye mask. Josephine shares the good news about George's proposal.

Millie, who is her usual three sheets to the wind, slurs, "I don't know why you want to marry that old man. He's always at the bar flirting with my friends. He's not good enough for you, Josephine." Thomas Sr. tells her to shush as he holds her around her shoulders to steady her.

"Mama, I love George!"

Millie could care less. "George, you're almost old enough to be her daddy, so you better treat her right."

George wishes Miss Millie would lay off the alcohol, and hopes her behavior does not foretell his wife-to-be's choices. But he remains respectful when he answers with a respectful, "I will, Miss Millie."

Millie responds with her trademark blank, glassy-eyed stare. Thomas Sr. tries to smooth over the awkward exchange by asking George what time Pastor Perryman will marry them.

"At ten o'clock in the morning. That is, if it's okay with you, sir." Thomas Sr. nods his head in agreement, while Millie shakes her head no.

Josephine, her eyes filled with joy, looks lovingly into the eyes of the man of her dreams. George returns her gaze, "Jo, I will give you everything I have, and work hard to give you everything you want."

Josephine coos, "George, you are everything I want."

Millie has had all she can stand, "Well, isn't this just so lovely. Can I go back to bed now?"

"Sure Mama, I wanted you to be happy for me. Do you need anything before I start packing?"

"I'm hungry. Are you too busy getting married to make me a sandwich?"

"Give me a few minutes, and I'll bring one to you." Josephine walks over to her daddy, "I'm going to miss you. Please let me know if you ever need anything; and Daddy, you're welcome to visit us anytime. And I mean that with all my heart."

"Baby, you've taken care of everybody your whole life. Let George take care of you now. He'll be your husband tomorrow, so don't worry about us. Stay focused on the joy you feel about becoming George's wife, and having his child. Thomas Jr. and Betty can help me out until your mama gets back to her old self. I don't know what happened, but I'm going to ask Mother Kirksey to put some anointed oil on her."

Josephine is so happy she thinks she's going to burst. "I've got to call Shirley—first she will scream and then worry me about what dress she should wear!" She takes George's hands and stares into his eyes. "June 28, 1940, what a glorious day to marry the man of my dreams!" George looks intently at her, takes her in his arms, and kisses and caresses the woman in his heart. He is blissful at the thought of her becoming his wife in just a few short hours. He feels like a young man in love, and doesn't know why everybody mentions their age difference—eight years isn't that much older.

Josephine and George settle into their eighth month of marriage in February 1941, with five-month old Pamela and George's eight-year old, Delores. George is out on the town, drinking and carousing with his cousin, Chad, and best friend, Deuce.

Chad's caramel-colored skin is a contrast to his chocolate-skinned cousin's. Average height, Chad is pleasing to the eyes; his handsomeness found breath-taking to many females. His wavy hair and warm smile that expose perfect teeth alignment, are a lethal combination. He claims the few extra pounds he carries give him character. Chad has the gift of gab and could easily sell ice water to Eskimos.

Deuce's sexy bedroom eyes, accentuated against his almond skin, invite even the most demure females to take a second look. Tall and cuddly, he looks like an overstuffed teddy bear. Outgoing and full of jokes, Deuce keeps people laughing—he and Chad are a party by themselves. Dressed in their stylish zoot suits, the men are out to have a great time. Pork pie hats and wing tip shoes complete their ensembles, as they aim to show the females the best of everything any woman could desire in a man.

Their eyes wander quickly from female to female, staring and flirting as much as possible before Josephine and her friends arrive. George feels real good after having a few drinks under his belt. "I'm trying to stick close to home, but I miss seeing these ladies. Josephine and her girl friends better hurry up before trouble switches over here and smiles in my face. Now, her friends are easy on the eyes, so you two will have to choose who's going to be with who. Try to act like gentlemen, and don't fight over the nicer looking one, okay? I know Jo is glad to get out—it's her first time since Pamela was born. But I've already popped her with another one—I'm trying for a boy this time."

Deuce shakes his head and laughs, but Chad is not amused. "Darn, George, why don't you give her a chance to catch her breath; she already has to take care of Delores and Pamela."

Deuce adds his two cents, "Because if he did, she might slip away from him. He's gonna keep her pregnant with no shoes to make sure she stays right in that house while he's out here looking at other ladies."

A woman walks by slowly and deliberately, and George's eyes are steady on her as he continues to talk to his cousin and friend. "If you're going to say it, say it right, Deuce. It's barefoot and pregnant. And Jo agreed to have a house full of babies. I'm not holding a gun to her head—I'm just holding her to her word—and close to me. Damn, that girl is shaking her money maker!" George winks and flashes his gold-toothed smile; and she winks back, smiling profusely.

Chad notices their flirtation, "George, you better watch yourself. Josephine will be here any minute, and you know she'll give you and that woman H-e double l."

George laughs, "Yes, she has her mama's temper, but look at it this way—this is a stage and the ladies are part of the scenery. I'm just enjoying the scenery."

Deuce spots Josephine, "Well you better close the curtain—Josephine and her friends just came in. Hmm…they look pretty good; I think I want the one on the left. She looks like she can hold on to a teddy bear like me."

Chad turns to get a better view, "They both look good to me, so let's see who they want. Good luck, Deuce—you know I'm going to get the finer one, so don't get your hopes up too high."

"We'll see, Chad. I'm not trying to marry anybody, I just want to have a good time; so either one will do the job for me."

"I told you guys not to fight over her friends. They both look good, but my baby is by far the finest," brags George. Josephine and her friends remove their expensive winter coats and hats, revealing their striking dresses underneath.

Deuce shakes his head, "Josephine should have waited until she reached the table to take off her coat. She looks extra, extra fine in that blue dress. George, you might need to go over there and escort her to the table—these men are staring a hole through her."

Chad agrees, "Yes, cousin, you got you something really special there. I can see why you keep her pregnant." George is not particularly pleased with their remarks about his wife, but forces himself to smile.

Josephine took special care when preparing herself for the evening. She's painfully aware of George's wandering eyes and wants to make sure they wander solely on her. Her time was well spent, as the low-cut, v-neck royal blue dress she designed fit her in all the right places.

The belt on her tiny waist gives no indication that she is with child; and although the bottom of the dress is loose, the material lays close to showcase her sexy body. As she glides across the floor, her presence commands attention from both male and female admirers. George can't help but notice men ogling his wife the way he ogles other women. But since Josephine is his prize, he takes pride knowing she will be going home with him when the evening ends.

The ladies arrive at the table, and Josephine introduces her friends. "These are my good friends, Vernette and Rita." Vernette's floral, cream-colored, v-neck dress has a lace collar that looks glamorous on her honey-colored skin. Voluptuous Rita looks sassy in her all-black three-quarter sleeve dress. Six buttons going down the front makes her outfit look even more alluring. "Ladies, this is Deuce and Chad. And we all know this handsome man here—he's mine."

Josephine kisses George, and the ladies sit across the table opposite the men. She notices George is a bit tipsy and tries not to envy him being able to drink. At 20, she's underage, but usually enjoys a gin and tonic—not tonight, or for the next seven months for that matter. She had a couple of drinks when she was carrying Pam, but her mama, Millie, of all people, has insisted she not drink with this one. Her morning sickness has been so bad she calls it all-day sickness; so alcohol is one less thing she has to throw up.

George sets up the first round, "Ladies, what are you drinking?" Vernette orders vodka and orange, and Rita orders scotch and water. Josephine is getting ready to order when George jokes, "Josephine, I know you want soda pop, since you're already popped."

Vernette is surprised, "Josephine, are you pregnant again already? Why didn't you tell me? Pamela's only five months, isn't she?"

Josephine laughs, "Yes, Vernette, I was going to wait until I got further along, but I see George can't hold his liquor or his tongue. We're expecting in November. And George, I'll take an orange soda pop for now. No, make it a ginger ale instead. I wouldn't drink alcohol anyway—lest I make your baby as drunk as his daddy."

They all laugh and get to know each other as Deuce and Chad

try to discreetly decide who's going to be with whom tonight. The woman George winked at earlier walks by the table and smiles at him. Josephine quietly observes as George smiles back at her. She cautions the flirting woman, "You just as well move that smile and your gyrations somewhere else—this one is mine. I only share him with our two children. And don't turn your face in this direction if you come back this way, either." The woman takes heed and walks away swiftly. Josephine turns to George, "I suggest you keep your wandering eyes on me. We don't want to get no mess started because we both know I'll finish it. I plan to have a good time, and I'm not going to let you disrespect me."

George is embarrassed but tries not to let it be obvious to the others, "Alright, Josephine, all eyes on you!"

Chad tunes in, "All eyes are on you, Josephine. The men have been steady watching since you strolled in. George you need to keep your eyes on your prize. These boys in here are looking at her like they're starving!"

Deuce adds, "Chad, we need to watch Vernette and Rita too. All three of these ladies are beautiful tonight." George laughs, realizing his wandering eyes have been officially retired—at least for now. He's fully aware that he has a pretty young thing—that's why he married her in the first place.

The evening continues and the coupling is complete—Vernette and Chad, and Rita and Deuce find common ground. They tell jokes, dance and have a great time. Two men come over and ask Josephine if they can buy her a drink, or if she would dance with them. The second man even adds that she is the most beautiful woman he has ever seen. George rearranges the seating and positions Josephine next to him, hugging her close. Josephine is pleased, as she knows George's wandering eyes saw there were plenty of eyes wandering on her. She laughs to herself as the old adage, "what's good for the goose is good for the gander," comes to mind. George is overly attentive to Josephine this evening, but her admirers still stare at her from across the room.

CHAPTER THIRTEEN

George is at his spot, The Black Stallion Bar, on this June evening in 1942. His brother, Mark, and co-worker friend, Raymond Moorehead, are having a few drinks after work. It isn't apparent when looking at George and Mark that they are brothers. George took after their darker-skinned mother, and Mark after their light-skinned father. Mark is tall, average looking, robust and caramel colored—contrasting his handsome, chocolate-dipped younger brother.

Raymond's gentle nature is cloaked by his appearance as he is tall, milk chocolate and athletically built. He grew up in the same neighborhood as George and Mark and frequented the gym as a child to watch George box. George boxed well, but Raymond, who is Josephine's age, later took up the sport and became a Golden Gloves champion—something George did not achieve. Raymond looked up to George, who attended his boxing matches to watch him compete. George, Mark and Raymond all share a garden, raise pigs and chickens and work together at the iron and steel factory, B&T Metals.

It has been a couple of months since George has been out with the boys; and he is overdue for a good time. "I'm glad we got out tonight! I've been confined too long—all that racket with two babies crying and Delores hanging on me was driving me crazy! It's more than a notion. I'm glad that's women's work. I'd take working in the factory any day over being stuck at home with babies."

"George, man, you got yourself a prize when you married Josephine. How long has she had you tied down? A year?" asks his brother.

"No, Mark, we've been married two years now. She had your nephew, Stephen, eight months ago, remember him? I know he was early, but he counts. I'm glad I got my boy, but it's hard enough having two babies in two years, plus Delores—don't put two babies on me in the same year."

Raymond adds, "It seems like yesterday, but me and Beatrice have been married for three years."

Mark considers himself a virtuous man and works diligently to preserve his image and his marriage. He doesn't miss an opportunity to hint to George to stop his womanizing ways and become a better man. He boasts, "It's been 10 for me and Grace; and we're still as happy as we were the day we married. I'm trying to get my little brother to follow in my footsteps."

George isn't paying attention; instead he flirts with a woman standing nearby. Mark continues, "George, are you listening?"

He doesn't answer—his eyes focus on the woman. "Man, that's a pretty young thing over there."

Raymond eggs George on, "These women are a sight to behold." He and George laugh, but Mark doesn't find their ogling or comments funny.

"George, I'd advise you to keep your wandering eyes on this table. You don't want Josephine to get wind of you looking at the ladies. She found out the last time," Mark cautions.

George ignores Mark and heads toward the woman, "I'll be right back! I need to talk to that pretty young thing."

He walks over to the table and whispers to her as Mark shakes his head with disapproval. "He has a jewel at home. I don't understand why he flirts so much."

Raymond smiles, "Yes, Josephine is as pretty as they come—she's a prize for any man lucky enough to have her in his life."

The woman giggles, writes her telephone number on a piece of paper, puts her lipstick imprint on it and hands it to George. He holds it in his hand like it's a medal, says a few parting words and strolls back to the table, grinning like he has won a prize at the county fair. Mark warns, "George, you need to throw that paper away. You'd better not let Josephine find it. You know she's ready to turn your wandering eyes into wall eyes as it is! And what are you trying to find? Josephine is prettier and classier than all of these women in here."

Raymond agrees, "Yes, she certainly is." George stares at the woman and ignores them. Raymond shakes his head, "Well, I'm going to turn in. George, don't get into nothing you can't get out of."

George is confident when he responds, "I always get in and out with no problem, Raymond. I can handle my business."

Raymond stands up, "Okay, I'll see you both in the morning."

Raymond leaves and George gets up from the table, ready to return to the ladies. Mark taps him on his arm, "George, wait a minute. I want to talk to you. Sit back down, please."

He reluctantly sits back in his chair. "Sure thing brother, but hurry up, I need to strike while the iron's hot."

"You better think twice before getting all tangled up with that woman. You know Josephine won't stand for no woman coming up in her marriage."

"I know that, Mark, but Jo doesn't want to go out with me anymore. But she goes out with Shirley and another friend I don't even know."

Mark senses his little brother's concern and offers him counsel. "You need to spend more time with her. When she wants to go out again, have Mama watch the babies and you take her out. And control your eyes."

"You're right, I need to change my ways. Rome wasn't built in a day, you know. But I'll be right back, the lady's calling my name."

George stands to head back over to the lady. Mark grabs his shoulder, "Come on, let's go home to our families. Come on, George."

"Oh alright, Mark, at least let me go say goodbye." Mark blocks him, "Come on, let's go!" George winks and waves at the ladies as he leaves the bar. He wonders when Josephine is going to fry the walleyes he caught last week. He laughs as he thinks it's better to have the walleyes served on a plate instead of his eyes on a wall.

It's July of 1943, and George leaves B&T Metals to head to the Black Stallion before he goes to the garden. He enters the bar and sees Raymond, who is singing "Ain't Nobody's Business," while dialing the pay phone. When he sees George, Raymond stops singing and hangs up abruptly.

"Hey Raymond, did I interrupt you?

"No, I was calling Beatrice to see if she needs me to bring anything home."

George laughs, "You look like you saw a ghost or something. Are you okay?"

Raymond wipes his brow, "I'm doing better now that we're out of that sweatshop, and you?"

"I'm better than a pig in slop! And speaking of pigs, ours are darn near ready for slaughter, and the chickens are laying plenty of eggs and gaining weight, too."

Raymond likes speaking with a British accent, "Yes, we're feeding our families in good fashion." He resumes speaking normally, "Glad we're in this together. We make a good team—Mark even does his share of the work—in between the free counseling sessions." They both laugh, knowing only too well how Mark takes every opportunity to offer sage advice, even though they don't ask, and many times don't want it. "So how are Josephine and the kids?"

George loves to brag about his family. "They're all just fine. I've been keeping my Jo busy—three babies in three years, plus my oldest daughter. Our baby girl is four months, so we'll have to get started on making another boy soon."

"Sheila's the baby's name, right?"

George is taken aback, "You don't know your own name half the time. So how is it that you remember Sheila's name?"

Raymond's response comes fast, "Beatrice talked to Josephine last night and they were talking about the kids. So, of course, Sheila's name came up."

George asks how Beatrice and their kids are doing. Raymond sips his beer as he gives the update on his family. George thought about the last time the four of them were out on the town and suggests they go out again when his Mama Rose can watch the babies. "Jo had a good time when she came to Beatrice's birthday party. She goes out with her friends sometimes; but I'm going to have to keep my eyes on my prize. She's a mother of four, but still one to adore. Does Beatrice ever go out with the girls?"

"The only place Beatrice goes is to church three to four times a week. She does so much volunteering that she barely takes time to sit down. I'm surprised she sits still long enough to hear the sermon on Sundays. She's definitely God's servant."

George counters, "Well, at least you know she's in a good place. And since you go with her, you can see what she's doing."

Raymond has other things on his mind. "Yeah, I guess. Hey, it's your day to go to the garden, right? I bet Josephine would like some cucumbers and tomatoes."

George asks Raymond how he knows what his wife wants, and suggests he concern himself with what Beatrice wants. He stands up and is confrontational. Raymond stands, "Listen George, I told you earlier Beatrice and Josephine were talking on the phone last night. Josephine mentioned the vegetables; that's how I know. Man, I won't say anything else about Josephine if you're going to get upset."

George swings his arms, as if to box. "You may be a Golden Gloves champ, but I still know how to throw a mean punch!" They laugh and play box for a minute. "Look, I have to go to the garden and get my Jo's cukes and maters. I see you're empty, are you leaving too?"

Raymond looks at his empty bottle. "No, I think I'm going to have one more. I'll see you tomorrow."

"Okay man, you better be sure to call Beatrice and find out what she wants you to bring home."

Raymond smiles, "I will. Don't work too hard at the garden—it's hot out there."

The moment George is out of his sight, Raymond uses the pay phone. "Hello baby. How was your day?"

Josephine replies the obvious, "Busy! But I took a nap when the kids took theirs so I could to be fresh when I see you tonight."

Raymond sighs, "I'm counting the minutes until I'm holding you close to me. Do you want me to pick you up?"

"No, Raymond, I'm going to have Shirley pick me up. I don't want Mama Rose to see you again. I had a hard time explaining why you picked me up the last time. You can drop me home though since George will probably be over her house watching TV. He always does that so she can help him watch the babies. It would do him good to watch them by himself and see how much it takes to handle four."

"Josephine, how's my baby doing today?"

"Sheila's fine. It's hard to believe she's four months already, and she looks more like you every day."

"I marked her well, didn't I?"

"Yes, too well. George is getting suspicious because I don't tell him everything like I used to. Hell, as many women as he fools around with, I don't feel bad about being with you. He keeps asking who my new girl friend is that I've been going out with." Her grin turns mischievous, "I should tell him her name is Raymona."

Raymond thinks about his earlier encounter with George. "I need to be careful when I talk to him. I said you wanted cucumbers and tomatoes, and he exploded like a stick of TNT. I told him you mentioned it to Beatrice last night, and she told me. We laughed it off, but it got heated."

"Raymond, you really do need to be careful and watch what you say to George. He looks at Sheila kind of funny sometimes, so he may see her resemblance to you. And he very well knows what you look like since he's known you all of your life."

"Okay, I'll be more careful." Raymond sighs, "Josephine, I think about you constantly. I can't help it—all I want to do is to be with you. I have since we met."

Josephine loves hearing Raymond express his affection for her. It seems the moment she and George said "I do" the romance in their relationship said "you won't." He acts like he owns her, and doesn't show her affection or attention—unless they're around people. And she's well aware of his womanizing ways, which causes her pain. Raymond is the exact opposite of George, as he is loving and affectionate.

"Josephine puts him to the test, "And just how long have you known me, Champ?"

"Fourteen wonderful months—May of 1942."

Josephine giggles, "I'm impressed. And just why do you remember that date so well?"

"We were out celebrating Beatrice's birthday, which turned out to be a birth day for me too as it was the day you and I met. When you walked in with George, it was like a thunderbolt struck me. I couldn't keep my eyes off of you. And you may recall that I made it my business to follow you to the bathroom; I had to talk to you privately. I'm glad I did, and I'm glad you felt something for me, too."

"I know I shouldn't have, but I had a strong attraction to you. George, he is my first love, but you are my second," Josephine confesses. Sheila begins to cry. "Look, Champ, I have to go. Sheila must sense that her daddy's on the phone and is vying for your attention. I'll see you at 8 tonight at the Black Stallion. Goodbye."

"Okay, I'll see you then, baby. Goodbye."

Josephine hangs up the phone, a part of her feeling like she's beating George at his own game. But she is well aware that the real reason Raymond is in her life is because of how amazingly good she feels when she's with him. She picks Sheila up and sees Raymond looking back at her. What have I done? she asks herself.

It's the end of January, 1945, and one-week-old Donna, baby number five in the Price household, coos loudly, making her presence known. George is out on the town with Deuce and Chad at their usual spot. George has been doing a fair share of introspection lately; and realizes he needs to settle down and bring a halt to his womanizing ways. Josephine has not been as affectionate toward him and seems less duty-bound about being his wife. George and Chad sit at the table while Deuce is at the bar.

Chad is in unusually high spirits, "I think I met the future Mrs. Chad." George is surprised, "Who is it, Chad? You always hide your women, so we probably haven't met her."

Chad laughs, "Her name is Gwen, and you are right, I didn't introduce her to you yet. She's the woman I've been waiting for my entire life."

"Well don't let her get away—make sure you keep her happy."

Chad is caught off guard, "Cousin, that's surprising coming from you, Columbus' number one married ladies' man."

Deuce returns, his hands filled with drinks. "Deuce, congratulations are in order! Chad is making an honest woman out of his woman friend."

Deuce reacts, "My man, Chad! Congratulations—I'm happy for you. I knew you would work your mojo on some mother's daughter."

Chad laughs, "I'm ready to settle down; there's not much out in these streets, but the streets themselves. Deuce, you're next. What are you waiting for?"

Deuce doesn't hesitate, "The right woman. I'm not in a hurry to get married. I'm taking a page from George's book on sowing wild oats. But, I'm happy for you."

Chad's words strike a chord with George. "You said a mouthful cousin; I'm getting tired of being out in these streets, and Josephine is slipping away from me. I tell her I've stopped looking at women, but she refuses to go out with me—it's been over a year. But she goes out with her friends, and lately she's been coming in later and later and is more tipsy."

Deuce chuckles, "Oh, she's giving you back your own medicine, huh?"

"Yes, and it's a hard pill to swallow. And I don't have the time or the energy to run the streets. That's why I asked you two to meet me tonight; I wanted to tell you I'm sticking closer to home. I need to settle down; my five babies need their daddy, and my wife needs her husband. Since she just had Donna, she'll have to stay home a few weeks to recuperate. I hope me staying in will help us get close again. And I need to see what's going on in my home. Lately, when I answer the phone, the person hangs up. I could swear it's a man."

Deuce rarely sees the softer side of George. "George, man, you've been in these streets a long time, and it's good that you're going to stay close to home. You have a lot of babies, and a wife that most men would kill to have at their side. How could Josephine have another man? She's lucky to get any time to herself after taking care of all those babies you've popped her with. A man calling your house; come on George, quit being paranoid. Now, back to you Chad, give us the low down on your woman friend."

"I won't tell you everything because she's mine, and I plan to keep it that way. Her name is Gwen, and she's a real good woman. She's sweet, fine and can cook up a storm. She doesn't run the streets, but she isn't stuck up in church all the time either. She even has me going to church with her on Sundays. She spoils me, and I spoil her right back. We've been seeing each other for nine months, and I'm going to pop the question next week. I hope she doesn't run away."

George says kiddingly, "Does she have all her fingers and toes? And does she know what she's getting in to, fooling around with you?"

"She's fine, George. You'll see for yourself—after she agrees to be my Mrs." George feels better that he made the decision to stay close to home and prays he doesn't have to eat his words. They enjoy what could be the last of their regular boys' nights out.

Josephine is at home and answers the phone. Raymond is on the line. "Hi baby, I called earlier, but George answered so I hung up."

"Oh, that was you. He was upset. I told him it wasn't anything he or I should concern ourselves with—it was obviously a wrong number. He's out with the boys now, probably flirting his ass off. I can't talk long, though, I'm getting the kids settled."

"I don't want to talk—I want to see you. Can we meet somewhere?"

"Raymond, I miss you too, but I need a few weeks to get myself together. I just had a baby a week ago, remember?"

"I know, but I miss you more than I can say. So, how's my baby?"

Josephine sometimes wishes he wouldn't ask, "Sheila's fine. She's bound and determined to look like a female you."

"That is music to my ears. Well, goodbye, baby; dream about me as I dream about you."

"I always do." says a hurried Josephine.

CHAPTER FOURTEEN

The latest addition to the Price family, Carolyn, is now one and a half years old. Born Christmas day in 1947, Carolyn's siblings were in awe when she arrived, saying they had their own baby Jesus. The Price family has moved to a double on the north side of town. Mama Rose lives on the other side of the double, and Delores lives with her to have her own room. Their newest abode is located across the street from Faith Ministries Church, and catty-corner to 11th Avenue Elementary School.

A large living room, with a cozy brick fireplace, is the gathering room, and the spacious dining room is the second most inhabited. Family pictures adorn the walls in the living room, and a big clock with Jesus' face in the background hangs above the ocean blue sofa. Josephine sometimes chuckles when she looks at the clock, recalling when she used to sit on Jesus' face on Grandma Kirksey's sofa cover. George's overstuffed chair with matching ottoman sits directly in front of the console television set in the living room—his own personal haven.

A large, dark mahogany wooden table, which easily seats 10, is the center of the dining room. A crystal bowl and platter hold a waxed fruit arrangement, complete with teeth marks from when the kids were younger and mistook them for real fruit is its centerpiece. The tall china cabinet holds Josephine's fine china and crystal keepsakes. A wall painting that likens the fruit arrangement on the table hangs on the largest wall in the dining room.

The kitchen walls are a deep, rich gold; the cabinets and baseboards are painted to match the white appliances. Four small floral paintings adorn the walls. A mirror hangs on the wall near the back door—a handy place to check one's appearance whether coming and going.

The four upstairs bedrooms and full basement allow more living space for the ever-populating Price family.

Pamela, Stephen, and Sheila attend 11th Avenue Elementary School, and Delores attends Linmoor Junior High. Donna is four, and Carolyn is 1 1/2 years old. George still works at B&T Metals and now works part time at The American Jersey Cattle Club. Josephine's job is non-stop, as she stays home and cares for the six children. Although Delores lives with Grandma Rose, she usually stays with her siblings until after dinner.

The family joined Faith Ministries due to its close proximity. It is one of Josephine's retreats from home and she serves on the nurses corps and sings in the women's choir. Josephine also enjoys drinking and dancing with friends at the Red Tavern and occasionally at the Black Stallion Bar. Dancing has always been one of her passions, and she has won several dance contests, which she attributes to Miss Wiley. She often reminisces about the love and support Miss Wiley showered on her; not only with dancing, but also with her desire to become a fashion designer. Josephine is certain she would have become a well-known designer had her parents listened to Miss Wiley and permitted her to attend fashion school. She allows herself to dream about it, since she's well aware that with marriage, six children and a lover, it is only a pipe dream at best.

Busy having babies and raising them, Josephine sees her daddy and mama only occasionally. She knows that when she visits, she has to wait on Millie hand and foot, so when she gets a break, she likes to get out of the house and far away from responsibility. Millie is more reclusive, and has been totally swallowed up by alcoholism. Thomas Sr. still works at the Columbus Malleable, and Thomas Jr. is a resident physician in cardiology in Atlanta, Georgia. Betty is married but doesn't have children yet. Grandma Kirksey continues to serve as an Associate Pastor at Shiloh Baptist Church, and is in relatively good health.

Josephine is meeting Raymond for drinks on this early evening in May of 1949. For the past seven years, they talk every weekday and see each other at the Red Tavern once, sometimes twice a week. On this particular evening, Raymond has Josephine meet him at The Black Stallion for a change of pace. She is welcomed by Dante Romano, a stocky, strikingly handsome Italian man. A touch of gray at his temples is the only hint that he's 45 years old. His thick, wavy black hair contrasts his golden olive complexion. Josephine's eye for fashion is quick to recognize his expensive, tailored black pin-striped Acquaviva designer suit. Several buttons on his black shirt are undone, revealing a gold medallion sitting atop a nest of hair on his broad chest. Josephine doesn't recognize the cologne he wears but finds it titillating. Dante has seen her in his bar a few times, always admiring her from a distance.

"Hello Miss, welcome to the Black Stallion. Would you like to be seated at a table or at the bar?" Josephine looks around for Raymond, but he hasn't arrived. She chooses a table for two. "What are you drinking this evening?" he asks.

"I'd like a gin and tonic on the rocks. I'm waiting on my friend, and he will pay for it as soon as he arrives."

Dante hopes he arrives later rather than sooner. "You don't need your friend to pay. This one is on me. I've seen you here before, but you're always occupied. I've not had the pleasure of meeting you. My name is Dante Romano, and yours?"

"Josephine," she answers, feeling slightly uncomfortable and wishing Raymond would walk through the door.

Dante has wanted to know more about this lovely creature for years and wastes no time seizing his golden opportunity to talk with her. "Josephine, I'm certain all the men tell you how very attractive you are."

She blushes, not anticipating his forwardness. "That is sweet of you to say." He fixes his eyes on her, and she nervously sips her drink, checks her watch and looks around the bar. She breaks the awkward silence, "My friend, Raymond, is running late for some reason. He'll be here anytime now, I'm sure."

"He must have something wrong with him to leave a fine woman like you waiting. I would never do that. Are you hungry?"

Josephine hasn't eaten much, and responds that she is slightly hungry. Dante offers whatever she wants from the menu, but she declines. "I wouldn't want to trouble you. I don't have much money with me, and if my friend doesn't get here soon, I'm leaving. I don't like being in places by myself."

"You're not by yourself—I'm right here. So what would you care to eat?"

She gets hungrier by the minute but is unsure if she should take him up on his offer. "Really, I couldn't take anything else from you. I don't want the owner to think you're giving away his liquor and food."

Dante chuckles and calls on his employee, "Eddie, do you think the owner would mind feeding this lovely woman?"

Eddie replies, "No, boss, I don't think he would mind. In fact, I think the owner wants to feed her."

Dante stares into her eyes, "Josephine, it's okay—I am the owner."

She is pleasantly surprised, "Oh, I see."

"You see, but you still haven't told me what you want to eat."

She takes him up on his offer, "Well, if it's not too much trouble, I would like a hamburger."

Dante is pleased Josephine allows him to cater to her and finds out how she wants her burger. When he orders it, Eddie informs him that it will take six minutes. Dante responds, "Make it five—I don't want to keep this beautiful lady waiting." He asks her about herself and her family, and as their conversation continues, she finds herself becoming comfortable. "Josephine, would you care for another drink?"

"No, that's okay. I haven't finished this one." He insists and tells Eddie to bring her another drink with her hamburger.

"Dante, you don't have to get me another drink."

He doesn't move his eyes off of her, "Trust me, it is my pleasure."

Josephine's head is swimming, but not from the alcohol. She finds Dante's conversation, appearance and cologne intriguing. Eddie brings the hamburger and drink, and Dante talks about his various businesses as Josephine enjoys the man, the drinks and the burger. She politely thanks him again,."The hamburger was very tasty. I feel I should use another word, or say thank you in another language. You've treated me very well, Dante."

"Your language and your mellifluous voice is soothing to my ears, Josephine; and feeding you is my pleasure. A hamburger is nothing close to what a beautiful woman like you deserves. You deserve to be treated like the queen you are."

"Do the Hucklebuck" plays on the jukebox and Dante invites Josephine to dance with him. He's seen her dance before and likes the way she moves. He laughs and promises not to show her up; and she cautions him that she's won awards for dancing. After some coaxing, she agrees to dance, and they playfully banter while on the dance floor. Once the record is over, Dante remarks, "If I had a trophy, I'd give you one for that dance—you really have the moves, Josephine!"

They return to their seats and continue talking. He orders her another drink, and she doesn't refuse it. The more they talk, the more intrigued they become with each other. "Ooo, I do enjoy you!" he says, kissing her hand. Josephine giggles, but much to Dante's dismay, Raymond hurriedly enters the bar.

"I'm sorry I'm so late, baby. Beatrice's car is in the shop and I had to pick her up from Bible study. Of all nights, they ran late. Forgive me?" He kisses her on the cheek and speaks to Dante. Dante had been so attentive, Josephine almost forgot she was waiting for Raymond.

"Yes, I forgive you. Dante's taken real good care of me."

Raymond musters a half-hearted smile, "Thanks for entertaining my baby, Dante."

Dante nods and looks at Josephine, "Trust me, I enjoyed every minute of it. Be late again, and I'm taking her from you!"

They laugh, but Raymond's is forced. "Well, I'll make sure that doesn't happen. Fix Josephine another drink. Baby, I'll be right back, I need to pay my water bill."

"I'll have my bartender fix it for her as he has the others." Raymond gives Dante an unfriendly glare, and Dante returns a nonchalant one. The moment Raymond is out of ear shot, Dante reminds Josephine, "I was serious when I said I enjoy you. I would like for us to spend more time together. Will you allow me? I'll give you my private number."

Josephine begs off, "I don't think so. I'm married with six children, and Raymond is my lover. So my dance card is pretty full."

"You're an attractive, vibrant woman. I'm still tingling from the touch of your hand. And your eyes sparkle like fairies glow." He gives her his business card, "Take my card, and at least think about calling me. I hope you give me a chance to show you another side of life." Josephine looks at the card and quickly puts it in her purse.

Raymond returns, "Okay Dante, back up, you've talked to her long enough. You know I'm a Golden Gloves champion. Don't make me put on my gloves and knock you out."

Josephine attempts to break the tension, "Raymond, don't be silly, he's been a real gentleman." The three of them laugh, but Raymond's again is forced. He plays "Smoke Gets in Your Eyes" on the jukebox and holds Josephine closer than usual as they dance. Dante retreats to his office, believing she will call him in time. As she is in Raymond's arms, Josephine smells Dante's fragrance on her, intoxicating her even more.

CHAPTER FIFTEEN

Two weeks have passed and Josephine is preparing to meet Raymond. She decides to take the purse she carried when she met him at the Black Stallion. Dante has crossed her mind more times than she cares to admit. She kept his card in the purse, purposely trying to resist the urge to call him. But she is so curious about the other side of life he said he'd show her. She talks out loud, *Oh, here's his card. Just tear it up and throw it away.* She holds the card in her hand, looking at it and thinking about calling him. She goes back and forth—should she call him or should she not. *You know you really want to call him.* She takes her inventory. *You're married with six kids, you have a lover—and a child by him—and you're thinking about yet another man. Are you crazy?* She thinks a little longer. *But you're just so intrigued about the other side of life he said he'd show you. Darn it, Josephine, what are you doing? Call Shirley—she'll talk some sense into you.*

She tries to be even keeled when Shirley answers. "Hello, Shirley, how are you?"

Shirley is always glad to hear from Josephine, "I'm fine, Bestest Friend, and you?"

"Girl, I'm alright, but I need you to stop me from making a big mistake."

"Okay, what are you doing now? I tell you—there's never a dull moment!"

Josephine hesitates, "Well."

"Oh Lord, we're in for a good one—that 'well' gives it away!"

"Shut up, and listen, Shirley. I need your help."

"Okay, spit it out—your counselor is in."

She tries not to talk as fast as her mind races, "Remember I told you Raymond had me meet him at the Black Stallion a couple weeks ago?"

Shirley finishes the scenario, "Yes, he was late and you ate, drank, talked and danced with the owner." Josephine can always count on Shirley to recall every detail about her life.

"That's right. But what I didn't tell you is that Dante gave me his private phone number and asked me to call him. I told him I didn't think it was a good idea, but he said so many things, my heart just about pounded through my chest! Shirley, he told me about the businesses he owns; and I can tell he's well off by the designer suits and jewelry he wears. And he is so charming. He wants to show me another side of life. I just can't imagine what that would be like."

"I see trouble up ahead."

"I really want to call him, but I know I shouldn't."

"That's right—you shouldn't. Listen to me. George is a good husband. He's settled down and doesn't go out chasing women anymore. He works two jobs and takes care of you. He's good to his mama and provides a nice home for you and your six beautiful kids. Now, you also have Raymond who loves you too. And might I add that one of the six kids is his. Josephine, quit writing more chapters to your soap opera life. Walk away from Dante. Can you hear me—walk away from Dante. You don't need any more drama."

Shirley proceeds to point out some of the pitfalls of Josephine getting into a relationship with Dante. "You're lucky George doesn't know about Raymond, and adultery is a sin you know, so leave Dante alone."

Shirley does a great job at convincing her not to call him, and Josephine's desire to call him wanes. "Thanks, I knew you would help me see the light. I better get off this phone before someone listens in on this party line. Plus, I need to fix dinner before George gets home anyway. I love you, Shirley. Goodbye."

"I love you too—and don't you dare call Dante. Bye bye," Shirley says, unsure of what Josephine is really going to do, as she hung up the phone a little too quickly. She realizes she can't save Josephine from herself. She can only try to guide her—which is a big job in and of itself.

Nanette Marie

Josephine holds Dante's card in her hand and starts to throw it away, but she remembers his smell, his conversation and his manner, and dials his number instead. As the phone rings, she thinks about the other side of life. When he answers, she almost hangs up. She takes a deep breath and finds the nerve to speak. "Hello Dante, this is Josephine. Do you remember me?"

He doesn't hesitate one second, "Josephine, the award-winning dancer, who could ever forget you? I was afraid you weren't going to call." Josephine cannot believe she is actually calling him.

Dante cuts to the chase, "When can I see you?"

She didn't see that coming, especially so quickly. "Whoa, that was out of the blue. I don't think that's a good idea, Dante."

"I know you don't have a lot of time, and neither do I; but I've thought about you constantly. I want to see you, Josephine. Why don't you come by the Black Stallion tonight at 7? Take a cab. I'll pay for it and anything else you desire."

Josephine waits for her heart to relocate from her throat, and once it settled back in her chest, she speaks. "I do need a break, so don't be surprised if I show up."

He entices her, "I won't be surprised, but I will be delighted. See you later, Miss Sparkling One."

"Miss Sparkling One, why do you call me that?"

"Because your eyes sparkle like fairies glow."

Josephine giggles, "Well, I may bring some pixie dust with me." She remembers George will be home soon, and she hasn't finished dinner. "I have to go now, Dante. Goodbye."

"Ciao, Josephine."

She hangs up and thinks out loud. Another side of life; that sounds so intriguing. I want to see him again. She struggles with her decision. *What did I just do? I can't believe I called him. Hmm…guess I do live a soap opera life. Well, let me pick out an outfit before the kids wake up, and I start running after them. I'll ask Mama Rose to come over and watch them until George gets home. I don't know what the other side of life is, but I'm ready to find out.* She finishes preparing George's dinner, thinking it ironic that it's lasagna.

Dante can hardly take his eyes off of Josephine as she strolls in, looking magnificent in her form-fitting red chemise dress and black patent heels. He fights his desire to pull her close to him. "Well, hello, Miss Sparkling One. I'm so pleased you came. Did you bring the pixie dust?"

Josephine likes his wit, along with everything else. "Yes, and I have my magic wand in my purse." She feels awkward but needs to tell him to pay the cab fare. "Dante, the cab driver is waiting to be paid."

"I'm sorry, I was distracted by your presence. Eddie, go pay the cab driver. Josephine, forgive me, I couldn't think beyond seeing you in that red dress. But I don't want you to ever hesitate telling me anything you desire because I will make sure you have it—and more. I believe a drink is in order for my fair lady. Let me make it for you; gin and tonic on the rocks coming up."

Josephine nods her head yes to the drink but thinks about his other offerings too. She can't believe she's actually with Dante, and involuntarily becomes a little uneasy.

He notices her change in posture. "Josephine, please relax. Trust me, I have no intention of hurting you—my only desire is to please you."

Dante handles a couple of business matters during the three hours she's there, but sticks close and keeps her in full view. Her fourth drink gives her the courage to ask, "Dante, why did you want me to call you?"

"Is that a trick question? Josephine, everything about you is fascinating. You're thinking too much. Let's get on the dance floor."

Josephine is tipsy, but she's aware enough to keep her distance, "Okay, a fast song though."

Dante agrees, as he's confident there will be other dances. "Fast it is." He selects "Chattanooga Shoe Shine Boy" and "Some Enchanted Evening." He outstretches his hand, "Come on, Miss Sparkling One, let's see who wins the trophy this time."

Dante hesitates when the record ends, as he knows the slow song is going to play, and he intends to hold her close. Josephine turns to sit down, but Dante takes her hand and asks for just one slow dance. She resists at first, and then moves toward him as he gently pulls her closer. As "Some Enchanted Evening" plays Josephine enjoys being in his arms; intoxicated by his fragrance and the alcohol. Dante whispers, "Josephine, enjoy me as I am enjoying you." Her body moves slowly in rhythm with his, and she stops fighting herself.

She whispers, "I knew I shouldn't have let myself get close to you." Yes, she has had just a nibble, but is indeed intrigued with the other side of life.

Donna and Carolyn are napping and the older children are in school. It has been three weeks since Josephine's evening with Dante. She has done well resisting the urge to call him; but now finds herself dialing his number. Dante answers and is elated to hear her voice, "Josephine, I've missed you. Is everything okay?"

She has butterflies, "Yes, Dante, all is well. I've purposely stayed away from you. We got too close the last time we were together, and we could have made a big mistake."

"Josephine, we're both adults, and we're attracted to each other. Why does it have to be a mistake?"

She hesitates, as it seems silly to state the obvious, "Because..."

He finishes her statement, "I know...you're married and have a lover, six children, including your lover's child, etcetera, etcetera, etcetera."

"That's right; that's my story."

Dante shares some intimacies about his life. "Life is what it is. You feel guilty about being in two relationships. I think it's possible to be in love with more than one person. I feel you love people in different ways and for different reasons. You see, I have two families. I have an Italian wife, and we have a home and two children; and I also have a home and family with my mistress. They're aware of each other, and I maintain both families and love them all. I want what I want, and I have what I want. I treat my wife and mistress like the treasures they are, and I would treat you in the same manner. So, I understand your needs. Please believe me, there are many reasons I am enchanted by you. And what I know is that I intend to find out why you have such power over me."

Josephine doesn't speak, as she cannot find the words.

He breaks the silence. "Josephine, are you still with me?"

"Yes, Dante, I hear you, but I don't know that I'm with you. You make it sound so simple, but I see it as very complex. George doesn't know about Raymond. I think he's suspicious, but he doesn't know for sure. If George found out, he would leave me, and I can't provide for myself or six kids. I'm a homemaker, and my role in life is to have babies, clean house and cook. There are already too many people involved, and they could get hurt—you, too, for that matter."

"I'm willing to take a chance. I hope you decide to take a chance on me too. I want to show you and give you things you've never dreamed of, Josephine. You wouldn't have to worry about anything financially either. You know I want to see you. Will you come by tonight or tomorrow?"

"No, but I'll think about what you said and work on making it simple. I'm going to go now. Goodbye, Dante."

Dante bets himself she'll call again soon. "Goodbye, Miss Sparkling One."

As soon as she hangs up, her phone rings, and it's Raymond. She thinks about keeping it simple as she talks to him. Decisions, decisions.

Josephine and Raymond meet at the Red Tavern on this July evening. Each time they are together, she is reminded why she cherishes his affection. They laugh and talk for hours. Raymond treats her like the woman she is and values what she says and does. George doesn't talk to her much and when he does, he orders her around as if speaking to one of their children. She reminds him that he is her husband, not her daddy, but it falls on deaf ears. Their lives together revolve around the children—a stark contrast to when they first met and spent so much time together, enjoying each other, and talking about their future. Although intimacy with George is not as frequent, it is still exhilarating. Raymond is a good lover, but Josephine has to give credit where credit is due. George is skillful at pleasing her, which is why their family continues to grow—at least for the most part.

Their evening over, Raymond drops her off in the alley behind her home. George looks out the kitchen window and sees the all-too-familiar scene of Josephine getting out of his car. He is angry with Raymond, but also with Josephine as she is tipsy which is becoming her usual state these days. The children are asleep, and George walks back to the living room as Josephine staggers into the house. He confronts her, "Well, you finally came home. How is your man?"

"What man? Look, George, I'm not going to argue with you tonight, so don't try it. I'm too tired to deal with your foolishness."

George is not going to be dismissed, "How's your man?"

Josephine maintains her innocence, "You think you know everything. I was out with my girlfriend."

He gets agitated, "You've been drinking four and five times a week and coming home drunker and later. The kids need their mother; you're turning into your mama." Well, he pushed her button with that accusation.

"I'll never be like my mama, and don't you ever say that to me again! I'll never be like her!"

"Somebody needs to say it to you. You're drinking almost daily, you don't cook like you used to and the house isn't clean. You're constantly on the phone talking to whoever—you say it's your girlfriends, but funny thing—when I answer they always hang up."

"You must think you're my daddy. You're not, so leave me alone, George! I don't need to hear you complaining about what I do, and what I don't do. I didn't complain when you were running around with your friends and fooling around with all those women. I don't complain about you just sitting in your chair and having the girls pamper and wait on you hand and foot, like you're a damn king. It's a lot on me to take care of six kids day in and day out. I don't complain, so when I want to go out and have some fun, I will. Life is just what you make it, and I'm going to live mine. And to make it totally clear, you're not my daddy! My daddy's name is Thomas Stewart, not George Price."

George sets her straight, "Your daddy's name is Clarence McElroy. And speaking of daddies, who is Sheila's daddy? She looks like Raymond, the man whose car you just got out of. Do you still want to talk about daddies?"

Josephine doesn't have the energy, nor does she want to continue this losing argument. "I'm going to bed. I'm tired, and I've been drinking, as you so well noted. But I'll say it again—you're not my daddy, so don't treat me like I'm your child." Once she is alone inside their bedroom, she calls George a son of a bitch several times as tears fall because of the jab he took about her daddy. It seems like it wouldn't hurt any more after all of these years, but it does. And that's the first time he's said Sheila looks like Raymond. She is not quite sure what to do. She is grateful the alcohol has numbed her, and sleep, her friend, comes quickly.

CHAPTER SIXTEEN

Thoughts of him occupy too much space in her mind, but Josephine has not seen or contacted Dante. She and Raymond meet only at the Red Tavern since Dante was so bold with his flirtations. Dante weighs heavily on her mind today; so, in spite of knowing better, she calls him.

He instantly recognizes her sultry voice when she says "hello." "Josephine, how are you? Why haven't you called?"

"I'm fine, Dante. I've been busy doing my usual—taking care of everybody."

"Would you like to be taken care of, Josephine? I would love to take care of you."

She finds him so charming. "That sounds good, but how would you do that?"

"Come by tonight and I will show you," he teases. "Take a cab, and I will have everything prepared to suit my queen. I think about you constantly, and you're thinking about me, too. It pleases me to know that I am in your thoughts."

"Yes, I do, more than I care to admit. I will take you up on your offer and come tonight around 7; I want to see how you're going to take care of me." She laughs, "And I want you to have my palatial palace, replete with staff, ready for my arrival. I'll see you later, Dante."

"Ciao, Josephine." He smiles as he knows she doesn't realize he will make her words come true. He calls the staff at his mother's mansion with instructions on how to prepare for this enchanted evening.

Josephine wears a stunning tangerine dress with short-sleeves and a high neckline. She used a Simplicity pattern; as gone are the days of having time to design her own clothes. Signs of her having birthed five children are undetectable as her belt accentuates her petite waistline. She wears white patent leather heels—probably one of the last times she will wear them this year since it is late August, and fashion dictates no white shoes after Labor Day. A white patent clutch and pearl earrings complete her outfit, which reflects the change of seasons—white, the brightness of summer, and tangerine, the color of fall.

Anxious to see her, Dante stands outside 10 minutes before she is due to arrive. His double breasted, six-button navy blue suit, with a red and gold striped tie on top of the off-white shirt, makes it evident that he is a man of means. His navy blue and white wing tip shoes and navy fedora makes him appear distinguished. Josephine arrives, and he smiles broadly when he opens the door of the taxi to assist her. She is instantly taken by the tantalizing smell of his cologne, which reaches her nose before he can touch her hand. He is so handsome she has to remind herself to stop staring. "Hello, Miss Sparking One. You look divine this evening." He pays the cab driver and motions him away.

"Hello, Dante, my loyal subject." she says, her eyes twinkling.

He joins in with her playful teasing. "Are you ready for your royal treatment, my fair lady?"

She nods her head yes as he carries on. "Well, my lady, if you would please accompany me to my car, which is across the street." He gestures to an expensive-looking car, but Josephine doesn't identify the 1949 silver dawn Bentley.

"Does this meet my lady's approval for transportation to our destination?"

She feels she is on a cloud and dreaming while awake. "Yes, my subject." She has no idea what is yet to come, but riding in the comfort of his luxury car is definitely a step in the right direction. She relaxes, feeling like a real queen. Dante is easy to talk to, and they have an engaging conversation during the short ride.

The long, circular driveway leads to a home so grand it could appear as a featured article in a Better Homes and Gardens magazine. Josephine feels she has arrived on an Italian movie set. Dante, the consummate gentleman, opens her car door. "My lady, we have reached our destination. Please be careful as I assist you in exiting the car."

He opens the elaborate door to the mansion. Josephine peers in, and jokingly asks if the maid and butler will be serving dinner. "Yes, they will attend to you shortly, but I made them aware that I would escort you in personally." *Pinch me please, I know this isn't happening,* she thinks. He offers his arm and escorts her to an expansive room three times the size of her living room, dining room and kitchen combined. An outsized table holds several trays; the one with alcoholic beverages has a bottle of champagne chilling in a crystal ice bucket. A second tray holds fruits and chocolates, while a third tray displays an array of hors d'oeuvres.

Classical music plays, seemingly out of nowhere. Dante fixes her gin and tonic and pours himself a glass of wine. He entices her to try the hors d'oeuvres by offering to feed them to her. She declines, but picks one she guesses to be caviar, and nibbles on it slowly. The conversation, the food and alcohol flow effortlessly; and she becomes more and more relaxed, thoroughly enjoying her dream-like surroundings. He suggests a tour and she readily accepts. He shares that he purchased the mansion for his mother, who is away visiting relatives in Venice, Italy. Josephine has never seen anything as magnificent except in magazines and movies.

The tour ends when Dante escorts her into the spacious room with a dining table that would easily accommodate thirty people. Lavish, gold-trimmed teakwood chairs with plush red cushions are positioned around the table. A delicate crystal bell sits on a tray of alcoholic beverages at the far end of the table. He pours another drink and rings the bell. Within seconds, a man wearing a black suit and tie and a woman wearing a maid's outfit appear and serve them wedding soup, hot rolls and salad. Josephine deduces they are without a doubt, the maid and butler. She reaches underneath the table and pinches her hand to make sure she's not dreaming. She feels the pinch, which lets her know this is all really happening.

Dante rings the bell again, and the service staff reappears with the main course—chicken marsala on angel hair pasta and asparagus with a cheese topping. She surprises herself with the large amount she consumes and savors every bite. An excellent cook in her own right, she has made her fair share of spaghetti and lasagna, but has never tasted such flavorsome Italian food. Josephine has just eaten one of the most delicious meals in her life and didn't have to shop, cook, serve or do dishes. Heaven must be like this, she thinks.

Soft jazz now plays in the background of the elegantly furnished living room. "Some Enchanted Evening" fills the air, and Dante stands, takes Josephine's hand and leads her to the center of the room. As they dance, she melts further into his arms. He holds her ever so tenderly, and she snuggles as close as their bodies allow. Dante has been attending to her every desire, treating her like royalty. He whispers sweet, sexy words in her attentive ears, describing his desire for her; she finds herself willingly accompanying him to a lavish bedroom befitting a queen.

He kisses her longingly, the kisses become more arousing. He carefully removes her shoes, his jacket and tie as they exchange steamy, wet kisses. As their passion intensifies, Josephine unloosens her belt and guides Dante's hands to unzip her dress. His eyes dance all over her beautiful body, as he removes his shirt and trousers. They fall on the bed as the intensity becomes fanatical. Their breath and bodies find the same rhythm, and they make slow, deliberate love for what feels like time without end. She doesn't need to pinch herself; if this is a dream, she wants to stay asleep.

On their way back to the bar, they remain silent for much of the ride; verbal communication is not necessary, only stolen glances and contented smiles. As she rides home in the taxi, she feels like she has incarnated Cleopatra. Dante did exactly what he promised—he showed her another side of life.

Josephine calls Shirley the following day to tell her about her magical evening. She knows her voice of reason is going to speak her mind, and most of it she doesn't want to hear. But she needs to tell somebody about her night in paradise. "Hi Bestest Friend, what are you doing?" she asks, hoping Shirley has time to talk.

"I just put the kids down for a nap. It's been a month of Sundays since we've talked. What have you been doing?"

Josephine wants to blurt it out, but stays calm, "I know it's been awhile, but I have something to tell you."

Shirley hears the muffled excitement in Josephine's voice, "Lord only knows what Josephine's drama is going to be today. Go ahead soap opera star, what happened?"

The blurting begins, "Girl, I had the dreamiest time of my life last night!"

"Really? With George? Are you two getting along better?" Shirley almost kills the joy of the moment with those questions.

"No, he's still complaining and acting like he's my daddy. But remember I told you about the guy that owns the Black Stallion?"

Shirley fears this is going to be more drama than she anticipates. "Yes, and I remember telling you not to call him."

Josephine is borderline defiant, "I started to tear the card up, but then I decided to call." Shirley sits down in a chair, and waits for the soap opera to continue. "Anyway, I've seen him a few times over the past three months, and I like being in his company. I've been sharing stolen moments in a world I never knew existed."

Shirley knows what she's done is most likely something she shouldn't have. "Josephine, what world are you talking about? You're going to have to explain what you mean."

"George and I have been arguing like cats and dogs, and I was sick of him and bored with Raymond. I called Dante and told him I was tired of taking care of everybody, and he offered to take care of me. I met him at the Black Stallion and thought we'd have drinks and dance as we've done several times before."

"Several times, huh? I'm afraid to ask, but I will—what happened next?"

"Well, he was standing outside when I arrived and told me his car awaited. Shirley, he drives a new Bentley Mark VI! His car costs almost as much as my house. Anyway, he took me to his mother's mansion as she was visiting Italy. I've never seen such luxury. I mean 26 rooms, swimming pool, crystal chandeliers, fresh flowers everywhere—it was like I was on the set of a movie."

Shirley knows her friend well enough to know there is more to the story. "Enough of the tour guide talk. What happened next?"

"Girl, there were trays of alcohol, fruit and hors d'oeuvres, and then the butler and maid served us dinner. A butler and a maid, Shirley! Can you imagine? I'm still pinching myself."

"Seriously? His mother must be loaded!"

"He said he bought it for his mother, so he's the one with the money. Anyway, we ate, we drank, we talked, we danced, and then...."

"And then what, exactly?"

Josephine blurts out, "Girl that man made love to me like I was a born-again virgin. He was so tender, I almost cried!"

"Josephine, you didn't!"

"Don't judge me. I've only been with three men my whole life."

"That may be true, but may I add that the first one is your husband—you know, the man you married. The second one is your lover, and you have his child, and now an Italian lover! I don't quite know what to say."

"You don't have to say anything. I'm almost sorry I told you. But since you're my bestest friend, I wanted to share. It was like I was in a dream. And I will see Dante again—he makes me feel like a natural woman."

"Josephine, you better quit messing around on George—he's a good man, and he's your man. Don't you forget that! You're married to him, and you belong to him! Remember the wedding vows you took? I wish you would treat him better."

"I don't mistreat George. I was so young when we met; I never got to experience other men like he did women—even after we were married.

He didn't worry about our wedding vows, so why should I? I'll settle down one day. Life is just what you make it, Shirley, and I'm living mine!"

"Be careful, Josephine. You're weaving a tight web, and I don't want you to get too tangled up in it. I love you, and I don't want you to get hurt."

"Trust me, I won't. I'm going to hang up and get some of this never-ending work done. I'll talk to you soon. Goodbye Shirley."

Shirley is completely blown away, and prays Josephine wasn't ovulating last night. Josephine sits a few minutes longer, thinking about how wonderful she felt in Dante's world. She smells his cologne and thinks about him being a man of his word. Without any doubt, she has seen another side of life—and she likes it. Carolyn's wail jolts her out of her dreamscape, and she sighs, leaves Cinderella behind, and returns to Josephine's real world. Where is her glass slipper?

Mamas' Drama

CHAPTER SEVENTEEN

The spring weather is picturesque this Saturday afternoon in May of 1950—the sky is blue, the grass is green and the flowers are in full bloom. All is well with the Price family. George continues his job as an anodizer at B&T Metals and his part time job at the cattle club. Josephine keeps up with their family and the household, as well as her steady relationship with Raymond. The attraction and romance with Dante has run its course, so she has only seen him on a few occasions. She has more than enough on her plate with her family and Raymond.

Delores is at the movies with her friends, and the rest of the children are playing in the backyard, except for 2 ½ year old Carolyn, who is napping. Josephine paces the living room floor as her contractions grow stronger. George paces with her, rubbing her back, and offering words of encouragement. Shirley and Aunt Susan sit on the sofa, waiting to assist with the delivery.

"Now, Josephine, you've been having those contractions since early this morning. I believe this baby is going to be here pretty soon. You just keep walking—it'll be over before you know it," her concerned Aunt Susan says.

Shirley adds, "Josephine, your stomach has dropped considerably, and your contractions are getting closer together—it should be anytime now!"

"My back really hurts, and I feel like I need to have a bowel movement. I hope you're right," says a hopeful Josephine.

Shirley, who has four children, advises, "That's a good sign, girl. Your baby is pushing down the birth canal trying to get out!"

Josephine thinks she is being funny and is not in a humorous mood. "Shirley, this is no time for your jokes."

"As many children as you've had, you've never felt like you needed to have a bowel movement when it came close to the baby being born?"

"I'm having contractions, not a bowel movement." As soon as she speaks the words, a sharp contraction hits. "Ow, that one hurt! Let me go to the bathroom. Shirley, you're doing all this talking about bowel movements, and now I feel like I need to go. Thanks."

"You don't have to thank me; I didn't do anything."

Aunt Susan, Shirley and George place playful bets about how soon she will deliver. George guesses twenty minutes, Shirley says ten and Aunt Susan, who has never had children, thinks two hours will bring her newest great grand niece or nephew into the world.

Shirley points out, "This baby is stubborn—already five days past due."

Josephine feels pressure when she sits on the toilet, but no bowel movement. The pressure gets more intense, and she realizes her baby's head is crowning. She steps into the tub, and they all rush in when she shouts, "The baby's coming!"

Aunt Susan is perplexed, "Josephine, why are you in the bathtub?"

Shirley sees the baby crowning and throws a towel to George, "Oh my God, catch the baby, George!"

George's nervous hands hold the towel while Shirley and Aunt Susan help Josephine breathe and push out the newest Price addition.

George is excited, but holds her carefully. "She's here. And she's a pretty little thing!" He then repeats Aunt Susan's question, "But Josephine, why did you get in the bathtub?"

Josephine playfully rolls her eyes at Shirley. "As much as I hate to give her credit, Shirley was right. I thought I was having a bowel movement, but it was Suzette instead. I didn't want her to fall in the toilet or on the floor, so here I am, in the tub."

Shirley laughs, "Well, this baby should be one of the cleanest on earth—born in the bathtub! You're good, Josephine—the last one a Christmas baby and now a bathtub baby! Only you, Josephine Price, only you!"

The children hear the commotion and are now waiting in the living room, anxious to see their newest sibling. George brings her into the room, and she is wrapped in a pretty pink blanket. "Your mama is fine and she's resting right now. You can see her in a little while. This is your sister, Suzette Marie; she was named after your great Aunt Susan. She must have decided she wanted a bath first thing, as she was born in the bathtub."

The children gather around to inspect their newest addition. Carolyn, now awake, joins her brother and sisters in welcoming the baby. George holds Suzette close to her so she can get a good look. "Daddy, is she really my sister? She looks like my doll baby," she says in all innocence.

George takes a long look at Suzette, and her bone straight hair and olive skin stand out from the others. He decides it is from his Grandpa Randall's Native American side of the family. "Suzette's not a doll baby; she's your sister. Hello my pretty little Suzette," he says, now looking at her somewhat questionably. Out of the mouth of babes!

The Price family celebrates Father's Day with a Thanksgiving-type dinner—turkey, dressing, mashed potatoes, gravy, potato salad, macaroni and cheese, greens, rolls and sweet potato pie. The children present their daddy with the traditional Hallmark card, but Josephine starts a new tradition and has each child share a special talent or gift. Delores reads a passage from The <u>Souls of Black Folks</u>; Pamela sews a handkerchief from an old pillowcase; Stephen crafts a fishing lure from a hook and a piece of his mama's broken jewelry; Sheila sings "God Bless the Child"; Donna draws a picture of her and her daddy; and Carolyn proudly presents a drawing of an interesting-looking Christmas tree. Five-week old Suzette's gift is that she slept during most of the dinner preparation.

Josephine hasn't seen or spoken to Dante since a couple of months before Suzette was born. Dante knew she was due in May and asked Raymond about her when he came in his bar. Raymond told him she had a baby girl and is doing fine. Dante can't understand why Josephine hasn't at least touched base with him. He has no way to contact her, as she didn't give him their home phone number. She learned her lesson from having Raymond call, and wasn't going to add insult to injury.

She doesn't care about Dante the way she does George and Raymond anyway. Dante shows her a fantasy side of life, and she loves his status. She has a good time when they see each other, but their affair was short lived, and they haven't been intimate in months. She doesn't drink when she is pregnant, so her visits to the bar became less frequent as her pregnancy progressed.

Josephine thinks about Dante more than she cares to admit, especially when she looks at her newborn. The day after Father's Day, she calls him, and he is thrilled to hear her voice. "Hello Josephine! Raymond told me you had a baby girl. Congratulations! I bet she is beautiful—especially if she looks like her Mama."

Josephine is straightforward, "She has bone straight hair and olive skin, Dante."

Initially dumbfounded, he recovers, "Hmmm…do any of your other children have straight hair and olive skin?"

"No, she's the only one."

Dante's thoughts scramble, and after getting nowhere fast or slow, he asks, "I'm trying to remember when we began having sexual relations."

"That's all I've thought about—it was August of last year."

Dante counts on his fingers, "So, if I do the math correctly, that was nine months ago. Josephine, is she my child?"

"I don't know, Dante. George and I had been fighting and weren't having sex regularly, and I wasn't intimate with Raymond during the time she was conceived. I just don't know. Maybe she'll change in a couple of months."

"But you said none of your other children have the same features." Josephine is silent. "What is her name?"

"Suzette Marie."

"Suzette Marie, what a pretty name. Josephine, do you think Suzette is my child?" he asks again, hoping she will give him a definitive answer.

"Dante, I told you, I don't know."

"I want to see her. Do you need anything—money, diapers, milk? I will give you anything—and I mean anything you need. Just tell me, and it's yours," says a shaken Dante.

"What I need, you can't give me—and that's peace of mind. You can't buy that, Dante. Look, I'll bring her by in a little while. Goodbye."

He says goodbye and hangs up the phone. He wonders if Suzette is his—the timing and description fit. He smiles in anticipation of seeing them both, a feeling inside tells him she is his daughter.

Josephine enters carrying Suzette, who is wearing a pretty lavender dress and white satin slippers and is in a lavender blanket. Josephine looks spectacular in her navy and white polka dot dress, having discarded most of the pregnancy weight. Dante makes his way to them the moment they come through the door. "Hello, Josephine, you look fantastic!" Josephine is subdued and half-heartedly thanks him before sitting down. She doesn't open the blanket quickly enough for Dante— his curiosity about Suzette ran rampant after their earlier conversation.

Dante beams at the sight of Suzette, "Oh, she is beautiful—she resembles my children by my mistress."

"What have I done? A second child outside of my marriage!" She breaks down and cries the tears she's held inside for the past six weeks.

Dante urges her to take a deep breath and try to calm down. He tells Eddie to bring her a drink, which she readily accepts. "Josephine, I want to see my daughter and will give you whatever you need. You can bring her here or to my mother's home, whichever you prefer. I want you to be comfortable while I visit with Suzette. She's so beautiful!" Josephine almost finishes the drink with one gulp. Dante continues, "And when she's old enough, I want you to tell her I'm her father."

She almost chokes, "I'm not going to do that. This is my doing—not hers. This is my shame, not hers. She may look different than the others, but there's Native American on George's side so I'll just say that's where her looks come from. She won't know—and neither will anybody else."

"Josephine, everybody should know where they come from—no matter the circumstances."

She recalls being told about Mr. Clarence. "That can be painful, Dante. Trust me, I know from my own experience."

He asks what happened, but she refuses to talk about it and adds that Suzette and Sheila will not go through what she went through. "They won't know, and that is better for everybody. As far as I'm concerned, George Edward Price is their father, just as he is to our other children. I'm ready to go. Are you taking us home or calling a taxi?"

"I'll take you and my daughter home. That way I can see her longer. Hello, my pretty little Suzette."

Josephine is only home for a short time when the telephone rings. It's Raymond calling from the phone booth, "Hi, baby, what are you doing?" She wonders that very same thing.

CHAPTER EIGHTEEN

Not much has changed over the past five years in the Price household. It's June, 1955, and George is still working two jobs, going fishing and sitting in his easy chair. Delores attends college, and the school age children are now 7 to 15 years old and attend elementary, junior and senior high schools. Suzette starts kindergarten in the fall, and Josephine is eight months pregnant.

Dante regularly offers Josephine money and reminds her to let him know if Suzette needs anything. She takes the money sometimes but won't allow Dante to give Suzette money as it brings back memories of Mr. Clarence and his bribes. She never heard from him since her family moved twenty years ago, and only halfway listens when Millie wants to give her an update on him. The old adage "out of sight, out of mind" works for him, and it works just fine for her too.

Josephine and George remain married, and Raymond is still her lover. Both Raymond and Dante have suggested Josephine tell Sheila and Suzette that they are their fathers, but she denies their requests. Josephine has been clear that she has no intention of revealing her secrets to either of her daughters. She is determined to protect them from the hurt that comes with having a biological father different than the daddy that raises you. She is convinced that is better for everybody; most especially the girls.

George is aware that the two girls aren't his, but not from Josephine's admission; he sees the obvious resemblance to their real fathers. He stays in his marriage and takes the bad with the good. He and Raymond no longer have the garden and animals, but they still work together. Whenever it starts to grate his nerves that Raymond is having the affair with his wife, George consoles himself that he stays with Josephine for the sake of their children. In reality he loves Josephine, and she does take care of him, the children and his household. He has no interest in starting over with a new family at this stage of his life.

Josephine did not resume an intimate relationship with Dante, but she takes Suzette to see him once a month. He wants to see his daughter more often, but Josephine is inflexible, and keeps the visits to a minimum as she tries to strike some semblance of fairness. Suzette is a pretty little girl, and unlike her sisters, has long straight hair and olive skin. Josephine has told her that Mr. Dante is mommy's friend, and they visit sometimes when they're in his neighborhood. She also lets Suzette know that seeing Mr. Dante is their secret because her sisters and brother would be sad that they can't go since they are in school; and daddy would be sad, too, because he has to work.

Suzette feels like a big girl since her mama trusts her with a secret; and she certainly doesn't want to make anybody sad. They arrive at The Black Stallion, and Dante hurries over to them, "Hello, Josephine, hello, pretty Suzette! How are you?" Josephine is cordial, but the romance is definitely over—no sparks, no embers—not even smoke remain.

"Suzette, do you want some potato chips and your special chocolate-cherry drink?"

Suzette answers politely, "Yes, please. Thank you, Mr. Dante." Dante checks with Josephine, and although she wants gin and tonic, she settles for a coke since she is in her usual state of pregnancy.

Dante loves his time with Suzette, "Suzette, are you going to be in kindergarten soon?"

"Yes sir, after my new brother or sister is born. I'll be a big girl and go to school with some of my big sisters. But I can't go now because I'm still the baby."

Josephine interjects, "But not for long. You only have a few weeks before you're a big sister too."

Suzette cheers, "Yay!"

Dante is proud of his daughter, "I bet you'll be the smartest one in the class. Your mother told me you go to Miss Catherine's class and stay with the third graders sometimes."

"Yes sir, Miss Catherine lets me color and write my letters and numbers with the big kids."

"That's good, Suzette. I know you'll enjoy being in kindergarten. Would you like to color now? I have your crayons and coloring book right here." Dante places them in front of her and walks a few seats away. He motions for Josephine to join him.

"She resembles me more and more each time I see her; my genes are strong. Anybody can tell she has Italian, not Native American blood in her."

Josephine regrets that she took those few steps to listen to him, as she does not want to have this conversation. "Well, they'll be guessing at best. I'm not going to tell her—I'll take it to my grave. When I die, my secret will go right in the casket and ground with me."

Dante tries to ward off her defensiveness, "I wasn't pushing you to tell her, but I do want to see my daughter more often than twelve times a year. Now that she's older, I want to expose her to her Italian side of the family."

Josephine completely ignores him, "I'm going back over to her now. I need to get home and fix George's dinner so he can eat before he goes to his second job."

Dante knows the conversation is going nowhere, "I'll take you home," he says, hoping for an opportunity to revisit their conversation. Unfortunately for him, Josephine purposely keeps Suzette talking during the entire ride home. What part of "I'm not listening" does he not understand?

Only litter in the streets remains of the 1955 Fourth of July holiday, which boomed with picnics, concerts, parades and fireworks. Josephine's high hopes that her seventh (their eighth) baby would arrive by the holiday didn't materialize. She's not due until next week, but was hopeful the expected bundle of joy would arrive early.

For weeks now, a desire to talk with someone to release matters of the heart has been fueling steadily inside of Josephine. She is unsure if this urge is strong because of raging hormones or the combination of her pregnancy and the intense heat. It has been heavy on her spirit, and she needs peace of mind. Her first thought is to talk to her life-long bestest friend who she loves and trusts. But this heart to heart needs to be with someone who has navigated life a little longer and has more experience from which to draw.

Josephine's maternal second cousin, Louise, is the person she feels compelled to talk to, as she has always felt a close kinship with her. Louise, 10 years older, is also a great listener who has lived through some difficult challenges by learning some of life's lessons the hard way. She fought a cocaine addiction for 15 years before putting the powdery substance away for good—at least that is her intent. Clean for five years, Louise works with a community program at The Columbus Urban League and helps people she readily identifies with in their struggle to conquer addictions. Other than signs of early aging, Louise doesn't appear as weathered as her addiction could have deemed. She is a pleasant woman, short and pudgy, with shoulder length, naturally-curly hair. She is a people pleaser and lives a somewhat healthy lifestyle, except for the cigarettes that seem to replace her cocaine addiction.

Josephine feels a wave of relief when Louise pulls up in a 1954 blue Chevrolet convertible. She struggles to stand up to greet her, but instead decides that staying seated is the better choice. She is willing, but with the baby weight she is carrying, she isn't able. Louise complains about the heat as she walks to the porch. She joins Josephine on the porch swing and as it sways, she feels a slight breeze that wasn't in the air before. "I was surprised you called; we haven't talked in a long time. Are you okay? I mean, I see you're good and pregnant, but what's going on, little cousin?"

"Other than wanting this baby to get here, I'm pretty much okay; but I need to talk. You've always shown me kindness and love; you were one of the first family members to accept George. I want to speak openly; and some of what I plan to share, I've never shared with anybody. Louise, I trust you, but I need your word you will keep our conversation confidential. Can I speak candidly?"

"You have my word and my undivided attention. I'm here for you; feel free to talk openly."

"This is very difficult, and I've held this inside for so long. But for whatever reason, I feel like I'm going to burst if I don't release it from my spirit."

"Just relax, Josephine, and start when you're ready. Mind if I smoke?" Josephine looks down at her belly, and then back at Louise. "Oh, never mind, if I feel like I'm going to have a nicotine fit, I'll walk away and take a few puffs," she says, hoping not to send Josephine any closer to the edge.

"Louise, let me ask you a question. As far as everybody in the family is concerned, who is my daddy?"

"Josephine, everybody knows your daddy is Thomas Stewart."

"Well, that's partly true. He raised me as his, but my biological father is Clarence McElroy."

Louise is shocked, "Huh? Where in hell did you get that nonsense?"

"Straight from the horse's mouth—or I should say the mare's mouth, Mama. She told me when I was about eight-years old. She had an after-hours business at our house; and Mr. Clarence, who was the mayor of Harriman, would visit and bring me money and gifts."

"Josephine, I had no idea. Millie must have kept that one to herself, because I'm sure if my mama had known, it would be common knowledge. You know how so-called secrets travel, and I can honestly say I never heard it before now. She must have left that one in Harriman when you all moved here, so it really comes as a surprise."

"Louise, let me keep going while I can. Now we come to my life and my choices. It seems after what I went through, I would have chosen to be with one man so there would be no doubt about the father of my children. But a couple of years after George and I were married, I found myself in an extra-marital relationship, and he is still my lover. And Louise, I…."

Louise interrupts, "You're talking about Raymond, right?"

"Yes, but how did you know?"

"I told you about so-called secrets. Everybody knows you and Raymond are lovers—including his wife."

That took the wind out of Josephine. "I had a feeling Beatrice knew, but I didn't realize it was general knowledge! But there's more—Raymond and I have a child."

"I know; it's Sheila."

Josephine is stunned, "How do you know? I've given birth to six children. How do you know Sheila is Raymond's?"

"Again, I say, what we think are secrets, are not secrets at all—somebody always knows. The reality is that if one person tells another person, then it's no longer a secret. Secrets only exist if nobody else is involved, which is rare because most secrets involve at least two people. George confided in Mark that he thought Sheila was Raymond's, Mark told Grace, and I heard it from one of her friends."

Josephine is unsure if it's the heat or the conversation, but she suddenly feels like she is going to pass out. "I am shocked; I thought it was my secret. So do you know my other secret that, if we use your logic, may not be a secret at all?"

"Are you talking about Dante being Suzette's father? You can look at that child and know she's part Italian."

Josephine thinks she will have her baby on the spot if this conversation lasts much longer. "Louise, how long have you known about Suzette?"

Louise is apprehensive, but honest. "Do you recall I visited you the day after Suzette was born? You probably don't remember Mama Rose commenting on her straight hair and olive skin. I knew you had met Dante the year before. I saw the two of you together at his bar, and it was obvious there were sparks between you. I didn't say anything—it wouldn't have served me to point it out anyway. Everybody talks about how different Suzette looks from your other children, but they don't say much about Sheila."

"I really don't know what to say. I feel so much shame for what I've done; but I want to protect them from the pain I experienced from knowing the truth. George is no fool; he knows Sheila and Suzette aren't his, and he hurls it at me sometimes when we argue. But he still stays—he'd have a hard time starting over with another woman anyway. Nobody would want him with seven children."

She looks down and rubs her belly. "We still enjoy making love from time to time, but I think we've hurt each other so much, we won't ever rekindle the love we had when we met. Our marriage is more out of convenience now, but I know he loves me, even though he doesn't say it. It seems like after we got married, he decided he didn't have to tell or show me much affection. But girl, I love that man's dirty drawers. There were times I would fight over my man!"

"Marriage takes work, and most people think that folks just say 'I do' and everything falls into place like in a fairy tale. I work to keep my 24-year marriage together. Sometimes Reggie gets on my last nerve, but other times I couldn't love him more." Josephine nods her head in agreement. Even though some of Louise's comments have been hard-hitting, she already feels a bit of relief.

Louise treads into forbidden territory. "Josephine, have you told Sheila that Raymond is her father—you're probably waiting until Suzette gets older before you tell her about Dante. By the way, are you still seeing them?"

"I take Suzette to see Dante from time to time, but I'm not intimate with him anymore. Dante was like forbidden fruit, but I don't care enough for him to stay in a relationship; I only see him because of Suzette. Now Raymond, I don't know what it would take to get me away from him. George is my first love, but Raymond is my second. I think I fell so hard for George because…

Louise can't help but interrupt, "Because he is fine."

"Well, yes, he's definitely fine—that hasn't changed, but I also think with him being older, he represented a father figure for me. Lord knows he tries to boss me around like he's my daddy. But Raymond, he's so affectionate, and always tells me how much he loves me. He asks me about me and listens, which makes me feel really loved. I can't tell you the last time George told me he loves me. But he loves the way I cook and wait on him hand and foot. But that's my husband, I love him, and I vowed until death do us part. I'm not miserable, but that's in part because Raymond fills the voids."

"So, have you told Sheila about Raymond?"

"No, and I will not tell either of them—not now, and not ever. I vowed I would carry their fathers' identities to my grave. And that's exactly what I plan to do."

"Really? Do you mind if I weigh in on what you just said?" Josephine feels a contraction and rubs her belly. She nods her head yes. Louise wishes she could light a cigarette or two after hearing Josephine's vow. "I think you should tell them—and the sooner the better. You know Sheila and Suzette look like their daddies. Don't you think they get the same kind of remarks you got when you were growing up?"

Josephine tries not to get upset, "I'm not going to hurt them. I just have to love them and live with the facade that George is their father. He doesn't treat them any differently than he does our other children; and we are a family. Sheila doesn't know about Raymond, and I don't let Raymond have a relationship with her. Sometimes I tell him where we'll be so he can just happen to be there and see her, but I won't tell her he's her father. Pretty soon I'm going to stop taking Suzette around Dante because I don't want her to put two and two together, or tell anybody that we go see him."

Louise notices Josephine is becoming tense, and rubs her back. "Josephine, I understand where you are, but you must realize that they will have the same experiences you had coming up because of the way they look. They should know who their real fathers are. It would help them when people make comments. You knew where you came from— why shouldn't they?"

"For that very reason, Louise, because it was hurtful knowing where I came from. I wasn't daddy's child; I was an accident, a bastard born from my mother's extramarital affair. My parents didn't make me on purpose, and I'm a product of my mother's guilt and shame. Sometimes I feel ashamed for even being alive." Josephine is upset,

"Louise, talking to you was a mistake. I thought it would make me feel better, but now I'm feeling worse. And I told you something that is very confidential, and I ask that you don't tell anybody about Mr. Clarence. I'm going to lie down for awhile. I feel like I'm having contractions, but it's probably because I'm upset. I'm sorry I bothered you, and I appreciate you coming over."

Louise continues to rub Josephine's back. "Josephine, I'm not going to tell anybody, I promise. It wasn't a mistake for you to talk to me; and it's good you got that out of you. I'm flattered you chose me to talk to about something so personal. I didn't mean to make you feel bad; I was only being honest and trying to help you see things from the girls' perspective. God doesn't make mistakes. You got here the way you were supposed to—and the same pertains to Sheila and Suzette. You are a beautiful person; you love people and treat them real good. I hope you think about what we've shared; and I pray you love yourself more and find peace about your own existence. I love you, and I am here for you anytime. You need to settle your nerves and go ahead and lie down. I'm going to smoke a cigarette and head back home. I have to get dinner ready so I can work on making it 25 years with Reggie. Girl, you look like you're dropping lower by the minute. I'm getting away from you. I don't want you having your baby on my watch!"

Josephine laughs for the first time since their discussion began. "Thanks, Louise. I love you too." Before she or Louise move to get up from the porch swing, Josephine feels a sharp pain in her stomach, followed by the familiar liquid rushing down her legs. "Uh, don't leave yet; my water just broke."

Louise is frantic, probably more so because of the absence of the cigarette she wants so badly. "Okay, what do I do? You want me to drive you to the hospital? Oh girl, I need to calm my nerves first! I've got to take me a quick puff."

Josephine ambles to her feet, "Get Mama Rose. She'll call George and either drive us to the hospital or come over and stay with the kids, if George gets home quick enough." Louise sees Mama Rose's screen door open and shouts, "Mama Rose, we need you," while helping Josephine into the house. She dashes back to the porch to take a few much-needed puffs of her cigarette.

As Louise draws the smoke in and slowly blows it out, she replays their conversation in her mind. It was revealing, and she thinks Josephine understands there are very few, if any, real secrets. She hopes Josephine understands that she is subjecting her girls to the same hell she went through. The only difference, as hard as it may be for Josephine to accept, is her mama told her the truth. Sheila and Suzette deserve to know the truth about who they really are, and what they do with it is for them to decide. She prays that when Josephine thinks about withholding the truth about their fathers from them, she realizes it is not a secret, but an outright lie.

Mama Rose calls George and is over to Josephine's in less than two minutes. "Baby, George is on his way home; how far apart are your contractions?" Josephine answers that they're about seven minutes. "Well, we have time to wait for George. I'm sure he's driving 90 miles an hour—I'm glad he's not far away. It's something else that they want you to go to a hospital to have your babies, instead of just having them at home."

Louise calls Shirley, who is there in what seems like seconds. "Josephine, what trick are you performing with this baby? You missed the holiday, and you're not in the bathtub!" They laugh as Josephine playfully rolls her eyes at Shirley, glad to see her bestest friend, who is always at her side.

George arrives, "Well Josephine, it's time for you to have the fireworks you wanted last week. Let's get you to the hospital." Five hours later, little Audrey makes her entrance wailing to the top of her lungs. She's a tiny, chocolate bundle of joy. Grandma Rose looks at Audrey and is happy to see a reflection of herself.

CHAPTER NINETEEN

By early October, 1958, Josephine has given birth to her eighth child, and the Price brood has reached a total of nine children. Jeff, barely three-weeks old, shares the same day of birth as his only brother, Stephen, who is 17 years older.

Delores is in her second year of nursing school. Pamela has graduated and works full time in retail. Stephen is a senior, Sheila is a junior, Donna is in junior high and Carolyn and Suzette are in elementary school. Audrey, now three, loves being a big sister to her newborn baby brother.

George continues to work his full and part time jobs, and enjoys going fishing and hunting in his spare time. Mama Rose is in good health and takes the children fishing. Thomas Sr. passed away a year ago, leaving Josephine and Betty the task of caring for their reclusive mama. Grandma Kirksey is barely able to help herself, but oftentimes will stay with her daughter, praying to God to heal her broken spirit.

Giving birth, raising kids, and running her household for over 18 years has been Josephine's claim to fame. The older children are now old enough to watch the younger ones, so Josephine gets away whenever she chooses. She lives her credo, "Life is just what you make it," as much as possible—much to George's chagrin. In Josephine's drama-filled life, she finds her escape several times a week by playing Pokeno, going drinking and dancing with her girlfriends and spending time with Raymond who no longer tries to convince her to tell Sheila he's her father. He is happy to still be in Josephine's life.

Josephine stopped taking Suzette to visit Dante after she entered kindergarten three years ago. Suzette kept their secret about their visits and didn't speak about him to anybody. Dante misses Suzette a great deal, but Josephine will not budge on the issue. Although he has the resources and could easily force her to let him be in his daughter's life, he decides to let Suzette grow up without him. He is willing to acknowledge and support Suzette; but he cannot make Josephine agree to allow him to have a relationship with her. Dante regrets his daughter will grow up not knowing the Italian side of her family, but is respectful enough of George to not press the issue.

On this particular Saturday afternoon George watches television with Stephen, while Donna and Carolyn play Scrabble and Suzette plays Solitaire. Suzette is waiting for her mama to return so they can play Scrabble. Playing with Mama is more fun than playing with her siblings; and she likes having her mama's full attention whenever possible.

Josephine and Sheila return home after shopping. As they walk through the door, Sheila comments about how much she likes her new dress and all the fun she had. Josephine agrees and tells her she will be the prettiest girl at the dance. She has every reason to be biased but isn't by herself with that opinion, as the store clerks told Sheila the same thing.

Sheila thanks her mama for going shopping, and then says, "Mama, I don't believe you asked if I thought Mr. Raymond looked like my daddy. He's not half as fine! Right, Daddy?" Sheila walks over and teasingly rubs George's hair.

As dark complexioned as he is, George's face turns red, and Josephine quickly changes the subject. "Sheila, show your daddy your dress." Sheila pulls the prized dress out of the bag and shows it to him.

"That's nice, Sheila. Now where did you see Raymond?"

His voice is a little edgy, and Sheila hesitates, "Oh, we saw him at the...."

Josephine interrupts. "We've been running all day and I needed to catch my breath; so we stopped at the Red Tavern for a few minutes. Raymond was there."

George snaps, "You could have kept going. I'm hungry, is my dinner ready?"

Josephine picks Jeff up and kisses him. "I don't know, George; as you can see, I just got home. I told Pamela and Donna what to fix for dinner, but I see they didn't. Pamela and Donna, get in the kitchen and get dinner fixed. Sheila, go help them please. Look, George, I'm not as young as I used to be, and I just had your son three weeks ago, remember? So would you give me a minute to get in the house before you start on me? Is Audrey sleep? I need to check on her. She was fussy earlier, and I want to make sure she's okay."

Stephen sees the waters getting troubled and disappears into his bedroom. He is always the first to retreat when their parents argue. He doesn't like to see his dad go through the arguments he feels his mama always starts.

George raises his voice, "You've had most of the day. You found time to go shopping and to the Red Tavern to see your man! You're always going to bars. Stop taking our kids with you, they don't belong there! You need to keep this house better and get back to cooking like you used to. I work two jobs to support this family—the least you could do is have my dinner ready at a decent time!" Sheila asks if she can take Jeff, and Josephine carefully hands him to her. Sheila then gives their infant brother to Carolyn and tells Suzette and Audrey to go to their bedroom.

"Get off my back, George! I wish I had time to run to bars like you say I do."

The children are all painfully familiar with how ugly their parents' arguments are to hear and watch. They don't have to look for the handwriting on the wall—the tension in the room can be cut with a knife. They know when it starts, it's best to get the smaller kids, and themselves, out of the way and hope it doesn't escalate too much.

Josephine moves so close to George that she would be eyelash to eyelash if she were taller. She continues her rant, "Let me tell you a few things I do. Now, where do I start? I know, let's start with the kids. I get the younger ones up and out to school. I clean the house as best I can, there is a three-week and a three-year old here; and I'm the one who has to take care of their needs all day—and all night long. And I try to keep up with the laundry. I fix dinner, go over homework and make sure the younger kids get to bed at a reasonable time. I volunteer for the PTA to stay close to their teachers. Plus, I actually enjoy working with the March of Dimes every year. Being on the nurses corps and singing in the choir lets me give some time to God. George, I try my damndest to do everything you expect of me, and I'm tired of you and everybody else pulling at me all of the time! I don't need your mess tonight. Just leave me the hell alone!"

"You have so much more support than I do. Daddy's dead, and Mama's alcoholism is a pain for all of us. Grandma Kirksey's health doesn't allow her to help me at all—I have to help them in addition to everything I do around here! I take care of you, the kids and them. Thank goodness Aunt Susan keeps the girls once in awhile. But other than her, I don't have any elders to talk to or help me. It's convenient your mother lives next door; and she helps, but I help her too. And George, I know I'm your personal servant, and I try to get your dinner ready on time since that's so important to you. But I have to do for everybody, and who's doing for Josephine? Oh, please allow me to answer that—no damn body!"

Stephen blares his music to drown out his parents' bellowing voices. Pamela, Sheila and Donna come in at different times and beg them to stop arguing. Their pleas go unanswered, and the argument escalates. It is always nerve-wrecking for the older girls, who are scared themselves, to have to console Suzette and Audrey, who are scared and crying.

Donna knows her mama may fuss at her later for calling the police, but they rely on the police to stop them before somebody gets hurt. She calls the operator for help. "My parents are yelling at each other, and when my mama gets mad, she fights my daddy! He doesn't usually fight her back, but they argue really bad! Can you please hurry and send the police?" The operator gets their address, assures her they will send the officers out, and tells her to let them in when they arrive. She also cautions Donna to stay out of her parents' way so she doesn't get hurt. Donna tells her she thinks she can sneak past them and get to the front door. "Please hurry," she says pitifully. The operator reassures her that the police will be there in a few minutes. Donna thanks her and stays as far away from her arguing parents as possible while cautiously moving toward the door.

George is fuming, "Woman, you better get out of my face! You talk about everything you do. The older girls help with the meals and the household chores, so you don't do them by yourself. You do go out drinking and screwing around with your men Raymond and Dante— that's why things don't get done around here. You're lucky I stay married to you—especially after you bringing those babies into our marriage! You whore!"

Josephine completely loses control and screams. "You're calling me a whore?! You, the biggest whore in town until your ass got too old to keep up with the women. Shut the hell up and leave me alone!" Two policemen arrive, and Donna lets them into the house. Josephine is still screaming in George's face and doesn't notice them. She swings at George and one policeman grabs her arm, but doesn't get a firm grip. Blinded by rage, she turns to him, grabs him and rips his shirt. The second policeman grabs her arms, holding them tightly behind her back, "Ma'am, you better calm down! You tore the officer's shirt! We could arrest you for assault!"

George speaks up for Josephine, "Officers, she's a spirited woman and has been through a lot lately; our newborn son is only three weeks old. But she'll calm down, won't you Josephine?"

Josephine glares at George, rolling her eyes, "Yes, I will." She looks at the officer and is apologetic, "I'm sorry I tore your shirt, officer. I didn't realize you were here, I thought you were my son, and I wasn't going to have him in our business. I'm genuinely sorry, and I promise it won't happen again, sir."

The policeman is rightfully upset. "Alright ma'am, but you better keep your hands off of police officers! We'll let you go this time, but you will go to jail next time, and you can count on that. Your kids shouldn't hear, much less see either of you behaving this way. Look how upset and scared they are. You need to find another way to work out your differences." He looks at George, "Sir, are you sure everything is alright?"

George is relieved that they don't arrest Josephine. "Yes, officer, I'm sorry you had to come out. Everything is alright now." As they leave, the officer looks at his partner, "Man, you're a better one than me. If she had put her hands on me, she'd be handcuffed, in the back of the wagon and on her way to the station. I don't care if she just had a baby."

After the officers leave, George gives the girls their marching orders, "Sheila and Pam, go finish dinner. Donna and Carolyn, bathe Audrey and Jeff, and then take your baths. Suzette, go tell Stephen to turn that music down. Be sure to take your bath when it's your turn. I'm going to sit in my chair. Josephine, why don't you go lie down?"

Josephine answers sarcastically, "Yes, Daddy. Suzette, get me some ice water and bring it to me, baby." Suzette feels sorry that her mama gets so upset, and is glad she can be near her before she goes to sleep. "Yes, Mama."

Josephine goes upstairs to her bedroom, and the phone rings. George waits until she answers, picks up the phone in the living room and listens with his hand over the receiver. Raymond is calling from the phone booth. "Hi, Josephine, I just wanted to hear your voice one more time before I went home. It was good seeing you and my Sheila earlier. I'm glad she liked the dress I bought her." Josephine doesn't respond. "Josephine is something wrong?"

"No, I'm just tired. I'll see you tomorrow, Raymond."

"Okay, baby, get some rest. I'll call you tomorrow," he says, sensing it's not a good time for her to talk.

George winces, hangs up the phone, and stands still, praying for the guidance to sit down in his chair instead of going upstairs for round two. He thinks this has to be payback for the womanizing he did early in their marriage. George never thought the shoe would be on the other foot, and he would be the one to bear the brunt of betrayal.

CHAPTER TWENTY

August of 1962 brings hot fun in the summer time. Carolyn and Suzette are spending the weekend at Aunt Susan's house. Aunt Susan is the only remaining elder on Josephine's side, as Millie succumbed to alcoholism and depression in 1959; and her mama, Minnie, passed two years after losing Millie. It is a treat to go to great Aunt Susan's house, as there are only two or three people there at one time, which is a far cry from the usual eleven at the Price residence. Aunt Susan is tall and stout like her sister, Minnie Kirksey, and is a devout Christian as well. At 80 years old, it is difficult for her to get out to church regularly, so she loves radio and television evangelists.

She has listened to her favorite evangelist, Oral Roberts, since he started on the radio in 1947. She is a devoted follower and found it a blessing when he became a televangelist in 1954. She is listening to his radio program, dipping snuff and spitting in the old Maxwell House coffee can she keeps nearby.

She wants the girls to hear some of this good religion. "Girls, come in here so you can hear the Reverend Roberts preach. You can always learn something from a man of God." Suzette and Carolyn reluctantly join their favorite aunt, hoping they can get away after a short time of pretending to listen. They ask why she listens to him so much, and she explains, "Well, babies, I can't get out to church like I used to, and this is a true man of God. He preaches the word straight from the Bible."

Suzette is not impressed. "He sounds kind of boring to me. Do we have to listen to him?"

"Yes, you do have to listen; and girl, and I rebuke that spirit in you— Reverend Roberts is an anointed man."

Carolyn whispers to Suzette, "He's a boring man," and they both laugh.

Aunt Susan scolds them, "Your mama should make you all listen to him. Truth be told, she should listen to him herself. She needs to learn how to honor her wedding vows. Josephine has a good husband and doesn't do right by George. She ought to be grateful he stays. Why Suzette, he takes care of you and treats you like you're one of his own. I tell you, that George is a good man, and Josephine better change her ways! She probably thinks he won't leave because of you nine kids. But Josephine doesn't treat George right, not at all."

Suzette is stunned and wonders if she really heard Aunt Susan say Daddy isn't her daddy. The words felt like Aunt Susan stuck a knife in her heart and twisted it. She feels tears coming and quickly excuses herself, "I need to go to the bathroom." Aunt Susan doesn't notice Suzette is upset, as she is enraptured by the word. "Well you go on—and be sure to wash your hands after you flush."

Luckily the bathroom is only a few steps away, as Suzette barely reaches it and closes the door before she sobs uncontrollably. She flushes the toilet a couple of times, hoping it will mask the sound of her crying. She gets on her knees and prays, "God, Aunt Susan really hurt me when she said I wasn't Daddy's child. Mama's never said that to me. I thought Aunt Susan loved me. Why did she have to hurt me so badly? Why, Lord, why? What did I do to deserve this pain? What did I do?" She finally stops crying; but the sharp words have already penetrated her heart.

After the toilet flushes a couple of times, Aunt Susan calls out to Suzette and asks if everything is okay. Suzette finds a voice to say "yes ma'am" and wipes her face with a cold, wet washcloth. She checks in the mirror to make sure her eyes aren't noticeably swollen. They are slightly red, but she is prepared to say soapy water accidentally splashed in them if Aunt Susan asks. She probably wouldn't notice anyway; she's so engrossed in her reverend.

For the rest of the weekend Suzette pretends to be her happy-go-lucky self, but is sad at times. She can hardly wait to get back home to her mama, as she knows she would never hurt her like Aunt Susan did. Suzette feels like she is suspended in time. She is grateful when Sunday afternoon arrives, and her daddy picks them up to take them home.

Josephine likes getting an occasional break from her children but is always glad when they return. She is in the kitchen cooking dinner, "Well girls, how was your weekend? Did Aunt Susan fix her special creamed hamburger on toast like she always does?"

Carolyn answers, "Yes, ma'am, she did—and it was delicious as usual." Suzette is unusually quiet and doesn't react. Carolyn continues, "Mama, I'm going to go upstairs and unpack my suitcase. Suzette's been awfully quiet this weekend, but she won't tell me what's wrong with her." Josephine kisses Carolyn and tells her to come back down to help with dinner once she finishes unpacking.

She doesn't need Carolyn to tell her something is wrong with Suzette—she saw it on her face when she walked in. Suzette struggles to hold back tears, feeling better now that she's home with her mama who truly loves her. "Mama, Aunt Susan said something that really hurt my feelings." Josephine asks what it was, and Suzette shares what Aunt Susan said about her daddy. Josephine is not expecting to hear this today or any day in this or the next lifetime. Her mind races to think good thoughts so her face would not convey her horror.

"Mama, is it true? Is Daddy really not my daddy?"

Josephine struggles to mask her rising anger, "I don't know why she would say something like that, baby—she certainly doesn't know what she's talking about. No, Suzette, it isn't true at all. Your daddy, George, is your real father."

Suzette sighs with relief, "Thanks Mama, I don't know why she said that to me. That was so mean, and I didn't even do anything to her."

Josephine's inside temperature is at the boiling point, but she remains cool on the outside. "I'm sure she didn't mean that, sweetie. She's getting old and doesn't always realize what she says. I'll talk to her, but don't let it hurt you anymore, okay?"

Suzette knows if anybody would tell her the truth, her mama would, and she feels better. "Thanks Mama, she really hurt me. I hope I don't get old and hurt people."

Josephine wants to cuss, but laughs instead, "I hope you get old, but don't hurt anybody. Now why don't you go upstairs and unpack your bag? When you get finished you can help me with dinner too. I love you, and I'm glad you're home, baby."

"I love you too, Mama! I'll be right back. I don't understand how Daddy wouldn't be my daddy anyway—you've been married for over 20 years, and I'm only 12. Aunt Susan needs to take some math classes."

Josephine cringes, "That's right—22 years to be exact! Now you go on and unpack your bag." Josephine hugs and kisses her, as the tidal wave of guilt floods her spirit for lying to Suzette.

The moment Suzette's feet hit the stairway, she dials Aunt Susan. "Praise the Lord, Susan speaking."

Josephine speaks through clenched teeth. "Aunt Susan, I need to talk to you about you saying George isn't Suzette's father. Why in hell would you say something so crazy?"

Aunt Susan isn't fazed, "Because it's true. Why, I would think you would have told her by now." Josephine is livid, but Aunt Susan remains calm and continues to make her point, "You can look at that child and easily tell she's different from the others—even more so than Sheila. Suzette looks like her Italian father—a blind man can see that. When are you going to tell the truth and shame the devil?"

Josephine wishes she could reach through the phone. But if she did, she would be imprisoned for homicide—death by choking! "I'm not going to tell her. George is Suzette's father, just as he is to our other children. And I would appreciate it if you wouldn't say that to her again, she's just a child."

Aunt Susan sticks to her guns. "Josephine, Suzette is 12 years old, and she's old enough to hear the truth from you."

Josephine counts to ten; her teeth clench so tight her jaws hurt. "Suzette is mine, and I decide what she needs to know. I decide what to tell or what not to tell my child. It's not your place or your responsibility. You don't have children, and you have no right to say something so hurtful to mine."

Aunt Susan counters, "God didn't bless me with children. But if he had, I would at least tell them where they came from. I'm sorry I hurt Suzette, and I won't mention it to her again." Aunt Susan's religious side slips just a tad, and she condescendingly adds, "Your secret's safe with me, Josephine. The Lord is my witness; your secret's safe with me."

Josephine retorts, "Goodbye, Aunt Susan. And the next time you praise the Lord, be sure to ask him to forgive you for breaking my child's heart."

Aunt Susan feels badly that she hurt Suzette with the truth. She also feels badly that Josephine lies to her child and won't tell her the truth. "May the Lord bless you real good, Josephine." She hangs up the phone and shakes her head, "She truly needs Jesus."

Suzette returns to the kitchen to help her mama cook, hopeful they will play Scrabble after dinner. Josephine tells her that she and Aunt Susan talked, and Aunt Susan is real sorry about what she said.

Suzette is pleased, "That's good, because she really hurt my feelings. I was crying so hard I kept flushing the toilet so she and Carolyn wouldn't hear me. I was looking at the bathtub, and then I was trying to figure out why I was born in it. Mama, tell me again why."

"Because I thought I had to poop, but it was you instead." Suzette is disgusted, "Mama, I know babies and poop come out of different places. I can't believe you thought I was poop."

"When you're having contractions and there is pressure down there, it's hard to know exactly where the pressure is coming from. Don't get your feelings hurt again; some things you can only fully understand if you go through it. You may one day when you have children of your own; it's hard to explain otherwise."

Suzette giggles, "I kind of like the idea of being born in a bathtub—I was clean when I got here."

Suzette gets her wish when Mama pulls out the Scrabble board after dinner. She thinks everybody should have a mama who loves them like hers does. She's happy to be safely at home where she is loved.

CHAPTER TWENTY-ONE

There has not been a new bundle of joy in the Price family for six years, so nine is likely the final count for the Price children. Josephine and Suzette play Cooncan in the kitchen. Suzette is a mature 14-year old, who often asks her mama questions about the family. It is 1964, and today is no exception. "Mama, you don't look very much like Uncle Thomas and Aunt Betty, but they resemble each other. Was Grandma Millie married before?"

"No, Suzette, your Grandma Millie was only married to Grandpa Thomas. Why do you ask that question?"

"I just thought maybe she was, and you had a different father since you are the oldest."

Suzette has hinted before about how different Josephine looks from her siblings, so Josephine isn't surprised. "My parents were married two years before I was born. I'm going to tell you something that none of your siblings know, and I want you to keep this to yourself, okay?" Suzette nods her head yes. "My biological father is a man named Clarence McElroy, and he was the mayor of Harriman, Tennessee where I was born. He and Mama had an affair, and that's how I got here."

Suzette is floored, "Oh, I didn't know that! Did you know him when you were little?"

"Yes, I saw him regularly. Mama had an after-hours business at our house, and he would visit and bring me money and gifts. She told me he was my daddy, and it was a secret I wasn't supposed to talk to anybody about it. People always asked me if I had a different father, just like you're asking now. I wish Mama hadn't told me because it broke my heart to know that my daddy, Thomas, wasn't my biological father."

"I'm sorry, Mama, I hope I didn't make you feel bad. But at least you knew the truth. I think everybody should know where they come from; I would want to know."

Josephine measures her words, "I think if something is hurtful, there's no need to say it and create heartache for somebody. I would have been fine if I hadn't known about Mr. Clarence. We moved here when I was around your age, and I never saw nor heard from him again. And that was fine by me."

"Does it bother you that he is your father and not Grandpa Thomas?"

"Sometimes; but as your great Grandma Kirksey always said, "God is my true father.""

"I think it was your right to know about your real father." She pauses before daring to say her next words. "Mama, is Daddy my real daddy? People say Dante Romano, the Italian man who owns the Black Stallion Bar, is my real daddy. Is he?"

"Suzette, George Edward Price is your real daddy. People run their mouths just to hear themselves talk. Life is just what you make it, so I try not to let much bother me. I suggest you do the same," Josephine says matter-of-factly.

Suzette pushes, "Mama, are you sure?"

"Suzette, I've told you the truth. Now it's your turn to make a word; go ahead and make it." The tidal wave of guilt didn't hit Josephine this time; she was absorbed in the hurt she felt about her own daddy.

The phone rings and Suzette answers, "Hello. I'm fine, but who is this?" She hangs up and is amused as the voice is a familiar one. "Huh, that man thought he had his woman on the line. "Hi baby, how are you?" she says in a deep voice. She laughs and the phone rings again. She starts to answer it, but Josephine intervenes.

"That's okay, Suzette. I'll get it this time. 'Hello.'"

Raymond is happy to hear Josephine's voice, "Hi baby, how are you?"

"I'm fine, and you?"

"I'm okay, but I'd be better if I saw you. Can I pick you up soon?"

Josephine replies, "Sure." Raymond suggests thirty minutes, and she responds "yes."

She hangs up the phone and Suzette asks, "Was that a man on the phone? It's probably the same one that just called." Josephine says he had the wrong number, and Suzette responds, "But you talked to him for awhile."

Josephine covers her tracks, "It was probably the same man. He asked how I was and then must have realized he had the wrong person. He asked to confirm the number he was calling and I said 'sure.' Then he said the number, and I said 'yes,' and he apologized for calling. I'm going to the store and pick up a couple of items for dinner, but I'll be back in a little while." Suzette wants to go with her, but Josephine tells her to stay home and keep an eye on Audrey and Jeff. "I want to get some fresh air anyway."

"Okay, Mama. Can we play Scrabble again later?" Josephine agrees, and hurries to get ready to meet Raymond.

Donna comes into the kitchen and Suzette whispers, "Donna, you won't believe what Mama just told me. She totally blew my mind!"

"What did she tell you?"

Suzette is skeptical, "Now, you can't say anything because she said it's a family secret, okay?"

"Suzette, you and your secrecy crap. Quit whispering. Now what did Mama say?"

"She told me her biological father isn't Grandpa Thomas—it's a man named Clarence McElroy. Did you know about him?"

"No, I don't know anything about him. Are you playing with me? Really, Suzette, why would you make up something like that?"

"I'm not making it up; that's what she just told me."

"I'm going to ask the older siblings if they know anything about him. Why would Mama tell you a secret like that anyway—you're not one of us older ones."

Suzette regrets saying anything to Donna. "I don't know why—she just did."

"Yeah, right. Look, I'm going to get my magazine. Now don't you go finding out anymore family secrets while I'm gone, okay?" Donna shakes her head and laughs as she leaves the kitchen. She knows Suzette doesn't normally lie, but that story is too far-fetched. As one of the older ones, she would certainly know if their mama had a daddy other than Grandpa Thomas. She thinks Suzette is playing a prank, and gives her credit; because she almost fell for it. But she is not going to ask her mama, that's for sure. So that secret, if it is true, is safe with her.

Suzette is relieved when Sheila comes into the kitchen. She is anxious to find out how things went last night at the Jamaica Club. Sheila saw Etta James, a rhythm and blues icon. She is proud of her big sister's determination to make it to the big time in her singing career. Sheila even talks about moving to New York. Who knows, Suzette may even get to visit her there one day, if she's lucky. "Sheila, how was the Jamaica Club last night? Did you see Etta James?"

"I certainly did. Not only did I see her, I sang with her."

"You sang with the famous 'At Last' Etta James?"

"Yes, Suzette, there's only one Etta James."

Suzette feels like her big sister has already made it to the big time. "Wow, I know that was a trip!"

"Yes, it was. She invited me to hang out with her and the band members afterwards. They had food and plenty of alcohol. They were really fine, but Etta did a good job keeping them away from me. I think she wanted them all to herself. I can't blame her—they were fine!"

"She probably did, but they may have wanted some choc-o-lot."

That comment doesn't set too well with Sheila, who is sensitive about her browner complexion. "Right, after all, she is high yellow, like you."

Suzette doesn't understand Sheila's gruffness. "Sheila, why are you calling me high yellow? You say it like there's something wrong with my color."

"Well, there's nothing wrong with you being high yellow, but I don't appreciate you calling me dark!"

Suzette is confused, "I wasn't calling you dark. I just said you were choc-o-lot. I think you're beautiful, good Lord!"

"Well, I think you're half white, half Italian or whatever you are!"

"Well, I think you're stupid, dark and ugly, Sheila!"

Sheila shrills at the top of her voice, "You little bitch, you'd better quit talking to me like that!"

Suzette screams back, "You'd better quit talking to me like that! I don't like being called yellow, just like you don't like being called dark! I was only kidding about Etta James; I wasn't trying to insult you!"

The girls exchange a few other unpleasantries before Sheila decides to calm things down. Suzette is unafraid, and Sheila has never seen so much fire in her little sister. She takes a deep breath and touches her arm gently. "Okay Suzette, we are totally out of control! Let's take a deep breath. I apologize for jumping on you like that. We're sisters, and our color doesn't matter."

Suzette takes a deep breath, not believing she got so angry with her big sister. Sheila is much taller and stronger than Suzette, so she must have temporarily lost her mind to stand up to her. "I'm sorry, too, and I really wasn't trying to hurt your feelings." She pauses before talking again and decides to ask a question that has been on her mind. "Sheila, sometimes when Mama and Daddy argue, he says two of us aren't his. And from the looks of things, I would say it's you and me. Do you think Mr. Raymond is your daddy?"

Sheila cannot believe her sister is asking this question after what just happened. She has to work hard to maintain control. "No, I don't think, neither do I care about Mr. Raymond because Daddy is my daddy.

Suzette, why are you asking me this?" As sarcastically as she can sound, she asks, "Do you think Dante Romano is your real daddy?"

Suzette knows her sister is angry, but she has wanted to have this conversation for some time, and since they've already squared off and she survived, she's ready for whatever comes next. "Well, as much as I'd like to say no, sometimes I do think he is. I mean, I really don't look much like any of you. But when I ask Mama, she always says, 'George Edward Price is your daddy,' almost like it's a recorded message. I try not to think about it, but people are always asking if I have the same daddy as you all."

"Suzette, I can't believe you. Did Mama slap the cowboy piss out of you when you asked her that? You're brave, girl! I wouldn't have the nerve to ask about Mr. Raymond."

"Well, as Daddy says, 'that's the difference between me and you.' Why shouldn't I ask her—everybody is always asking me. I just want to know because I get tired of trying to convince people that I'm part of this family. And I have a right to know. Mama gave me life, but it's my life; and I should know the truth, just like you should know."

Donna returns to the kitchen. "What were you two arguing about? You're lucky Mama's not here."

"It was nothing, Donna, we're okay now," Suzette says.

"Donna, Suzette had the nerve to call me dark, and then got all upset when I called her high yellow."

"Sheila, I didn't call you dark, I said you were choc-o-lot. Geez, there is a difference you know."

Donna laughs, "Suzette, you really need to be quiet, sitting over there looking like the mailman delivered you to the wrong address."

Donna and Sheila laugh and Suzette gets upset. She slams the rest of the Scrabble pieces in the box and gets ready to leave the kitchen. "Donna, that's not funny!"

"Well, it was meant to be a joke. You know Daddy's not your father, so you might as well take a joke—or the truth for that matter," Donna says.

Suzette is hurt and angry but blinks the tears away, "You always tease me about being different, like I want to hear it. It's hurtful in case you haven't figured it out! I wish you would shut up and keep your smart ass comments to yourselves!"

Sheila taunts Suzette, "Suzette, you should live in Egypt because you're in 'da Nile!'"

"Well, Mama says I'm Daddy's, and she's the one who knows. So I'm not going to accept or worry about what anybody else says, and that includes you!" Suzette fights the tears and doesn't want her sisters to see how hurt she is. She doesn't think they care anyway, as they always tease her about her long straight hair and color. "I don't even want to be in this family anymore. You are my big sisters, and you're supposed to love and protect me. But instead you enjoy teasing me about the one thing that hurts me the most. Donna, I wish you would quit being so mean; and Sheila, you are in the same boat with me. You look like Mr. Raymond, so you're in 'da Nile' too!"

"I know you're not going there with your bi-racial self. At least I look like my siblings!" Sheila says, trying to hurt her little sister who just pushed her buttons for the second time. She has dealt with the same issues Suzette has and is relatively sure Mr. Raymond is her daddy, but she has no intention of asking, as she is unsure if she could handle the truth. She is somewhat envious of Suzette for being brave enough to approach the subject with their mama. Sheila is angry about the situation, but she would just rather not think about it and maybe it will just go away.

"You may look more like them than me, but you can tell you're different too. So shut up Sheila; I'm sick of you!" an exasperated Suzette screams.

Sheila is not going to deal with any more of Suzette's drama. She needs to get ready to go back to the Jamaica Club anyway. And she makes up her mind that she is not going to let Etta James keep the band members away from her tonight. After all, this is a free country, and they're not her property. She is going to sing with Etta and talk to her fine band members too.

Donna tries to tell Sheila about Suzette's new-found secret about Grandpa Thomas, but Sheila tells her she has had her fill of drama for today and needs to get dressed. Donna is disappointed, but only for a short time, as she really doesn't think it's true. And she's certainly not going to ask their mama—enough said.

CHAPTER TWENTY-TWO

Suzette is at work on this blustery winter day in 1970. She works at The Columbus Urban League, the same community organization her Mama's cousin, Louise, worked at more than two decades ago. She answers the phone, and when she hears the tone in her mama's voice, she knows something is troubling her.

"Hi, Suzette, how are you?"

"I'm fine, Mama, but you don't sound too good. Are you alright?"

"I'm slow but sure. I have some bad news, though."

"What is it Mama, what's wrong?"

"A good friend of mine passed away, and I'm really sad. You should be sad too."

Suzette wonders who this person is that she should be sad about. It seems Mama would have said the person's name before saying how she should feel about them dying. "Who died?"

Josephine sighs, "Dante Romano."

Suzette is caught off guard, "Dante Romano? Why should I be sad about him dying?" Suzette finds herself getting angry at her mama who would tell her she should be sad about his death, but never confess that he was her father. She repeats herself, "Why should I be sad about him dying? Hmm…is it maybe, just maybe because he's my biological father?" Josephine doesn't speak. "I'm not sad about Dante dying. Sorry if that disappoints you. He must mean something to you, but he means nothing to me. Why should I care?"

Josephine thinks for a moment, "Because he was my special friend."

"Well, I don't care about him. I'm sorry you lost your friend, but don't tell me I should care about him dying. Your other friends or family members you call me about are people I know, and should feel sad about. So why are you calling me about him?"

Josephine has said as much as she can, "Baby, I'm sorry I called you. I usually call when I'm sad, but I'm sorry I bothered you."

Suzette reaches deep down to find some compassion, "Well, I'm sorry your friend died." She changes the subject and starts talking about one of the clients. Josephine isn't responsive, so Suzette tells a slight fabrication in order to get off of the phone. "I have to check on an applicant. I'll call you later. I hope you feel better, okay?"

Josephine is almost inaudible when she mutters, "Okay. I love you Suzette."

Josephine says goodbye in her and her mama's special way, hoping it will make her feel better. "I love you too, Mama. Boo boo."

Josephine responds mechanically, "Boo boo."

Suzette thinks how perfect of an opportunity this was for Mama to tell her the truth. The man is dead. Well, maybe she will tell her when she's on her own death bed, which she hopes won't be for a long, long time. Even though she's angry with her for not telling the truth about Dante, she wants her mama around as long as God will allow. Josephine is the only person Suzette feels is wholly hers.

Josephine thinks out loud, *I wish I had the courage to tell Suzette that Dante is her father. Lord, forgive me.* She takes another drink of gin and tonic and gets lost in watching her favorite soap opera, "As the World Turns." Josephine's life story could outdo her favorite soap opera, but she's not even remotely aware of it.

October, 1979 finds Josephine and George still married, and she and Raymond still lovers. All nine of the children are out on their own. Josephine continues to go out drinking with her friends and Raymond. George has retired and has more time to fish and watch television in his easy chair. Delores is a librarian, has a daughter and is divorced. Pamela is married with two young daughters, and she and her husband work at Westinghouse. Stephen, who has four daughters and a son, is retired from the Air Force and works at the Civil Rights Commission. Sheila lives in Sweden, has two daughters and is an international gospel singer. Donna is divorced, has two sons and works for the city. Carolyn, a single mom with a daughter, works for an insurance company. Audrey is married and works with a realty office. Jeff is single and in the Army. Aunt Susan passed away four years ago. She had pronounced that God was calling her home. She went peacefully, and the last television program she was known to have watched was Reverend Oral Roberts. Suzette is married to David and is two weeks past due with their first child.

Suzette has been up several times during the night feeling a strong urge to use the bathroom. She awakens around 5 a.m., and it dawns on her that the urge to poop is what caused her entry into the world via the bathtub. She thinks about her mama trying to explain this phenomenon to her years ago. Soon after David leaves for work, the contractions begin. She packs her bag, calls the doctor and then her husband. The elevator music playing while she is on hold is annoying, and she paces as she waits, enjoying the excitement of knowing she is a few hours from becoming a mom.

David answers, "Hi honey. Are you okay?" Suzette tells him she is wonderful and their baby is on the way. "Did you call the doctor—are you ready?"

"Yes, and yes. Bag is packed, and I'm ready to go. Be careful though, we have time; my water hasn't broken yet."

"I'm on my way! Now don't you get nervous—everything is alright, baby."

"David, it feels like Christmas in October! I can't believe I'm having our baby!" She laughs as she thinks about him asking her a few weeks ago what he was going to eat when she went into the hospital. Being the good wife, she made and froze chili and spaghetti so he could survive her being away for a of couple days—having his baby, no less.

David arrives home in minutes, and they make it to the hospital in plenty of time as Devon Michael Henderson is born six hours later.

David is a proud daddy, "Honey, he's a healthy, handsome boy—and at 9 pounds, he's sure to be a football player like me!"

Suzette agrees, "I think so. He has your build already—looks like a defensive tackle!" They laugh, happy their son is here and in perfect condition.

David says jokingly, "Suzette, he looks a little on the white side, though. I'm glad you told me about your daddy situation because I'd have some questions if you hadn't."

Suzette tries to take David's kidding in stride, but on a day that is one of the most special in her life, his offhanded comment steals a piece of her joy. She thinks about what she's had to suffer through because of her mama's extramarital affair with Dante. Suzette promised herself she would not repeat the actions of her mama and grandma; and has been monogamous in her relationships. "David, I told you my father was likely Italian, even though Mama still hasn't owned up to it. Two generations before me are enough of the family secrets and lies. The "mama's baby, daddy's maybe" curse is officially broken. I could never have a child and be uncertain about who the father is; you should know that about me."

"Don't get upset, honey, I was just playing. I love you, and I trust you. I know Devon is mine. Thank you for giving me a handsome son."

"I love you too, David; and I couldn't be happier that we have a child—our son, Devon. Wow!"

As they enter the hospital room, Josephine walks ahead of George. At 66, George moves slower, his advancing age and recently-diagnosed bladder cancer take their toll on his health. Josephine rushes over to see the newest addition to their family. "Congratulations Suzette and David, we are so happy for you. Let me hold my grandson! Oh, he's handsome—George, look how built he is already."

David's chest expands, "Yes, he took after his daddy."

"Mama, I had to think back to what you told me about me being born in the bathtub to realize I was in labor. I used to secretly resent you for saying you thought I was a bowel movement. Resentment gone, reality present, I understand perfectly now. Guess I did act like a little shit at times, though, huh?"

George and Josephine laugh, and Josephine answers, "Yes, you did, but that's alright." George smiles and nods his head in agreement. "George, look at his broad shoulders. What a cutie pie!"

George pats David on his back as he congratulates them. "David, you have a fine-looking son. Suzette, how does it feel to be a mother?"

"It feels real good, Daddy. We're so blessed."

Audrey enters the room, "Hi everybody—let me see my nephew! Oh! Congratulations new parents!" She looks at Suzette. "Suzette, why is your hair and makeup done? Didn't you have a baby a few hours ago? I'm telling you." She gets a whiff of Suzette's perfume. "And you're even wearing perfume!" Audrey looks around the room, "Where is the camera crew, or are the cameras hidden somewhere? You must think you're being filmed for a special for women on how to look like a beauty queen hours after having a baby. Girl, you're a trip."

Suzette laughs, "Audrey, you're funny! I wasn't going to be looking like 'Woo Woo' because I gave birth. I had to get myself presentable— you know that's how I roll! Just because I'm a mama doesn't mean I can't look good. But all kidding aside, I'm feeling so blessed. Thanks for being here everybody, especially you Devon. Welcome to our world, baby boy!"

Mamas' Drama

CHAPTER TWENTY-THREE

The summer of 1995 is egg-frying-on-the sidewalk hot. Suzette works at Ross Products in the contract marketing department. She and co-worker, Angela Colatrulio, have developed a good rapport, and Suzette has been instrumental in training her. Angela is an attractive Italian woman in her 40's, olive complexioned, with short, dark hair that is a little scarce in places. Her smile is engaging, and she easily takes center stage with her outgoing personality.

Angela is at her desk when Suzette arrives for work. After their morning greeting, she says, "Suzette, do you have a minute? I'd like to ask you a question, if you don't mind."

"Sure, Angela, this job has its challenges. I remember how overwhelmed I was when I started in this department a couple of years ago. What's your question?"

"Well, it's not job related—it's personal."

"That's okay, ask away!"

"Are you part Italian?"

Suzette couldn't believe her ears. She doesn't mind personal, but she didn't realize it was going to be to-the-bone-marrow personal. "No, I'm not; I'm Black."

"Really, all Black?"

"Yes, all Black. Both my mama and my daddy are Black."

Angela is straightforward. "Suzette, your mama may be Black, but your daddy is Italian."

Suzette is taken aback, "So exactly what makes you say that? Do you know something I don't?"

"I know what I see. I'm Italian—a proud one too—and I know one when I see one. You have Italian blood in you. Black—yes, half—but the other half is Italian. So if your mama is Black, your father's Italian."

Suzette has to keep in mind that she is at work in order to maintain her composure. "Unbelievable! What makes you so sure of yourself?"

"I've looked and looked at you, and I see keen Italian traits—your skin, hair, and features—even your mannerisms. I feel a bond with you, and you remind me of my two closest friends, Mona and Natalie; they're sisters."

Suzette wonders if her head is swirling around, or if it just feels that way. "Okay, guess I will share something since you're so convinced. I've always been told by siblings, relatives, friends—even strangers—that my biological father is Italian. My mother always denies it, though. Trust me, I've asked her many times. But you are more than likely correct with your observation."

"More than likely? I know I'm correct. Like I said, I'm a proud Italian, and I know one when I see one. Would you like to meet Mona and Natalie? We're going to dinner this week. Care to join us?"

Suzette tries to figure out if she's really having this conversation, and decides to answer just in case. Is God playing tricks on her or is He trying to tell her something she's supposed to know? "Sure, why not? You can show me the Italian side I've missed out on." She laughs, although she feels like she would imagine a punch-drunk fighter feels when he gets hit hard, but remains standing.

"It would be my honor to teach you. I'll call them and set it up. Does Thursday work?"

Suzette says "yes" and makes a plan to escape before her head pops. This woman didn't ask, she just told her she was part Italian. Wow, this has to be God! "Angela, I need to return some calls; I'll see you later."

Suzette needs to hear her mama's voice and calls her as soon as she reaches her desk. "Hi Mama, how are you?" They exchange small talk. Josephine tells Suzette her daddy and Uncle Mark went fishing, and Suzette talks about her drive to work. Suzette wishes she could tell her mama why she's really calling, but can't take hearing her lie. Josephine has a feeling there is something on Suzette's mind and wonders what she's not saying. She usually doesn't call her the first thing in the morning, especially from work. Suzette breaks the silence, "What are you doing today, Mama?"

"I'm watching Phil Donahue right now. Did you just get to work?"

"Yes ma'am. I had an interesting conversation with a co-worker a few minutes ago that made me think about you. So I'm just checking in."

"That's good. What was the conversation about?"

Suzette cannot answer and keep her workplace persona. An Italian woman just told her she is part Italian. She is in shock, but strangely not in denial. "Oh, nothing much, but I'd better get back to work. I just wanted to tell you I love you."

"I love you, too. Why don't you come by and get you some fish? I know they'll be bringing back a trunk full of them."

"Will do, Mama. Boo boo."

Josephine loves their special way of saying goodbye. "Boo boo, Suzette."

Angela approaches Suzette's desk as she's hanging up the phone. "I talked to Mona and Natalie. How about 6 on Thursday evening?"

Suzette checks her calendar. "It works for me—6 it is."

"Good, then we're on. I hope I didn't rattle you too badly earlier, but I know what I know."

"I'd be lying if I said you didn't, but a slap of reality is good I guess. You just hit me with truth as you see it."

Suzette attempts to change the subject and asks Angela to tell her more about her friends. Only too willing to do so, she tells her they had grown up next door to each other, and she, Mona and Natalie are like sisters. Feeling very comfortable, she talks about their father, who owned several successful businesses years ago when the girls were young. She talks about him having an Italian family and a family with his Black mistress too. Both families had the whole shebang—houses, cars, credit cards, etc., and he lived with both until he died in 1970. Angela drops another bombshell, "You remind me of his children with his mistress."

So much for changing the subject. "Wow, you just keep knocking me upside my head! I'm going to call you Gap Band pretty soon." Suzette sings the chorus from "Whoops upside my head!" and laughs nervously.

"Maybe I shouldn't have been so hard on you, but when you came off so 'Miss Black,' and I was looking at an Italian, I couldn't stand to hear you deny that part of you."

"Angela, until it comes from my mama's mouth, I will always be uncertain. And anyway, what if you're wrong?"

Angela finishes the conversation. "And what if I'm right?" Suzette just looks at her, knowing she probably is.

Suzette looks forward to dinner this evening with Angela and her friends. Angela talks a great deal about the Italian culture as if she is teaching Suzette an Italian 301 college-level course. Suzette has been listening, but hoping Angela will soon have her fill of trying to catch her up on her perceived Italian heritage.

Angela, Mona and Natalie await Suzette at The Marble Gang Restaurant. The band is in full swing when Suzette arrives, and Angela talks loudly to make introductions. "Ladies, I'd like you to meet Suzette, my Italian in denial. Whoops, I'd better say part Italian before she breaks out with her 'I'm Miss Black attitude!'" They all laugh at Angela's candor.

Mona is a beautiful woman with strong Italian genes. Her long dark auburn hair frames her non-blemished olive skin. She has a pleasant personality and laughs easily. Natalie is the younger sister and has medium-length brown hair with a nice golden complexion. She is somewhat quiet, which Suzette perceives as shy.

Mona speaks first, "It's a pleasure to meet you, Suzette."

Natalie chimes in, "We've heard so many wonderful things about you."

Suzette feels as though she knows them; not because of Angela's incessant history lessons, but the connection is strong. "You look familiar, but I can't put my finger on it. Maybe I've seen you here before." It is Mona's first time at the restaurant, and although Natalie has been there a couple of times, she doesn't recall seeing Suzette. "Oh well, hopefully it'll come to me where I know you from; maybe it's another lifetime," she says, knowing inside she feels strangely connected.

The women order adult beverages and dinner. Suzette finds herself feeling very comfortable, as if with close friends. She wonders why, but eventually dismisses it from her overly-active mind and continues to enjoy the evening. Dinner is wonderful, the music is great and the company, superb. The ladies plan to get together again in the next week or so; and as they bid farewell, agree to set another dinner date soon. On her drive home, Suzette is happy she met and spent time with the Italian connection and actually looks forward to seeing them again.

Suzette stops at Angela's desk Friday morning, and Angela asks her what she thought about Mona and Natalie. Suzette tells her she really enjoyed them and felt she knew them for some strange reason. "I'm looking forward to going out again," she admits. Feeling comfortable with Angela, Suzette shares her ultimate secret. "Angela, since you and I both think I have Italian in me, I want to share something else with you."

"Alright, go ahead Italiano."

"I've been told my biological father used to own the Black Stallion Bar on Champion Avenue. Do you possibly know who owned it back in the late forties, early fifties?"

"What a small world," Angela says. "We lived on Champion Avenue during that time. I don't know, but I'll call Mona. She may know since their dad was a businessman." Angela calls Mona, but she isn't in. "Well, let's try Natalie. I'll put us on speaker phone in case she answers." Natalie answers, "Hi Natalie, how are you? Did you enjoy dinner last night?"

"I certainly did. Suzette was so much fun. I'm looking forward to going out with her again—let's do it soon."

"We were just saying the same thing. We'll get Mona's schedule and set something up. Hey Natalie, I have a question. Do you know who used to own the Black Stallion Bar on Champion Avenue in the late 40's, early 50's?"

Natalie's response is like the shot that was heard around the world. "Daddy did, why do you ask?"

Suzette and Angela stare at each other in total disbelief. Angela takes the phone off of speaker, "Oh nothing, we were just talking about our old neighborhoods, and it came up. Natalie, I have a call coming in— I'll talk to you later."

Angela hangs up the phone like it suddenly burned her hand. Suzette stands there, stunned. Angela looks at Suzette with an expression that would freeze hot water in seconds. "Suzette, I don't want anything further to do with this."

Suzette is in shock. It is all she can do to nod and murmur "okay" as she somehow finds strength to walk away. She tries to make sense out of what just happened, but she can't. If she recalls correctly, Angela brought the matter up and doted on Suzette being Italian. Angela embraced her, and welcomed her into their Italian world. But when it becomes probable that Angela's best friends are Suzette's half-sisters, it doesn't matter at all that she is part Italian—Angela is finito.

Suzette feels the same stabbing pain she felt 33 years ago when Aunt Susan told her about her daddy. In a soft voice she whispers, "God, Angela just drove a stake through my heart. Why is there always pain for me? I guess you wanted me to know the truth, huh? This hurts."

She sits silently for a few minutes, struggling to keep the tears at bay. The phone rings, and she is grateful it's one of her favorite customers, Mr. Cleamons, as she direly needs a distraction from her confusion. Suzette now understands exactly why she felt so strongly connected to Mona and Natalie—she met her Italian sisters last night.

A few days later, Suzette drops by to visit her parents to cut her daddy's hair and trim his moustache. She has become his personal barber over the past few years, and he is still a satisfied customer. She also wants to check on the results of his recent visit to his internist, as his battle with cancer continues.

She doesn't play favorites, as she is her mama's personal hairstylist too. Josephine has grown accustomed to Suzette doing her hair since Shirley had to stop years ago due to poor health. Suzette loves spoiling her parents and does her grooming tasks with love and gratitude. Josephine already has the Scrabble board out, since her hair is still fresh from last week. After Suzette completes her barber duties, they play in the kitchen, while George is content watching television in the living room.

Suzette asks what the doctor said, and Josephine tells her that they removed more polyps from his bladder. He has lost weight, but he and the doctor agree that he is doing fine. Suzette is relieved, "That's good. I thought he looked a little gaunt, but I wasn't going to say anything. I just did my job and got him all trimmed up."

Josephine laughs, "You know your daddy doesn't want anybody fussing over him."

"Yes, I know, but it's hard not to; you taught us to pamper him since we learned to walk, and I'm not going to stop now. He loves it—even if he doesn't say so."

Suzette has wanted to talk face to face with her mama since she met Mona and Natalie. She makes a word on the Scrabble board, takes a deep breath and prays for strength to start the discussion—or at least to try. "Mama, remember when I called and said I thought about you after a conversation with a co-worker?"

"Yes, but you didn't tell me what it was about."

"I couldn't go into it then, but I'll tell you about it now."

Josephine makes her word. "I'm listening."

"Okay." She pauses for a minute before continuing. "An Italian girl who works in my department asked me what race I was. I told her I'm Black. She then asked if both of my parents are Black and I said 'yes.' She asked if you both were my biological parents, and I said 'yes.' She was adamant that since you're Black, my biological father is Italian."

"Well, when you told her your father and I were both Black, that should have ended the conversation. She doesn't know you!"

"There's more, Mama. Angela told me about her best friends; two Italian sisters who lived next door when they were growing up. She also talked about their father who had their family and a family with his Black mistress. Then she straight out said I look like the children by his mistress. I went to dinner with Angela and her two friends, and the sisters really looked familiar—especially Mona."

"Oh, you think you've seen them somewhere before?"

"I thought so. But they looked and felt—familiar."

"Well, all that means is that you've probably seen them before. Whose turn is it to make a word?" Josephine says, trying to end the conversation.

"Mama, I told Angela that I've always been told my father owned the Black Stallion Bar. She called Natalie, and guess who owned it— their father, Dante Romano. Mama, they are my half sisters!"

"That's not true, Suzette. Dante isn't your father; George Edward Price is!"

Suzette remains calm, hoping Josephine will decide to tell the truth. "Mama, it's okay to tell me; so many people say Dante is my father. I remember like it was yesterday when Aunt Susan, even though she didn't say who my father was, said daddy wasn't my father. But you said she didn't know what she was talking about. Mama, please be honest with me, please; I'm begging you!"

Josephine is adamant, "Suzette, George Edward Price is your father, not Dante. You tell your co-worker and anybody else that says that to you, they're a popeyed lie and to quit saying that nonsense. You are not Italian!"

Suzette pushes, "I wish you would tell me. I won't be angry—I just need to know. Please tell me the truth. I'm 45-years old, and at this point in my life, I would just like to hear the truth from you. I would respect you for having the courage to tell me."

Josephine is dismissive, "There's nothing to tell—George Edward Price is your real father. It's your turn to make a word, Suzette, go ahead."

Suzette is frustrated and knows she's reached yet another dead-end conversation on the subject. She feels like her mama is Peter, and the cock has crowed three times. She looks at her letters and smiles broadly, placing them on the board. "Wow, God is all up in this game! I can't believe I have this word—s-e-c-r-e-t, secret!"

Josephine quips, "I wouldn't have believed that one if I didn't see it with my own eyes. I'll be back, I need to use the bathroom." She knows Suzette is upset about their conversation, and tries to make her laugh, "And don't look at my letters while I'm gone."

Suzette gets a small dig in when she replies, "I won't look at your secret letters," more so under her breath than audibly.

George comes into the kitchen for a cup of coffee and on a whim she decides to talk about Dante. "Daddy, can we talk about something real quick?"

"Yes, Suzette."

"I love you so much and I'm thankful for everything you've done for me. You know the truth, and Mama won't tell me. Daddy, are you my biological father?"

George feels uncomfortable and unprepared to answer her; and stammers, "Suzette, I love all of you kids, and I know you are..." Josephine re-enters the kitchen at that defining moment, and George stops mid-sentence.

She asks what they're whispering about, and Suzette responds they are talking about his visit to the doctor. George fixes his coffee and looks relieved as he escapes from the kitchen—and Suzette's question. He doesn't want to tell her—he feels that's for her mother to do, since it was her decision to have an affair with Dante. He has provided for Suzette; and, even though he doesn't know that Aunt Susan told her over 30 years ago, he does love her as if she is his own.

Josephine sits down, "Let me make my word." She takes her time looking at her letters and compares their scores. "You're way ahead of me; I need to make a high-scoring word. Hmm...out of all these letters, I cannot believe the only word I can make is deceit. Deceit! Well, I'll be damned; you're going to win this game."

Suzette doesn't verbalize it, but she disagrees, as she feels Josephine has already beaten her. And the words played on the Scrabble board did what her mama couldn't do—they told the truth.

CHAPTER TWENTY-FOUR

The Price brood, with the exception of Sheila and Jeff, arrive at their parents' home. Sheila and Jeff are not aware of the meeting since they don't live in town. Everyone is curious about the urgent meeting called on this windy March day in 1998. Josephine did as George instructed—she called, asked the kids to meet, and did not answer any questions while on the telephone with them. She was torn apart because of what she knew, but abided by her husband's wishes.

George begins, "You all know I've been fighting cancer for over 20 years, and I've been winning. I got the news yesterday that the cancer has spread throughout my stomach."

Donna interrupts, "So Daddy, when are they going to start you on chemotherapy?"

"Donna, they aren't going to do chemotherapy. The cancer is too far advanced."

In an instant Donna becomes hysterical. "Daddy, then what are they going to do?"

"There is nothing they can do. The doctors say I have six months to live."

They all gasp in disbelief, and Pamela screams, "This just can't be. Daddy, are you sure?"

George, feeling numb more than anything, remains calm. "Yes, Pamela I'm sure." Donna, Delores and Pamela cry, and Audrey and Carolyn sit quietly in shock. Stephen paces as he fights back tears, while Josephine sits motionless in her chair.

Suzette also fights tears, "Daddy, what do you and Mama need us to do?"

"I'm still here; I feel alright, and things are okay for now. One thing I want everybody to know is that I don't want to be put in a nursing home, even toward the end. I intend to stay in my home and pass on right from here." The patriarch of the Price family made his announcement with an air of authority none of them have heard from him before.

Everybody is crying, hugging their daddy and telling him they love him. Suzette looks across the room and sees that Mama is almost catatonic. She walks over and holds her, wanting her to know that she is supported too. "Daddy, please let us know what we need to do. And Mama, you know we're here for both of you."

Josephine speaks for the first time since George gave his heart-breaking news. "Yes, baby, I know. We just need to take care of your daddy right now."

The family talks more about how they will move through the upcoming months. Their children leave, and George watches television from his favorite chair. Josephine fixes him a cup of coffee and a ham and cheese sandwich before going upstairs to their bedroom.

She calls Shirley. "Hi Bestest Friend, how are you? It feels like a month of Sundays since we talked." They laugh, almost to tears, as they catch up on the latest escapades with their children and grandchildren.

Josephine gets quiet. Shirley calls her name but there is no response. "Josephine, what's wrong?"

"George found out yesterday that his cancer has spread through his stomach. Shirley, the doctors say he only has six months to live." The tears she's been holding flow like an angry waterfall. "I'm doing everything I can to be strong, but it drains me to watch what he goes through. He's been fighting and winning for years, and now they don't give him any hope to live beyond six months. He's losing weight, and I know he's in pain, but he doesn't talk about it. You know how prideful George is."

Shirley tries to comfort her grief-stricken friend. "Oh Josephine, this is devastating; I am so sorry to hear about George! Please give him my love."

"I will, but keep us in your prayers; we'll get through it somehow.

I just needed to tell you. Shirley, I'm so lost. George has been at my side since I was 16 years old." Josephine cries again when she hears the bleak reality of her own words. Shirley speaks comforting words as Josephine pulls herself together—at least for the moment. "Well, I have to call Sheila and Jeff, and then I'm going back downstairs to watch TV with George. The kids are gone, and I know he could use somebody to sit with him. I just needed to talk to you." Once they hang up, Shirley prays for George, Josephine and their entire family. She knows Josephine and George's marriage has been turbulent, but she is well aware how deeply Josephine loves him.

Josephine is content that the kids were there to love and support their daddy earlier. She calls Sheila and Jeff and tell them the sad news. She feels so helpless that she can only comfort them with words, and is not able to hug them as they cried for their daddy. They talk to George and promise to visit soon.

For the first two months George's health doesn't noticeably change, but by June his health begins to show a decline. In August, he is not only losing his fight against cancer, but the fight to maintain his dignity. George's strength wanes, and he becomes so weak he is challenged to go up and down the stairs. The bedroom and bathroom are located upstairs, but unfortunately his strength will only allow him to climb the stairs once a day.

He has no choice but to wear adult diapers, and finds refuge lying on the living room sofa. His bladder continues to fail him, and the adult diapers don't hold the urine until he finds strength to change them. His urine oftentimes soaks through the diapers onto the protective padding on the sofa. Because of his pride, he only allows Josephine, who is always at his side, to help him change some times. She has to maintain an uneasy silence while watching her husband of 58 years suffer cancer's debilitating blows. Hospice offers a hospital bed, which would be more comfortable and make it easier to care for him, but George doesn't permit Josephine to accept it. They all plead with him, but he only allows Hospice to administer pain-killing drugs.

It's hard on everybody to see their husband, father and grandfather decline from the ravage of the disease. It is mid-August, and Suzette is leaving in a couple of days to take Devon to Morehouse College. She drops by to visit her daddy, and is appalled to see him lie on the urine-soaked pad, barely able to move. He still refuses the bed; and most times Josephine's help, even though he has little strength to help himself.

Suzette knows her mama has been forbidden to call Hospice and begs him to change his mind. He refuses, but Suzette boldly calls Hospice and requests the bed. She then lovingly but firmly tells her daddy the bed will be there tomorrow, and he will accept it. She reminds him that everybody loves him too much to see him in that condition.

George Edward Price, a man of extraordinary dignity and pride, relents as the reality that he can't manage his urine, or much of anything else at this point, is evident. Being able to place the onus on Suzette makes it easier for him to accept his fate. The hospital bed arrives, and George settles in and finds it surprisingly comfortable. The bed also makes it easier for Josephine and the visiting nurses to properly care for him.

George's will to live begins to leave him; and he can only lie in the hospital bed fully aware of what is happening, yet helpless to change it. His sharp mind is the only part of his body that remains unaffected by the disease. He lie there day and night, wishing his mind would shut off, as he feels the humiliation of his wife, daughters and strangers having to care for him and change the adult diapers he no longer has the strength to change himself. Watching George suffer through his last days on earth is taxing on everyone's spirit. He loses weight rapidly and has no desire to eat, taking only a few sips of nutritional liquid from time to time to appease his family. It is as if George's body accepts the doctors' six-month prognosis, as he passes away peacefully at home in September, 1998.

A week after George's funeral, Stephen calls a meeting at his home to discuss George's will. Suzette is supposed to take Josephine, but notices when she calls to remind her of the time she's picking her up, that she is intoxicated. She thinks it better that Josephine not go, and calls Stephen for his opinion.

"Hey Stephen, I'm getting ready to come over. I know you want me to bring Mama, but she's been drinking and is pretty tipsy; so I don't think she should come."

"Go ahead and bring her, Suzette. She needs to be here to discuss Dad's will."

"I really don't think she needs to be there in her condition."

He chuckles, "She's fine—she's been that way most of our lives. Go ahead and bring her." Suzette reluctantly agrees, but has a strong feeling things will go awry.

She calls Jeff and talks to him about the situation. "Sister Dear, she's our mother and Dad's widow. She should definitely be there. I think you should take her; it'll be fine."

"Okay, but I really don't want to—something tells me it's a big mistake. When Daddy told us he only had six months to live, he didn't tell us if he had a will. So me, Audrey and Pamela agreed to work together to make sure he had one. Come to find out after he died, Brian had written one back in June, and Pamela never told us about it. She claimed it was on their kitchen table for months, but Mama didn't even know about it. Daddy told me he didn't have a will, which is why Hospice suggested one. I don't get it."

"So, anyway, there are two wills—the one Hospice suggested where everything is left to Mama, as it should be, and the one Brian, who is not a lawyer, wrote that leaves part of their double to Carolyn." Suzette needs to get off the phone to get Josephine. "Jeff, I better get going so I can pick Mama up. Probate Court will straighten everything out so this meeting really doesn't matter. But I'll go ahead and take her. Give the family a kiss for me. I love you."

"I love you, too, Sister Dear. Call me later."

Delores, Pamela, Donna, Carolyn and Audrey sit at the dining room table, while the in-laws, Brian and Christie, are in the living room.

Stephen, the self-proclaimed patriarch of the family, sits among his sisters, perched to lead the discussion about the wills. He is annoyed that Suzette and Josephine are late and thinks back to how his dad was always hurt because his mama would come in late after being out with her lovers. Suzette and Josephine interrupt his thoughts when they arrive and join them at the table.

Stephen voices his frustration at their lateness, and Suzette suggests he get over it and get on with the discussion. He begins, and as Suzette predicted, drama ensues. The first point Stephen brings up is that Dad left Carolyn half of the double owned by his parents. Suzette challenges him as to why he thinks Carolyn, who is one of nine siblings, should receive half of their mama's house. His authoritative response is, "Because Dad wanted her to have it."

Josephine looks at Carolyn, "Carolyn, he was your daddy, but he didn't want you living next door to us when he was alive. He didn't like the way all of those men paraded in and out when you lived there. I don't know why George would have a will that says that, or why you think you should have half of my home."

Pamela chastises Josephine, "Mama, stop talking to Carolyn like that!"

"I'll talk to her anyway I want. And Pamela Ann, I'm the mama, not you. You didn't have chick nor child—I did." She rolls her eyes at Pamela and Carolyn. Stephen glares at his mama and asks her to go into the kitchen with him so they can talk privately. Josephine gives Pamela and Carolyn a menacing look as she grabs her walking cane and follows him. Audrey takes a quick break to go outside and smoke a cigarette.

Stephen and Josephine are in the kitchen just moments, when his voice bellows, "Don't you dare talk to my sisters like that! I'd better not hear you disrespect them in my house again!"

Suzette and Donna look at each other in disbelief, and Suzette is immediately on her way to the kitchen. Donna hurries closely behind her while the others talk and act as if nothing is wrong. Josephine screams for Stephen to get his hands off of her. As Suzette enters,

Stephen has Mama's wrists pinned to the arms of the chair and is straddled across her, hollering in her face. He looks like a big black bear waging an attack on a defenseless fawn. Josephine struggles to get free while Suzette tries to help her, screaming for him to let her go. Donna joins in the fracas, and she and Suzette fight to get their mama to safety. During the melee, none of the others, including Brian, the only other male present, go to aid the frail Josephine.

Stephen hollers for Suzette and Donna to get out of the kitchen, saying that the matter is between him and Mama. Suzette counters, "You have lost your mind! Get away from Mama!"

"Suzette, she's hurt you all of your life, and you defend her after what she's done to you? Having you by that damn Dante!"

"Stephen, shut up you asshole; you don't know what you're talking about! And I forgive her for whatever she's done to me. Now get away from us and our Mama!"

Donna and Suzette fight to free Josephine from Stephen's assault, and battle their way through the dining room to the foyer. Stephen, who is in a rage, circles them, pacing frantically, like a hungry, uncaged animal. Josephine flails her three-pronged cane, trying to defend herself from Stephen rather than supporting herself to walk. "Stephen, I just lost your daddy and you attack me? Big man, huh?"

Audrey is coming back inside as they reach the front door. Surprised to see the flurry of activity, she asks, "What's going on?"

Suzette responds, "He attacked Mama!"

Audrey's quick glance shows everybody seated but Stephen. Her mind cannot process that he would have attacked his own mama. "What? Who attacked Mama?"

Suzette screams, "Audrey, please, let's just get out of here!"

Audrey, Donna and Suzette help Josephine down the front porch steps and into Suzette's car. Audrey follows Suzette on the drive to their mama's home. Donna is so shaken up that she heads home to calm down. All of the other siblings remain inside.

Suzette asks, "Do you want to go to the hospital?"

A tearful Josephine is no longer intoxicated, but scared. "No, I'll be okay."

"Mama, I can't apologize enough for what Stephen did. He never should have put his hands on you." Suzette looks over at her mama, who is a nervous wreck, and tries to think about something to help calm her down. She knows Mama loves music and asks if she would like to hear a particular song. Josephine says "Oh Happy Day," so Suzette puts in Quincy Jones' CD and plays her favorite song. Josephine manages to smile through her tears. Suzette fights tears as she drives with one hand and gently strokes her mama's hand and wrist with the other.

Audrey follows them and pulls up in the parking space within seconds behind Josephine and Suzette. They help Josephine walk down what seems to be an endless sidewalk to the back door of her home. Once inside, they settle on the sofa, one on each side of her, and sit, hugging and massaging her arms and wrists.

Audrey is beside herself, "Suzette, what happened? I could barely stay focused on the road!"

Audrey is stunned as she listens to Suzette's account of the drama that occurred in the few minutes she was outside.

"Not one of the others even tried to help me and Donna get his big ass off of her! They just sat there looking smug—like it wasn't their own mother being attacked! I wouldn't expect Christie to do anything, but Brian's weak ass just sat in the living room like he was oblivious."

Audrey is remorseful, "I shouldn't have gone outside. I could have helped you."

"Don't blame yourself, Audrey. Who would have known Stephen would sink that low and hurt his own mama? I guess since Daddy is gone, He forgot that Daddy told him not to put his hands on her."

Josephine speaks up, "I can't believe Stephen attacked me! I'm almost 78 years old…and I am his mother! I'm afraid of him now, and I don't want to be alone with him. I know he doesn't visit much, but if and when he does, I'd feel safer if one of you or Donna were here with me. I just don't want him to hurt me again."

Suzette feels sick to her stomach at the thought of Mama being afraid of her own son. "Mama, I don't want you to be afraid," she says, feeling helpless for not being able to protect her."

Josephine continues, "But he's too big for us to handle. He held me down in that chair and I couldn't get loose. We barely got him off of me! I don't know what he would have done if you and Donna hadn't come in there."

Audrey is angry at her brother and herself. "Well, if I had been in there, the three of us would have dusted him! I can't believe the others didn't help! I don't know what's wrong with them!"

Suzette tries to console her injured mama. "Mama, are you really afraid that he will hurt you again? Do you want me to call the police and get a restraining order?"

Josephine refuses, "I don't want to get anybody else involved, but I don't want to see Stephen anytime soon. His daddy and I didn't raise him to put his hands on women. I don't know what possessed him to turn on me."

Audrey's anger escalates, "I think he is possessed! Nothing else makes sense. What a big punk ass! Mama, it hurts my heart to see you in so much pain. I am so sorry—you don't deserve to be mistreated. Are you sure you don't want to go to the hospital?"

Josephine rubs her wrists and shakes her head, "No, baby, I'll be okay." She drops her head. "I just lost my husband, and now my oldest son attacks me. I can't tell you which hurts the most—my wrists or my heart." Josephine cries, and Suzette and Audrey join her. Audrey gets the liniment, and she and Suzette lovingly rub their mama's wrists, hoping it will help to remove some of her physical and emotional pain. Suzette thinks that while their mama may have done some hurtful things, she doesn't deserve to be attacked by her own son. What kind of man attacks his mother? A twisted, weak one is the only answer she can come up with. A real man wouldn't have touched his mama in anger—only in love.

Suzette and Audrey stay with Josephine for several hours. Suzette asks Mama if she is hungry or wants them to do anything else for her. "No, baby, Raymond said he's coming by, and he should be here soon. You go on home now and get some rest; this was hard on you, too. I'm just going to sit and watch television anyway." Suzette and Audrey reluctantly leave, after hugging and kissing their mama like there is no tomorrow.

Shortly after they leave, Raymond is at the door with White Castles, Josephine's favorite hamburgers. He notices Josephine rubbing her wrists, and asks her what is wrong. She tells him about the attack, and Raymond is ready to go give Stephen a piece of his mind—and his fists. Raymond is outraged that Stephen put his hands on his mama, and that all of the kids didn't come to her aid. He wants to take Stephen on man-to-man; certain he would be a much better match than his defenseless Josephine. He paces back and forth, pounding his fist in his hand.

Josephine asks Raymond to calm down; and makes him promise to stay away from Stephen, which he does after some persuading. He cuddles Josephine in his arms, feeling guilty that he wasn't at her side to protect her. Raymond stays longer than usual that evening, not caring that Beatrice is home waiting for him. His love for Josephine runs deep in his heart, and he needs to be with her as much as she needs to be with him. Josephine feels safe in the arms of her lover of over 55 years. He is her reigning Champ.

CHAPTER TWENTY-FIVE

The year 2000 marks the change of a century. George has been deceased two years, but Josephine's extramarital relationship with Raymond is very much alive. He and Beatrice are still married, but he calls Josephine daily and visits at least four times a week. He usually calls from a phone booth, but sometimes steals a few minutes to call from home to see if she needs him to bring anything.

Donna is at Josephine's enjoying a game of Cooncan with her mama. The timeless card game brings back fond childhood memories for Josephine, as she recalls the fun times she had when playing with Thomas Jr. and Betty. Josephine laughs as she lays her cards down, winning for the fifth time in a row. She chides Donna that she's purposely letting her win.

Donna laughs and reshuffles the cards. "I didn't let you win; you beat me fair and square. But I'm having fun in spite of getting my butt whipped." She notices Josephine hasn't eaten much of the food she brought her and asks if she is going to eat more.

"I ate a piece of chicken and some mashed potatoes—that's plenty for now. Raymond's bringing White Castles, so I'm saving room for them. I'll finish eating the food you brought me tomorrow or later this week. You know I don't have much of an appetite anymore."

Donna bristles at the sound of Raymond's name and looks in the opposite direction and rolls her eyes. Her mind flashes back to when she was a little girl and would hear her daddy complain about Raymond being her mama's man. She didn't understand what he meant; but she knew her daddy's feelings were hurt, and he got mad about it sometimes. As she grew older, she realized her mama was having an adulterous affair, which left a permanent mark; as she was hurt and angry at her mama's betrayal. She always wished Josephine would stop the affair and still resents Raymond for being in her life. Donna was her "daddy's girl," and Raymond was always an unwelcome interloper—as he is even now, at least in her eyes.

Once she gets her eye rolling under control, Donna turns back to face Josephine. "Okay, as long as you eat—that's all I care about." She thinks for a minute. "Mama, I know Daddy's been gone a couple of years, but I still don't appreciate your relationship with Raymond. He was a source of anguish for Daddy, and I feel betrayed when he's around. Daddy would complain to us all the time about Raymond—wishing he wouldn't call our house, and you would stop going out with him. And then you had Sheila by him—that was bold! But Daddy was a good man, and he stayed with you, and us, anyway. Why didn't you ever stop seeing Raymond? He's still married, too. It's so wrong on so many levels, Mama."

"Donna, you don't know what you're talking about. I've never said Sheila is Raymond's, so you can take that out of your mouth. And you can feel any way you want, but Raymond is my business. I loved your daddy, and it certainly wasn't my choice that God took him. But don't you get in me and Raymond's business. He's a good man, and if you spent some time around him, you'd see that for yourself.

Donna shudders, "I don't want to know anything about him. He's probably the last man on earth I would ever want to know!"

"That's your choice, Donna; but life is just what you make it—and I'm going to live mine the way I see fit."

"Okay, Mama, I see you're not going to change at this point. And I don't want to argue, especially about him. Do you want to play another hand—at least until he gets here?"

"I'm not arguing, Donna, I'm just telling you the truth, so you can understand he's not a bad man. We don't have to talk about Raymond. Go ahead and deal another hand so I can beat you again."

The doorbell rings as she deals the cards, and of course it's none other than Raymond. Donna answers the door and speaks to him in a tone that is not so friendly, but not quite rude.

"Hello, Donna, how are you this fine evening?" He looks over at Josephine and a cheek-busting grin comes on his face. Josephine's face lights up like the Christmas tree on the Whitehouse lawn. He looks back at Donna, who has to stop herself from rolling her eyes. "Donna, I thought I saw you drive by Long and High about an hour or so ago. Was that you in that green Toyota?"

Donna replies, "Maybe so, I was in the area around that time."

"You were moving fast. You must have been on your way here."

She puts the cards in the box and doesn't respond to him. She goes unnoticed as Raymond looks at Josephine, who is still all smiles. "Josephine, I brought the White Castles you wanted. Donna, there's some for you too, if you'd like."

Donna makes every effort to keep from cutting her eyes at him. "No, I'll pass. Mama, I'm gone; I'll see you tomorrow." She walks toward the door, and her back is to them, so she freely rolls her eyes, and fights the urge to shake her head in disapproval.

"Okay, Donna Lee, you have a good rest of the evening now." Josephine is giddy, and her attention is now on Raymond. She playfully motions for him to sit next to her, giggling and snuggling close to him. "You were calling me from the phone booth when you saw her, weren't you?" He nods yes. "You know I appreciate you checking in to make sure you bring me what I want, Champ, other than you, that is."

"And I enjoy bringing you what you want—including me," he says as he hugs her close, and watches her smile, contentment written all over their faces.

Devon is twenty and is a junior at Morehouse College. Very handsome, he looks more Italian than Suzette. Built like a stocky football player since birth, he is average height, with dark olive skin and silky hair. Suzette hasn't discussed their Italian heritage with Devon; instead she's told him what she's always been told—that they have Native American on her daddy's side of the family. Devon knows his dad has German and Native American on his side.

Devon is home to work during the summer break, and he and Lisa, his high-school sweetheart, find themselves rekindling their romance. Lisa is cute with flowing, thick hair. She is only inches shorter than Devon and is short waisted with long, Tina Turner-looking legs. Devon and Lisa have remained in contact with each other since high school. Their relationship gains traction quickly, and they are inseparable during the summer.

After the summer break is over, they return to college—Devon to Atlanta, and Lisa to Cincinnati. A month later Lisa discovers she is pregnant and delivers Devon the news that he is going to be a father. He is not sure how to present this news to his mama. He knows Suzette will eventually be okay after the initial shock, and he doesn't want her to think he is going to quit school. He promises Lisa he will support her during the pregnancy, and be at her side for the delivery. They stay in close contact during school and spend a good deal of time together when they return home for the holidays.

Suzette is guardedly happy when Devon tells her she is going to become a grandmother. One of her first reactions is to urge him to have a DNA test. "I'm not saying she's not your baby, but it's always 'mama's baby, daddy's maybe,' so the test will be good for everybody." Devon agrees to have the test done, as he sees from his mama's concern, how important it is to her. He knows there will be no rest for the weary if he doesn't have it. Suzette is fond of Lisa, but wants there to be no doubt about the paternity of the baby—more so for the sake of the unborn baby girl. With what she's experienced with the uncertainty of her own father, Suzette made sure she was monogamous so there was no question that David is Devon's daddy.

At six in the morning on April 23, Lisa is in labor and calls Devon. He hops on the road, hoping to arrive in time for the delivery. He had informed his professors that if he missed class for a few days without notice, it is because he is home for his baby's birth.

Devon calls Suzette to give her the good news, "Hi Mom, how are you?" He is excited and doesn't wait for an answer before telling her Lisa's in labor, and he's on the road home.

"Alrighty now, you're taking that nine hour drive—good for you.

You must be convinced the baby is yours."

"Well, we were seeing each other when she got pregnant, and she insists the baby's mine; so I'm going to do the right thing and stand by her. You taught me it's not only important to do the right thing; it's also important to do the thing right."

"I'm proud of you for stepping up, you Morehouse man in the making. That's what a real man does. You are going to have a DNA test, right? You said you and Lisa were off and on, so you need to be certain the baby is yours." Devon expected that, "Yes, Mom, we'll have a test after the baby is born."

Relieved, she asks how far away he is and he says five hours. He adds that since he's driving at full speed, he figures it will only take four and a half. "I have a sign in the window that says "having a baby," so if I get stopped, they'll know I'm on a mission."

Suzette laughs, but cautions him to be careful. "Watch your speed— you know the highway patrol is." Devon is heavy-footed, but he has travelled up and down the highway so often that Suzette doesn't worry about his safety. He is a smooth talker and has talked himself out of several speeding tickets. At least this time he has a valid excuse.

He laughs, "Yes ma'am." Four hours later, he arrives at the hospital and calls Suzette to let her know he will call when the baby is born. His beautiful daughter, Alexis Marie, is born the next morning. It's as though she waited to make sure her daddy was home before making her grand entrance. Devon is a proud daddy, and immediately sees her resemblance to him.

Suzette enters the hospital room, and it momentarily takes her breath away to see her son holding the baby. Alexis Marie Henderson looks like a doll with enormous cheeks and Betty Boop eyes. Her coal black, curly hair lays so perfectly on her head that it looks like she spent hours in a salon.

Devon hands her to Suzette, "Here's your granddaughter, Mom."

Suzette's heart melts from the sound of the word granddaughter.

"Devon, she is so beautiful." Alexis' eyes focus on Suzette's, and without blinking, she stares at her, seemingly looking deeply into her grandmother's eyes. "I can't believe how long she's looking at me—it's like she's trying to tell me something."

Devon interjects, "Mom, she just wants you to love her."

Suzette lets her guard down and enjoys the moment. "I already do. Hi sweetie girl."

Devon wishes Suzette wouldn't be so skeptical about him being Alexis' father. He wonders if it's because she thinks Lisa was with other guys during the summer. He doesn't know the true reason his mama is so adamant about having the DNA test. Suzette is trying to protect her potential granddaughter from the generational "mama's baby, daddy's maybe" curse she broke when she had him.

Alexis begins to cry, and Lisa feeds her wailing daughter. The three of them laugh and talk as Alexis reacts to their voices. Even though she already loves this beautiful little girl, Suzette can't help but wonder if she is really theirs; she certainly hopes so. Devon stays through the rest of the week and returns to Morehouse on Sunday morning. It is difficult for him to leave his daughter; but he knows he needs to finish his education to provide her a good life. She voluntarily keeps Alexis, and is readily available when Lisa wants some free time. Devon drives home a couple of times to see his daughter before summer break begins. He loves his little girl, which he has fondly nicknamed "Squirt."

It's mid-June, 2001, and Devon is now home to work for the summer and spend time with Alexis Marie. She is two months old and gets cuter by the day. Since he is home for a couple of months, Suzette reminds him about the DNA test. She offers to pay for it so cost won't be an issue.

Whenever Suzette talks to family and close friends about having the DNA test, they laugh, as the strong resemblance of Alexis to Devon and Suzette is obvious to them. She dismisses their laughter and reminds them that Lisa could have a baby by a gorilla and it would be cute.

They think Suzette is being overly cautious, but she doesn't care, as the test is really for Alexis to know the truth.

Suzette is surprised at Lisa's willingness to take the test. Lisa tells Devon she has no doubt that he is Alexis' father, and the DNA test will prove it once and for all. She doesn't appreciate Suzette thinking she is lying about Devon being the father of her baby, and will gladly prove to her that she is her granddaughter.

Devon receives the test results two weeks later. Suzette is in the kitchen when he comes in with the envelope, "Mom, I have the results of the DNA test."

"Wonderful! Do I need to sit down?"

Devon is beaming, which is a good sign, "I think you can take this standing up. Alexis is your granddaughter! The test shows that I'm 99.9% her father. Mom, I can't believe how much doubt you had. Everybody says how much we all look alike."

"What everybody sees is not always the truth. I know Alexis favors us, but looks can be deceiving. She needs to know the truth. I want her to go through life confident about who she is, and where she came from, without any doubt whatsoever." Suzette gives him a congratulatory hug; and for the first time, the baby pictures she's been looking at of herself, Devon and Alexis, look identical. Why couldn't she see that before?

Mamas' Drama

CHAPTER TWENTY-SIX

This late-summer day in August of 2003 in Winston-Salem, North Carolina finds Suzette visiting Jeff and his wife Alesia, while attending the National Black Theatre Festival. They're in the kitchen having a good time while Suzette makes her infamous made-from-scratch carrot cake with cream cheese icing. They drink adult beverages, and the conversation is light-hearted—the laughter almost non-stop. "I hope I'm mixing this cake right. These beverages are starting to go to my head. I'm not complaining, though!"

Alesia offers her support, "I'm sure the cake will turn out just fine, Sis. I tell you what, I'll be more than happy to taste test it for you."

Jeff asks about Mama. "Sister Dear, I talked to Mom a few days ago, but she seemed distracted. Is everything alright with her?"

Suzette tries to stay upbeat as she shares the latest about their mama's condition. "Jeff, Mama's health is declining, and she is starting to exhibit early signs of dementia. She doesn't have much of an appetite and rarely cooks anymore. When we can get her to go out to eat, and that's a job within itself, she only nibbles at best. She has home delivery meals and home aide services, but Audrey, Donna and I make sure one of us visits her daily to help. She's not able to do much for herself, and is low key most of the time. The only time I see her really come alive is when Mr. Raymond comes over—she perks right up when he's around."

Jeff's mood changes from concerned to aggravated. "I don't want to hear about him. He was always a thorn in daddy's side and embarrassing to me—picking her up and dropping her off when I was playing with my friends. They would tease me and say, 'I bet your daddy doesn't know!' The bad thing about it is that Dad did know. He hated it and always talked about Raymond calling and sneaking around with Mama. One thing I know for sure; when Mama dies, if Raymond is coming to her funeral, then I'm not!"

Suzette's head spins, but not because of the alcohol. "Jeff you can't be serious—she's our mother! How could you even think, much less say, you're not going to be at your own mother's funeral? That's cruel and disrespectful." Hurt and angry, involuntary tears form in Suzette's eyes.

Jeff retorts, "You're calling me disrespectful? Mama is the one. She disrespected Dad and still disrespects us. She was always talking on the phone or going out with Raymond, and I hated watching my father being tormented by their affair. So I'm very serious—if Raymond is going to be at Mom's funeral—count me out!"

Alesia is shocked at her husband's behavior, "Jeff, you shouldn't say that. You know you'll be at your mother's funeral." Jeff looks at her without speaking.

Even the alcohol doesn't help buffer the anger of his words. Suzette responds to him, "Jeff, Daddy should have stopped Mama from seeing Mr. Raymond, or vice versa. It wasn't fair that he complained to us; there was nothing we could do except what you're doing now, which is judge her. I can't believe you sit here and say you are not going to your own mama's funeral. That's so unfreakingreal! And Jeff, Mama is your mother, not your wife; so don't punish her for what she does as a woman. I promise you that when she dies, I will personally make sure Mr. Raymond doesn't come to her funeral. Does that work for you?"

"Yes, it does. Suzette, you act like it's okay for them to be together. You even admit to staying when he comes over her house. I can't believe you speak to that man, much less are friendly with him. Don't you remember what Dad went through?"

"Yes, Jeff, I do. But the affair between Mama and Mr. Raymond wasn't for me to deal with—that was her and Daddy's issue. We don't know what they went through in their marriage; maybe she took a page out of Daddy's book. Who knows? And as far as being friendly with him, Daddy's been gone for five years now; and Mr. Raymond checks on Mama daily and visits almost every day. Mama always says, 'Life is just what you make it,' and she can do whatever she chooses. I don't judge her for what she does or doesn't do. What matters to me is that she is happy and safe."

"Well, I'll take you at your word that he won't be at her funeral."

Suzette is floored but knows she's said enough. "That's not a problem, little brother. Now let's change the subject and mix up some more libations so we can get back to the laughter. I want to think about how much of a blessing it is for Mama to be alive at the age of 82 and not put her in the ground prematurely. I'm grateful for every day she's on this earth. When Audrey brought her down for Thanksgiving last year, she was so excited you would have thought she had travelled overseas. She loved every minute she was here."

A kinder Jeff responds, "I know, and I loved having her here. In fact, we all did. It was too short of a visit; but she was here, and that's what mattered."

"Well, keep those fond memories about your mother in your heart, and be grateful that she is still alive." Suzette sips more of her beverage— wishing the alcohol would render her semi-conscious. It feels like her mother is being assaulted again—only this time it is emotional instead of physical.

A year later, during a week-long business trip to New York, Suzette talks to Audrey and Josephine. They both mention that Raymond hasn't been over to Josephine's in a few days. Suzette ignores the gut feeling that tells her something is horribly wrong; although it gnaws at her the entire time she is gone. She returns from the Big Apple and checks in with Audrey, only to find that they still haven't seen or heard from Raymond. Suzette doesn't feel her mama is being forgetful. And she can't ignore the haunting feeling that something is awry. "Audrey, I hope it's not what I'm thinking it is. I know it sounds drastic, but I'm going to check the obituaries in *The Dispatch*."

"Suzette, quit being a drama queen; it's nothing that serious."

"This has been pulling at me for days. I pray he's alright, but the fact that he hasn't been in contact is not like him. I hope my gut is wrong."

Audrey stays on the line as she thinks it asinine that Suzette feels she will find Mr. Raymond listed in the obituary. Unfortunately, Suzette's instincts prove her right, as Mr. Raymond's picture and obituaries appear. "Audrey, this isn't good."

"What? What did you find?"

"Mr. Raymond passed away ten days ago, and his funeral was four days ago. Mama's going to be devastated! Audrey, we need to go over there after work and tell her."

Suzette devises a plan to present the dreadful news to their mama and asks Audrey a question, but she doesn't respond. "Audrey." Still, no response as Audrey's mind has taken a leave of absence. "Audrey, can you meet me at Mama's at 6?" After not receiving a response for the third time, Suzette looks at the phone's light indicator to make sure they're still connected. "Audrey, can you hear me?"

In a weak voice, Audrey finally answers, "Yes."

"Are you alright? Can you meet me at Mama's at 6?"

"Yes, I can meet you, but I need to go."

Suzette is talking to the dial tone when she tells Audrey she will let Mama know they are coming by. She had no clue Audrey would take Raymond's death so hard. Suzette dreads having to give her mama this awful news. She calls Josephine, "Hi Mama, how are you?"

Josephine's health may be failing, but she still has her sassy ways. "I'm slow but sure."

"Mama, I can't stay on the phone because I have so much work to catch up on, but Audrey and I want to come over around 6. Is that okay with you?"

"Yes, that's fine. I missed you while you were gone, and I haven't seen or heard from Raymond. That's not like him. I've been calling their house, but Beatrice answers, so I just hang up. She and I used to talk years ago, but we don't anymore. The last time Raymond was out of touch like this was when he got sick and went into the hospital. It took him a few days, but he called as soon as he was well enough to dial the phone. I hope he's alright. I'll just wait to hear from him; I know it'll be sooner than later."

Suzette knows better and strains to keep her voice calm. "Well, try not to worry, okay Mama? We'll see you in a few hours. Do you want me to bring you anything?"

"Just bring your lucky self," "Miss Sassy" responds.

Suzette laughs, but her heart aches for her mama. God, how is she going to tell her that Mr. Raymond is dead? "I love you, Mama. Boo boo."

"I love you too, baby. Boo boo." Josephine hangs up the phone and is happy she will see her soon. She's missed seeing Suzette and Raymond, two of her four closest companions.

Josephine, her mind a thousand light years away, is watching television when Audrey and Suzette arrive. Well, at least the television is on, and she's looking in its direction. Audrey reaches her first and hugs her, "Hey Mama, how are you?"

Josephine quips, "Hay is for horses. I'm slow but sure."

Suzette wonders how she is going to get the words about Raymond's death out of her mouth and to her mama's ears. She hugs and kisses her, knowing she will soon be devastated beyond imagination. She asks mama what she's eaten, and it isn't surprised when she says breakfast. Suzette wonders if she's had anything to eat. Because Josephine is in the early stages of dementia, her recall isn't always good; but she is still alive and sassy, and that's a blessing.

Suzette tries to convince Josephine to go out for something to eat—enticing her with White Castles; but she stands firm on staying home. "No, I'm not leaving. I'm waiting right here for Raymond. I don't want to miss him when he comes. It's just not like him to stay away this long and not call me." Suzette and Audrey look at each other and sit down, knowing this is going to be heartbreaking.

Suzette begins, "Mama, we need to tell you something about Mr.

Raymond." Josephine looks over at Suzette, and at that precise moment, a Crime Watch Alert comes on television. They show Raymond's picture as the announcer reads the grim news flash, "An 83-year old man was stabbed ten days ago during a robbery attempt at a telephone booth at Long and High. Witnesses informed that Raymond Moorehead initially beat the male assailant off with the telephone receiver, but the assailant returned with a knife within minutes and stabbed Mr. Moorehead multiple times. He was taken to the hospital where he later died. If you have any information about this brutal murder, contact your local Crime Watch Alert at the number shown below."

Suzette and Audrey, not believing their ears or eyes, stare at each other an undetermined amount of time. They did not know he was murdered! How uncanny that the crime alert would come on at the very moment they are telling their mama about his death.

Audrey asks, "Mama, did you see that?"

Josephine is indifferent when she answers, "Yes."

Suzette knows she didn't process what she saw. "Do you realize who they were talking about?" Josephine shakes her head no. Audrey starts to cry, and Suzette walks over to her mama, hugs her and tells her what happened to Mr. Raymond.

Josephine wails uncontrollably, "No! I can't believe it! That isn't true! When did he die?

Audrey replies, "It was a few days ago. I'm sorry, Mama, he's gone."

"When is his funeral? I want to go."

"Mama, they already had it several days ago," says Suzette.

Josephine agonizes as Suzette reads his obituary. "Oh God, no! "First George, now Raymond! What am I going to do?"

Suzette assures her, "Mama, we're here for you." She rubs her Mama's back as if trying to rub her pain away. "What can we do?"

"Just don't ever leave me."

Suzette reassures her, "We promise. Do you want to go out for a minute? We can go for a ride to get some fresh air."

Josephine nods her head yes, and Audrey helps put her shoes on. Josephine tries to stand, but is so lightheaded she has to sit back down. "I can't believe Raymond's gone. He didn't deserve to be killed. I just can't believe he's gone!"

Suzette calls Jeff later that evening and tells him he can come to his mama's funeral when she dies. She tells him about Mr. Raymond's murder. He thanks her for calling and says he is sorry for their Mama.

Mamas' Drama

CHAPTER TWENTY-SEVEN

Time moves slowly as Josephine grieves Raymond's death like it was yesterday. Making it through the last two weeks has been agonizing. She cries most of the night—sleeping only after waves of tears subside. When George passed, Josephine was sad for a long time, but had seen him gradually lose his connection to life. On the other hand, Raymond's demise was sudden and brutal, and she did not get to say goodbye.

Suzette calls Josephine on her way to give a presentation to middle school children. She has served as a board member and PR Director for a non-profit theatre company for four years and enjoys working with the arts. This is her first time giving a marketing presentation to school agers, so she has no idea what to expect from their overly-active and unpredictable minds.

Josephine answers after several rings, "Hello."

Suzette worries about her mama, and is relieved to hear her voice. "Hi Mama, how are you doing?"

Josephine doesn't give her usual "slow but sure" response, but says instead, "I'm doing all I can. I can't get used to Raymond being gone—and knowing he was murdered at the phone booth breaks my heart even more. I feel like I'm responsible for his death."

"I know it's hard on you, Mama; that's why we call and come over so much. I hope we're not overdoing it."

Josephine tells Suzette how grateful she is that they stay close, as she feels so alone. "George has been gone for six years, and I miss him every day. And now Raymond—it's just hard to believe. Did they catch the man who stabbed him?"

"Not yet, but they will."

Josephine laments, "I feel so lost." Suzette remembers her mama was this sad when Daddy died. She misses her daddy, too, and understands her mama's grief. Suzette wasn't close to Raymond, but she always appreciated the fact that he brought her mama joy and was a beacon of light to Josephine. He wasn't a bad man; it was their extramarital relationship that was bad for everybody—but them.

"I'm on my way to St. Philip's Episcopal Church to do a presentation. Do you want me to drop by afterwards?"

"No, you don't have to come by. You and Donna were here yesterday, and Audrey just left. My grief is to be expected, but I'll be alright."

Suzette tries to comfort her. "Have you thought about some of the good times you and Raymond had? That may help you get through some of your sadness."

Josephine chuckles, "Well, I thought earlier about how proud he was of his daughter."

Suzette is caught totally off guard, as Mama has never remotely had a discussion of this nature before. "Who is his daughter?"

Josephine replies, "You know who it is."

"No, I don't. I need you to tell me."

"It's Sheila. Raymond was so proud of her; he always said how much she resembled him."

Suzette takes a deep breath and can't pass up a golden opportunity to ask about Dante. It doesn't matter if it is the 999th time. "Mama, did Dante think I looked like him?"

Josephine hesitates for what feels like a month of Sundays before finally saying, "Yes, Suzette, your father, Dante, thought you looked like him; and he was proud of you."

Suzette wonders momentarily if she really heard what her ears transmitted to her brain. "Wow, Mama, I don't know what to say. That took you almost a lifetime to tell me." Suzette's mind spirals through many loops and twists, and she is grateful she's parked and not driving. She's always thought she would be prepared for the truth if and when her mama revealed it. But she honestly doesn't know what to say, think or do. She glances over at her briefcase, a reminder that she has a presentation to give. Josephine remains silent. "Mama, I have to go; I'm late, and the kids are waiting. I'll call you after I finish."

Suzette hangs up and stares at the cell phone; a feeling of being anesthetized overtakes her body and mind. After asking her mama all of her life, and always being lied to; she never expected to hear the truth. She is confused, and doesn't know what to do with this revelation. Suzette gazes out of the car's front window. People are doing everyday things—walking their dogs, getting in and out of cars, talking and laughing. Nothing has changed for them, but her entire world has been turned inside out. She remains frozen for a few more minutes, then shakes her head as if to shake herself back to the earth plane. Her mama just confessed that Dante is her father. Wow! She sits a few more minutes before her mind can communicate to her body to get in motion. She has to go inside and teach the kids. She needs to figure this out later, when she can sit with it for awhile. Right now, as they say in theatre—it's show time!

Suzette does her best to stay focused on her presentation, and is relieved her audience is children. She makes a few blunders, but smoothes them over without detection by their young minds. At the end of the presentation, the children go on their merry ways. Once in her car, she calls Audrey and they laugh as she recounts some of the children's antics. "I think at least three of the ten were listening. We may possibly have some future thespians in the making after all!"

She moves on to her big news. "Audrey, I called Mama earlier and she was grieving Mr. Raymond something awful. My head is shaking like a bobble head doll at what she said to me."

"A bobble head doll? You can usually handle anything. What did she say?"

"She told me Mr. Raymond was Sheila's father."

Audrey is hopeful, "She did? Did she say he was my father too?"

Suzette is thrown by Audrey's question. "No, she didn't. She started out talking about him being proud of his daughter and said I knew whose father he was. How would I know that—I wasn't there. Hell, that's her 'mama's baby, daddy's maybe' drama."

"I'm surprised she didn't say Mr. Raymond was my father. I've always thought he was. I think I look like him."

Suzette had no idea that Audrey thought Mr. Raymond was her father. "Audrey, she just said he was Sheila's father, and he was proud of the way she resembled him. You should ask her if he's your father."

"Suzette, unlike you, I'm not brave enough to ask."

"Well you should, Lord knows I've asked a thousand times. And you never know what she'll say—especially today. She told me something else that really blew my mind."

A disappointed Audrey hears excitement in Suzette's voice. "Really? What?"

"Girl, I put it out there and asked if Dante thought I looked like him. Sis, she said 'Yes, Suzette, your father, Dante, thought you looked like him; and he was very proud of you.' I can't believe she told me! You know how many times I've asked her about Dante and gotten nowhere." Audrey can only listen as she wonders if Raymond is her father. It seems Mama would have told Suzette when she was talking about him being Sheila's daddy.

"Audrey, I'm trying to figure out what to do, if anything. But I'm glad she told me—I just wish she had told me years ago. I could have accepted myself for who I am instead of denying the truth. I guess her grief for Raymond took her off her game—or maybe it's the dementia. I don't know. I'm feeling so many emotions right now; confused, dazed and hurt are the ones that immediately come to mind. I feel a sense of relief, but I'm in a fog. I'll deal with it; I just need some time to wrap my head and heart around this. Wow!"

Audrey sighs, "Suzette, that's deep, but at least you know—and the timing is perfect since you're going to Italy in a few months. I wish I knew the truth about my father."

"Well then, why don't you ask her while she's in the telling mood? She didn't say you were Raymond's, so you're probably daddy's. You look like Grandma Rose to me. You were only eight when she passed, so you may not remember her. Ask Mama to show you pictures so you can see for yourself."

"You're right. I barely remember Grandma Rose, but I will ask about the pictures. Mama probably won't ever tell me the truth. I guess I'll always wonder."

The wheels in Suzette's head turn so fast; she feels like she is going to derail if she doesn't take a few quiet moments to herself. "I wish I could help you Little Sis, but that's all she said. Hey, I need to get off this phone and call Mama back; unless you want to call her first. She might fess up."

"I'm not going to ask her; she wouldn't tell me anyway." Suzette knows Audrey is disappointed but needs to sit with herself right now. She thinks about the old adage, "The truth shall set you free," which begs the question—free from what, or free to do what? She trusts time will tell.

A million thoughts criss-cross Suzette's mind like a labyrinth, and she decides to visit Josephine instead of calling her. She needs to talk to Mama in person about Dante. She needs to hear why her mama has kept what she considers a secret for 54 years. Suzette has known in her heart that Dante is her biological father; but she chose to live in denial, especially when her Mama continued to lie. The observable physical traits between Suzette and her siblings were pointed out by everyone, from family to total strangers.

Josephine is sitting in George's old chair and begins to cry the moment Suzette walks through the door. Suzette's tears fall, and she holds Mama until they both stop crying. Suzette loves her and knows telling the lies must have taken a toll on her too. She is more hurt than angry, and has a million questions about Dante.

Suzette wants to hear about Dante from Josephine, as she didn't pursue a relationship with Dante's daughters when she met them ten years ago. Angela's hurtful dismissal helped her realize she was unwilling to put herself in a position to be rejected by Mona or Natalie. She is unwilling to take the chance to care if they would accept her. And what if, heaven forbid, Dante isn't really her biological father? It is all more than she is willing to risk emotionally.

Suzette approaches her mama gently as she realizes Josephine is fragile, physically and emotionally. Suzette asks why she didn't tell her the truth about Dante before now. Josephine cries harder and says she isn't feeling up to talking. She begs Suzette to wait until another time. Suzette tries coaxing her, but soon recognizes her mother is unable to have the conversation she's longed to hear for a lifetime. The long-awaited conversation is deferred, and the truth has not yet set her free.

CHAPTER TWENTY-EIGHT

Sparkling white snow covers the ground, and the glorious Christmas holiday season fills the air. The holiday music, decorations and lights are infectious, and people greet each other with a spirit of love. The seasons don't change much for Josephine, now 83. Her health slowly declines as the menacing grasp of dementia tightens its grip on her mind and body.

Suzette picks Josephine up to help her prepare dinner. It is more for company, as Josephine is not able to do much due to her frailties. Suzette's home looks inviting, and smells like the holidays. The fragrance of the live, six-foot white pine tree located in the living room is reminiscent of the smell of the Christmases Suzette recalls while growing up. The tree is beautifully adorned and lights up like Times Square; its lights illuminating the foyer and dining rooms. Josephine breathes in the smell of the tree and smiles as she fondly remembers when the fragrance was part of the many holiday celebrations in her home.

Josephine and Suzette settle in the kitchen; the aroma of the family's sweet potato pie permeates the air. As Josephine takes in its familiar smell, she recalls her childhood when her mama would make the prized pie, and how special it was when her mama and grandma carefully instructed her how to bake it. Her mind also reaches back to when her grandma would serve her a slice of pie and peach ice tea when she read Bible verses to her. She giggles as she thinks about apologizing to Jesus, and about all the stories Grandma Kirksey would tell her.

Josephine then recalls when she taught each of her daughters to make the pie. Some things they learned from each other, but instructing them on how to prepare the family pie recipe was a tradition that had been honored for generations. She had a sense of pride about passing that tradition on to each of her daughters.

Suzette is delighted to have her mama all to herself. She cleans mustard and kale greens and Josephine handily folds plastic shopping bags. "Mama, I'm so happy you're here. It's not often it's just you and me. Call me selfish, but I love spending time alone with you."

"I love spending time with you, Suzette. We always have so much fun." Josephine foregoes her gin and tonic as Suzette mixes the traditional eggnog and brandy drink they typically enjoy during the holidays.

It has been four months since Josephine's confession to Suzette about Dante. Josephine has avoided the conversation Suzette craves. She desperately needs clarity to heal from a lifetime of secrets, lies and deceit. They talk about many things, including Suzette's harrowing trip to Italy just weeks after the big reveal.

When Suzette and her nieces arrived in Rome, the sight of the airport police holding automatic weapons was frightening. The person they were to stay with never met up with them; and after spending eight hours at the airport, they had to find a hotel. Having no money to cover the unexpected hotel costs, the majority of their time was spent frantically making arrangements to return home. The highlight of the trip was a six-hour tour of picturesque Rome.

"The piece of Rome we saw was beautiful, and the food was delicious. But you know, the trip to my 'Fatherland' mirrors the journey I've been on with Dante being my father. When we landed, the airport security was frightening; and the trip was filled with disappointments; yet Italy itself was beautiful. To me, the parallel of the trip and my life is that although I have gone through much heartache and turmoil, I can still find beauty in being me."

"Yes, you can, Suzette."

"Mama, I need to ask you about something else."

"Okay."

"Why did you tell me years ago about Grandpa Thomas, but didn't tell the older ones? They called me a liar because they didn't know about your biological father."

Josephine is acquiescent, "Because I felt it would help you."

"Help me how? Being truthful about Dante being my father would have helped me."

"I told you about your Grandpa Thomas because I wanted you to know you weren't the only one raised by a daddy that loved you as his own. Our lives mirrored each others in many ways, and it was the small piece I was brave enough to share with you."

"But why did you deny that Dante was my father? Why did you lie?"

Josephine pauses. Hearing Suzette say the word "lie" shakes Josephine to the core of her being. She always felt having Suzette by Dante was a secret she was entitled to keep. But Suzette's anguish forces Josephine to admit that her secret is in fact, a lie. After years of deceit, Josephine's response to her wounded daughter is truthful, "Suzette, I didn't want to hurt you."

Josephine takes a long sip of her spiked eggnog, and lets it move slowly down into her belly before she speaks again. "I should have been truthful with you and Sheila, but I couldn't hurt you like Mama hurt me."

"My daddy was my heart, and I was a daddy's girl. I felt so special being his daughter; only to find out that I wasn't—I was a result of Mama's affair. I felt ashamed for being born, and I was always fearful Daddy would stop loving me since I wasn't his blood. I didn't want you to feel the same way I did—like you could be abandoned by your daddy one day. I thought I was protecting you from the pain I suffered from knowing about my biological father."

"I know my choices hurt you deeply, and I am so sorry I didn't tell you. Your father, Dante, was a good man. He was charismatic, handsome, and witty. He was a very successful businessman and showed me a side of life that was like living in a fairy-tale world. Our relationship didn't last long, but I stayed in touch with him because of you. Do you remember going to his bar when you were little?"

"I vaguely remember going to a place where a man would fix me a chocolate-cherry milk drink and let me color. Was that him?"

"Yes, baby, it was. I stopped taking you to see him when you went to kindergarten. He wanted to be more involved in your life, but I wouldn't let him. I didn't want to confuse you and disrespect your daddy anymore by taking you around Dante. I should have thought about how being so different from the others affected you. I just thought having the Native American blood in the family would be enough to explain your appearance when people asked."

"I am so sorry, Suzette. Instead of protecting you, I subjected you to the same pain I went through. The big difference is I knew the truth about my father, and I denied you the truth about yours. The decisions I made at the time seemed right, but I realize now that I was wrong. I was wrong to lie to you. Please try to understand, and find it in your heart to forgive me."

Suzette hugs her mama, and then puts her heart—the broken heart she has shielded for a lifetime because it couldn't withstand the pain—on the table. "I am trying to understand, and I love you. But all I ever wanted and needed was the truth about who I really was, and where I came from. And I needed to hear it from you, Mama. Just like you, I have been hurt over and over again because of the way I look. People closest to me found it amusing to tease me about my Italian side. You not telling me Dante was my father didn't stop the hurtful things I went through. It didn't stop the curiosity and comments from people. It was worse for me because I completely denied a part of me in order to prove them wrong."

"I've felt like an intruder—a misfit in this family. That's been such a difficult place to be, and it's been a lifetime struggle. If you had told me who I really was, I could have accepted myself and felt good because I knew the truth about me—Suzette. I wouldn't have had to pretend to be somebody I was not. I could have loved myself for who I was, instead of hating myself for who I wasn't."

Grateful to finally release some of the hurt that's been embedded like a knife in her heart, Suzette takes a deep breath and exhales slowly. "Until Devon was born, you were the only person that was wholly mine; nobody else, only you. I felt betrayed because you wouldn't tell me the truth. You had so many opportunities, but you chose to lie instead. Your lies gave me the only reason I needed to live my life in denial. I've been the brunt of jokes, insults, jealousies and curiosity just because I was born. I stuffed the pain deep inside where it's festered my entire life. I needed—and deserved—to know the truth, regardless of what you went through, or felt I would think about you. Mama, keeping the identity of my biological father from me was never your right, and it was never a secret."

"When David and I started having problems in our marriage, I was surprised we lasted the time we did—I thought he would have abandoned me long before the problems started. I don't regret getting the divorce because we had become two very different people, and didn't have the same things in common anymore. But I was surprised that we lasted for over ten years."

"Mama, I've always felt I was a mistake, and was unworthy of love. I've chosen men that I knew weren't available so I wouldn't have expectations for them to stay. I've pushed good men away because I convinced myself they couldn't possibly love or care about me. I told myself they would abandon me because I wasn't good enough. I thought I couldn't trust men to love me; but I came to understand that I didn't trust or love myself. I had to come to terms that my feelings of unworthiness came from the pain inside of me, not who was on the outside of me.

Josephine reaches out to hug her daughter close to her, hoping she doesn't pull away. "Baby, I am so sorry for the heartache I caused you, and I regret I didn't tell you the truth before now. I tried to tell you many times, but I just couldn't. I was ashamed of the extramarital affairs; but please don't misunderstand, I am not ashamed of either you or Sheila. You came into this world the way God intended you to, and I love you both very much. It wasn't just my shame that made me not tell you—I couldn't risk losing your love. I wish I could take all of the pain from your heart and put it in mine. Can you ever forgive me?"

Suzette welcomes the healing tears that flow down her face; the tears that will help her release some of the pain she's endured for a lifetime. She is grateful to have this conversation with her mama. She never thought she would hear the truth from her, or have a chance to share her heart with her. "Yes, Mama, I forgive you, and I love you even more because you found the courage to tell me the truth from your own heart, and your own lips. I will hold these words close to my heart—always. And I want to thank you, Mama; thank you for giving me life. Thank you for loving me and doing the best you could as my mother and best friend."

"Suzette, I can't imagine my life without you. I'm grateful for being on this earth for so long, and for everybody and everything that has been a part of my life. And baby, there is one thing we know for certain, and that is by whatever vehicle or vessel, relationship or encounter, the Creator is our true father. I pray you continue to find the joy that's here on earth. Live your life like its golden; be sure to live each moment like it's the golden time of day. Be a lover of people—and treat yourself—and somebody else, real good! Remember what I always say, life is just what you make it!"

Suzette is unashamed of the tears that cover her face. Her heart is filled with gratitude. She holds her mama close and forgiveness that matches her unconditional love fills her heart. "I love you, Mama."

"I love you too, Suzette."

Suzette cuts a slice of pie for each of them, and they venture into the living room. They drink their holiday eggnog and sing Christmas songs. Suzette sings "Santa Baby," and Mama gets up and does her own rendition; moving around without her cane. They settle back down on the sofa; and Suzette thinks about her mama's words of wisdom, "Life is just what you make it." She cherishes each moment they spend together, as she realizes that only too soon she will eat the prized sweet potato pie without Mama at her side. Suzette has forgiven her, and looks forward to healing.

Josephine eats her pie, savoring every bite. Suzette takes a bite of her pie, but for her, after swallowing the family secret, the taste of the pie is still delicious; but the taste of the family secret, is bittersweet.

THE END

Our family's Sweet Potato Pie Recipe, in Mama's handwriting

Sweet Potato Pie

2 cups cooked mashed potatoes (4 med)
3 tablespoon butter — — 2 eggs
7/8 cup sugar — — — 1/2 teaspoon salt
1 teaspoon Cinnamon — 1 cup milk
1 teaspoon allspice — 1/2 teaspoon Vanilla

Add butter, sugar, & spices to hot potatoes. Separate the eggs. Beat the egg yolks. Add the yolks, salt, milk and vanilla to the potato mixture. Fold in the beaten egg-whites. ~~Pour~~

Pour in a pie dish lined with unbaked pastry. Bake a 375 °F. for 1 hour. When cool serve with whipped cream. Less calories —

Margaret & Johnson

Even today, when I bake the family pie, I pay homage to Mama. I am learning that being free means moving through life being content with yourself, whoever that self is. No matter your situation, "life is just what you make it!"

Book Club Discussion Questions

1. What influence, if any, did Josephine's situation with her fathers have on her as she grew older?

2. Do you think people are justified to keep the truth from those that are directly affected by the "mama's baby, daddy's maybe" condition? Why, or why not?

3. Did any of the characters evoke anger, compassion or any other strong emotions in you? If so, which emotions and why?

4. How do you feel about Clarence insisting that Millie tell Josephine he was her "real" father, and his demand to tell her before she turned eight?

5. What do you think lead to the depression which caused Millie and Josephine to turn to alcohol?

6. Do you think Josephine was justified to continue her affair with Raymond for so many years? Please explain.

7. What was Josephine's reason for keeping Suzette from Dante? Why didn't Dante threaten Josephine the way Clarence threatened Millie?

8. Do you think Sheila was justified in becoming angry with Suzette for the 'choc-o-lot' reference to her color? Does "colorism" still exist? (Why, or why not?)

9. Why do you think Suzette withheld her true paternity information from Devon?

10. Did Suzette cling to her Mama? Why or why not?